PENGUIN MODERN CLASSICS
The Princess and the Political Agent

MAHARAJ KUMARI BINODINI DEVI (1922–2011) was an award-winning writer from Manipur, in North-east India. She was the youngest daughter of Maharaja Sir Churachand Singh of the erstwhile kingdom of Manipur and his queen Maharani Dhanamanjuri Devi. Besides her Sahitya Akademi Award–winning *Boro Saheb Ongbi Sanatombi* (*The Princess and the Political Agent*), she wrote short stories, radio plays, dance dramas, essays and song lyrics. She wrote original film scripts for features and documentary films and adapted several of her works into screenplays for films like *My Son, My Precious* (1981) and *Ishanou* (1990) that premiered internationally at Cannes and the Museum of Modern Art. She was also a translator of Bangla literature and a sculptor who studied at Santiniketan. She held political office and used her writing for environmental, civil and women's causes. She was the founder of LEIKOL, the Manipuri women writer's collective and a founding member and president of Roop Raag, an arts organization of Manipur.

L. SOMI ROY is the translator of his mother Binodini's works from their original Manipuri. He is the founder of Imasi: The Maharaj Kumari Binodini Devi Foundation in Imphal. A film curator from out of New York, he has curated for US institutions like the Museum of Modern Art, Film Society of Lincoln Center, the Whitney Museum of American Art and Asia Society. He has written on film, theatre and photography for *Artforum*, *Drama Review*, the British Film Institute and International Documentary Association. He has given talks at the National Geographic Society, the Smithsonian, Harvard University and the Royal Asiatic Society of London, and has taught at New York University and Manhattan Marymount College. His translations of Binodini include *Crimson Rainclouds* (2012) and *The Maharaja's Household: A Daughter's Memories of Her Father* (2015). He is a promoter of international polo in Manipur and works for the preservation of the Manipuri pony.

BINODINI

The Princess and the Political Agent

Translated from the Manipuri by L. Somi Roy

PENGUIN BOOKS

An imprint of Penguin Random House

PENGUIN BOOKS

USA | Canada | UK | Ireland | Australia
New Zealand | India | South Africa | China

Penguin Books is part of the Penguin Random House group of companies
whose addresses can be found at global.penguinrandomhouse.com

Published by Penguin Random House India Pvt. Ltd
7th Floor, Infinity Tower C, DLF Cyber City,
Gurgaon 122 002, Haryana, India

First published in Penguin Books by Penguin Random House India 2020

Copyright © L. Somi Roy 2020

All rights reserved

10 9 8 7 6 5 4 3 2 1

ISBN 9780143446514

Typeset in Minion Pro by Manipal Technologies Limited, Manipal

www.penguin.co.in

Your Highness, my aunt,
Please forgive my breach of courtesy.
I have taken your royal name
In this book I have written.
The Princess and the Political Agent
I dedicate to you.

—Binodini

CONTENTS

HISTORICAL EVENTS TIMELINE

The Kingdom of Manipur in the 19th Century

1819	Occupation of Manipur by the Burmese.
1825	During the First Anglo-Burmese War, Prince Gambhirsingh and Prince Narasingh expel the Burmese from Manipur with British help. The British establish a presence in Manipur.
1825	Princess Sanatombi's great-grandparents Maharaja Gambhirsingh and Maharani Kumudini, Lady of Meisnam, ascend the throne.
1833	Maharaja Gambhirsingh dies, leaving behind his two-year-old son Chandrakirti. Crown Prince Narasingh rules as regent.
1843	Princess Sanatombi's great-granduncle Maharaja Narasingh ascends the throne.
1844	Grand Queen Mother Kumudini, the Lady of Meisnam, flees to India with her twelve-year-old son Chandrakirti.
1850	Princess Sanatombi's grandfather Maharaja Chandrakirti becomes king.
1886	Death of Maharaja Chandrakirti.

| 1886 | Princess Sanatombi's father Maharaja Surchandra becomes king. |
| 1886 | Death of the Grand Queen Mother, the Lady of Meisnam. |

Events of the Anglo-Manipuri War (The Battle of Khongjom), 1891

SEPTEMBER 1890	Princess Sanatombi's uncle Prince Koireng leads a rebellion against her father Maharaja Surchandra.
SEPTEMBER 1890	Maharaja Surchandra goes into exile in Calcutta.
SEPTEMBER 1890	Princess Sanatombi's uncle Maharaja Kulachandra becomes king.
MARCH 1891	The British try to capture Prince Koireng. Five British officers including Political Agent Grimwood are massacred.
APRIL 1891	The British attack Manipur and the Anglo-Manipuri War breaks out. The British prevail in the Battle of Khongjom.
APRIL 1891	Major Maxwell arrives in Manipur. He raises the Union Jack.
AUGUST 1891	The British imprison Maharaja Kulachandra in India and execute Prince Koireng.
SEPTEMBER 1891	Princess Sanatombi's cousin, seven-year-old Churachand, great-grandson of Maharaja Narasingh, is installed as king.

NOVEMBER 1891   Death of Princess Sanatombi's half-brother Prince Lukhoi, the only son and heir of Maharaja Surchandra and Queen Maharani Premamayi.

DECEMBER 1891   Princess Sanatombi's father Maharaja Surchandra dies in Calcutta.

The Princess and the Political Agent

1892   Princess Sanatombi elopes with Political Agent Maxwell.

1892   Lt Colonel Maxwell is transferred from Manipur.

1894   Maxwell returns to Manipur as Political Agent.

1894   Princess Sanatombi becomes the consort of Political Agent Maxwell.

1895   Maharaja Churachand is sent to boarding school in India.

1896   Maxwell is transferred to India. Princess Sanatombi goes with him.

1897   Political Agent Maxwell and Princess Sanatombi return to Manipur.

1897   Maxwell and Princess Sanatombi move into the new British Residency.

1901   Viceroy Lord Curzon visits Manipur.

1904   Princess Sanatombi offers a *ras* dance at the British Residency.

1904   Burning of the bungalow of J.G. Dunlop, Assistant Superintendent, precipitating the Women's War against the British.

| 1905 | Princess Sanatombi's cousin Maharaja Churachand weds Maharani Dhanamanjuri, Lady of Ngangbam. |
| 1905 | Maxwell leaves Manipur for good. Princess Sanatombi dies soon after. |

IMPORTANT CHARACTERS

In Alphabetical Order

ANGANGMACHA, YOUNGER LADY OF NGANGBAM: Step-grandmother of Princess Sanatombi. She is a queen of Maharaja Surchandra, and sister of Maharani Premamayi, later the Dowager Queen.

BAMACHARAN MUKHERJEE: Indian clerk, first in the palace and later for the British.

BORACHAOBA, PRINCE: The chieftain of Yaiskul. Son of Princess Sanatombi's great-granduncle Maharaja Narasingh. Cousin and childhood friend of Maharaja Chandrakirti.

CHANDRAKIRTI, MAHARAJA (CHILD KING 1833–43, REIGNS 1850–86): Grandfather of Princess Sanatombi. He is the son of Maharaja Gambhirsingh and Maharani Kumudini, the Lady of Meisnam, later the Grand Queen Mother.

CHANDRAMUKHI, LADY OF THOKCHOM: Youngest consort of Maharaja Chandrakirti.

CHAOBIHAL, BRAHMIN MOTHER: Her daughter Mainu is Princess Sanatombi's companion.

CHIEFTAIN OF YAISKUL: See under Borachaoba.

CHURACHAND, MAHARAJA (1891–1941): Cousin of Princess Sanatombi. He is the great-grandson of Maharaja Narasingh. Installed as king at the age of seven by the British in 1891 after the Anglo-Manipuri War.

DOWAGER QUEEN: See under Premamayi.

GAMBHIRSINGH, MAHARAJA (1825–33): Great-grandfather of Princess Sanatombi. He and his cousin Prince Narasingh expel the Burmese from Manipur in 1825 with British help during the First Anglo-Burmese War.

GRAND QUEEN MOTHER: See under Kumudini.

GRIMWOOD, FRANK ST CLAIR: Political Agent of Manipur starting in 1887. He is one of five British officers killed in 1891 by the palace guards of Manipur.

JASUMATI, LADY OF SATPAM: Mother of Princess Sanatombi and Princess Khomdonsana. She is one of the queens of Maharaja Surchandra.

JILASANA, PRINCE: Uncle of Princess Sanatombi; youngest son of Maharaja Chandrakirti.

JUNIOR SAHEB: Assistant Superintendent J.G. Dunlop, whose bungalow is burned in 1904, precipitating the Women's War of 1904.

KHEMA, SANASAM: Love of Mainu, the companion of Princess Sanatombi.

KHOMDONSANA, PRINCESS: Younger sister of Princess Sanatombi. Daughter of Maharaja Surchandra and Queen Jasumati, Lady of Satpam. Married to Arambam Meino.

KOIRENG, PRINCE: Uncle of Princess Sanatombi. Half-brother of Maharaja Surchandra. Also known as Bir Tikendrajit. He is executed in 1891 by the British after the Anglo-Manipuri War.

KOUSESWARI, ELDER LADY OF CHONGTHAM: Step-grandmother of Princess Sanatombi and fourth queen and first love of Maharaja Chandrakirti. She is the mother of Prince Koireng.

KULACHANDRA, MAHARAJA: Half-brother of Maharaja Surchandra and Prince Koireng. Reigns 1890–91 until he is deposed after Manipur's defeat in the Anglo-Manipuri War of 1891.

KUMUDINI, MAHARANI, LADY OF MEISNAM; GRAND QUEEN MOTHER: Great-grandmother of Princess Sanatombi. She was the powerful queen of Maharaja Gambhirsingh and the mother of Maharaja Chandrakirti.

LAMPHEL, CHANCELLOR: A powerful, young nobleman; son of General Thanggal.

LUKESWARI, YOUNGER LADY OF CHONGTHAM: Step-grandmother of Princess Sanatombi and third queen of Maharaja Chandrakirti; younger sister of the fourth queen, Kouseswari.

LUKHOI, PRINCE: Half-brother of Princess Sanatombi. Only son and heir of Maharaja Surchandra and his Queen Premamayi, the Lady of Ngangbam, later the Dowager Queen.

MAINU: Companion to Princess Sanatombi.

MANIKCHAND, NONGMAITHEM: Husband of Princess Sanatombi. A wealthy trader from a distinguished family.

MAXWELL, HENRY ST PATRICK, LT COLONEL, CSI: Arrives as Major; British Political Agent of Manipur. Consort of Princess Sanatombi. Serves in Manipur: 1891–92; 1894–96; 1898–1905.

MEINO, ARAMBAM: Brother-in-law of Princess Sanatombi; husband of her younger sister Princess Khomdonsana. Powerful official under both the monarchy and the British.

MERI, CHANCELLOR: Musician and love of Princess Phandengsana, aunt of Princess Sanatombi.

MOIRANG, KING OF: Father of Maharaja Churachand.

NARASINGH, MAHARAJA (REGENT 1833–43, REIGN 1843–49): Great-grandfather of Maharaja Churachand. War hero and cousin of Maharaja Gambhirsingh. As princes, the two expel the Burmese from Manipur in 1825 with the help of the British during the First Anglo-Burmese War.

NOT GUILTY: Orderly to Princess Sanatombi.

PREMAMAYI, MAHARANI, LADY OF NGANGBAM; DOWAGER QUEEN: Also called Leihao, she is the stepmother of Princess Sanatombi. She is the powerful Queen of Maharaja Surchandra and mother of their only son and heir Prince Lukhoi.

PAKASANA, PRINCE: Uncle of Princess Sanatombi. Younger blood-brother of Maharaja Surchandra and rival of Prince Koireng, his half-brother.

PHANDENGSANA, PRINCESS: Aunt of Princess Sanatombi; she is the daughter of Maharaja Chandrakirti.

PHEIJAO: Horse handler for Prince Pakasana. Later works for Maxwell.

SANATOMBI, PRINCESS: Consort of British Political Agent Maxwell. Married to Manikchand. Oldest child and daughter of Maharaja Surchandra. Favoured great-grandchild of the Grand Queen Mother. Cousin of Maharaja Churachand.

SURCHANDRA, MAHARAJA (1886–90): Father of Princess Sanatombi. Succeeds his father Maharaja Chandrakirti and is deposed in 1890 by his half-brothers led by Prince Koireng.

TEMBI: Maid of Princess Sanatombi.

THANGKOKPA, PRINCE: Son of Maharaja Debendra (r. 1850), the younger brother of Maharaja Narasingh. He is Princess Sanatombi's granduncle.

THANGGAL, GENERAL: Warrior in service to the monarchy after the expulsion of the Burmese in 1825. Executed along with Prince Koireng by the British in 1891. Father of Chancellor Lamphel.

TONJAO OF MOIRANG: Brother-in-law of Princess Sanatombi after he marries her younger half-sister. Nobleman and ally of Princess Sanatombi and her family.

HISTORY, FAMILY AND FICTION

A Note from the Translator

My mother Maharaj Kumari Binodini Devi, who wrote under the single sobriquet of Binodini, published her only novel, her Sahitya Akademi Award–winning magnum opus *The Princess and the Political Agent* in 1976. The historical novel is a love story of a Manipuri princess and a British officer of the Raj. It is set in fin de siècle Manipur. It spans the years before and after a watershed year when a palace insurrection precipitated the Anglo-Manipuri War of 1891. The dramatic backdrop of the love story is the loss of sovereignty as the Tibeto-Burman kingdom on the mountainous seam of South and South East Asia is annexed into the British Indian Empire. The title of Binodini's historical novel in the original Manipuri, or Meiteilon to use its endonym, is *Boro Saheb Ongbi Sanatombi*. It translates literally as 'Sanatombi, the Wife of the Big Saheb'. As Binodini wrote in her author's preface to the original edition, 'One big question was, why, when the British had just newly conquered Manipur and the pain of being subjugated was still raw, did the daughter of Surchandra become the wife of the enemy?' The enemy–husband here, one half in the romance, is Lt Colonel Henry St Patrick Maxwell, the first Political Agent of Manipur under British rule, who falls in love with Princess Sanatombi, the daughter of its deposed king, and takes her as his consort.

Now largely forgotten around the world, the Anglo-Manipuri War grabbed international headlines in 1891. A scandal of imperial avarice and colonialist policy, it sat on the front pages of the *London Illustrated Newspaper*, the *New York Times*, and the *Statesman* of Calcutta, to name but a few, for the better part of the year. A Reuters correspondent came to Manipur and flashed updates from the field around the world. Avid readers in Australia, New Zealand, Singapore and France followed the events as they unfolded.

The Princess and the Political Agent therefore uncovers a lost chapter in the history of the British Raj—a diplomatic storm that had pitted Empress Victoria against Viceroy Lansdowne, imperialists against nationalists, empire versus kingdom, and had been hotly debated in the British Parliament. But it does so through characters, historical and fictional, high and low, that Binodini brings to life, telling her story through the eyes of the defeated and through their loves and sorrows at home and in the palace.

Binodini's own father, Maharaja Churachand, a cousin of Princess Sanatombi, was installed by the British in 1891 as the king of Manipur. The fatherless boy-king was promptly packed off by Maxwell to boarding school at Mayo College in distant desert Rajasthan, the Eton of the East as it used to be known. The India-born Scotsman, in Binodini's novel, assumes a quasi-parental role in grooming her father into a modern king.

With her own father as a major character in the novel, *The Princess and the Political Agent* was a very personal book for

Binodini. Growing up in privilege in the palace as a princess herself, Binodini veered into leftist ideology in college in Shillong, then further broadened her horizons as a humanist and artist as a student at the art school in Rabindranath Tagore's Santiniketan. Her writings until *The Princess and the Political Agent*—short stories, plays, essays and lyrics—were about ordinary folk. Her novel took Manipur by storm upon its publication. A part of the reason was that her own relatives frowned upon her airing a family scandal long-thought buried. But it was also because it evoked for the first time, and in painterly detail, an insider's portrait of the vanished splendour of Manipur of a bygone age. Moreover, it was about 1891, a date that still stings Manipuris today as the year when the kingdom lost its sovereignty and, with it, its identity.

For all the story's foundation in Manipur's history and its author's deep first-hand knowledge of the milieu and mores of its courtly culture, Binodini was clearly emphatic in her original author's preface that *The Princess and the Political Agent* 'is not biography, it is not history', but a work of fiction. Binodini's most important historical source was the court chronicle of Manipur. She wrote, 'Someone had said to me that this was a book of record, and that I would not get much material from it for the story. But for me, if the chronicle had not existed, this book would not have been possible.'

Binodini gleaned incidents and characters from the most fleeting of records in the court chronicle and other documents. She melded them with family lore and memory to fictionalize the palace and social realities in her story. Only Binodini knew precisely—and was careful not to divulge—which parts of her novel were from these sources, oral or text, and which were the creation of her imagination.

The essential framework of the novel is a flashback, or rather, a series of flashbacks, that come back time and again to the setting of her opening chapter right to the very end. The story of Sanatombi and Maxwell slips in and out of two historical periods. The first is the period of early alliance with the British after the First Anglo-Burmese War of 1825. The second, and more pivotal to the novel, is the reign of her grandfather and her father in the second half of the nineteenth century. This was the era of amicable Anglo-Manipuri relations that ended with the disastrous war and British victory in 1891.

In brushing in historical and political character to her portrait of Sanatombi, Binodini forefronts two major women characters. Sanatombi's wilful childhood and youth centre around Binodini's portrayal of the formidable Grand Queen Mother, a boldfaced presence in Manipur's court chronicle like no other queen. A second remarkable woman, the deposed Dowager Queen, one of several queens Binodini rescues from the mists of history, unpacks the internal intrigues of the palace and Anglo-Manipuri politics around 1891. In Binodini's hands, the former also becomes the key to Sanatombi maturing into an astute and political young woman.

The kings of Manipur were allowed multiple queens. Polygamy was common in Manipur, a practice no doubt further boosted by the loss of men during the seven-year occupation of the kingdom by the Burmese from 1819 to 1825. Women are allowed to remarry through a ritual of social recognition called *loukhatpa* that did not involve a formal marriage. Women in relations with married British men, who often left their wives and families back in Britain as Maxwell did, were called native wives during the Raj. But in Manipur, and in accordance with local custom, women in loukhatpa relations are recognized simply and fully as wives. Hence, Binodini's reference to Sanatombi as Maxwell's wife in the Manipuri title of her novel.

Binodini is an entertaining yet exacting writer. Her prose demands a response from the reader, asking them to piece together the incidents she sometimes narrates in non-chronological order. Some of these foreshadow while others are under the pall of the present of the story. She requires the reader to hold on to these untimely fragments, for surely, she revisits them later to flesh out backstories, as in her tale of the love affair of Sanatombi's maid. This style also mimics memory and oral storytelling. It is from her mother Maharani Dhanamanjuri Devi, a great storyteller, that the young Binodini heard first-hand stories of Sanatombi. Those who knew Binodini will tell you that she was a captivating conversationalist with a talent for storytelling. The conversationalist shines through in her dialogue, a skill honed by her many radio plays. The storyteller, first observed in her award-winning short stories, also entertains readers of *The Princess and the Political Agent* with anecdotal asides that could almost stand on their own as discrete short stories.

Binodini was also a well-known essayist in Manipur. In her collection of late-life postmodernist essays *The Maharaja's Household: A Daughter's Memories of Her Father* (2008) we see Binodini as a self-reflexive writer, regularly prefacing her memories with qualifying phrases like 'I heard . . .' 'I remember . . .' 'She told me . . .' 'I seem to recall . . .' until she arrives at the conclusion that memory is an act of creation. A modernist and a literary stylist—and an admirer of Virginia Woolf—Binodini was an artist aware of the workings of the mind, her own included. She had once consulted, in the late 1950s, with her closest friend's husband Mrinal Barua in Calcutta, one of a handful of psychoanalysts in India then, about some mind-blanking episodes resulting from a creative block she was experiencing. Her observation of the human mind, coupled with her mining of memory, found further expression in discursive memory and stream-of-consciousness techniques in *The Princess and the Political Agent* in addition to the non-linear exposition of her narrative.

An artist who had studied painting and sculpture, Binodini also uses a range of graphic devices that become apparent upon reading the book. The original edition, which this translation uses, is peppered with little graphics—sketches of a hookah, an elephant procession, a cannon, or a dragon boat with rowers—to introduce unnumbered sections, chapterized in later editions. Furthermore, Binodini uses idiosyncratic punctuation and paragraph spacing as additional graphic literary devices. I remember working with my mother on her liberal use of ellipses in the first edition, not just at the end of sentences but also sometimes at the beginning. It is only now upon reading and rereading that it strikes me that these ellipses, along with her insertion of additional spacing between paragraphs on one hand, and the elimination of conventional line spacing on the other, were Binodini's means of exercising control over the reader's progression upon the page. They instil pauses, shifts in trains of thought, or beginnings of digressions. Binodini is a strong-willed narrator, and these graphic literary devices make for changes in dramatic rhythm, and, in turn, the pace of reading and comprehension. The pauses that they impose upon the reader create an almost palpable rhythmic breathing of the prose. I have tried to keep these devices intact to retain the effect of Binodini's purposeful layout of her narrative upon the printed page. I have also occasionally stretched her graphic gaps with new pages within chapters to denote the more significant time-shifts. I trust this will be helpful for the reader not privileged with an information bank of Manipuri history like the average Manipuri reader, while remaining true to the novel's literary style. For further help, at the suggestion of my editors at Penguin Random House India, I insert a historical timeline and a list of dramatis personae to guide the reader through the plethora of characters and historical incidents.

Many memories came to me as I translated my mother's novel. Reading it, I often delved into my own recollection of family lore—where and from whom Binodini has gathered and stitched together images, words and incidents to create the imaginative pastiche that brings her characters to life and propels her story. It has been a translation project I had been meaning to take up for many years now, punctuated at intervals by my mother's gentle nudging. Rarely did she allow translations or adaptations of her work, and in my youthful foolishness, I had always translated her short stories and screenplays more as a chore fulfilling a parental command. It is now, after her death, that I find myself approaching the translation with the passion I wish I had had the maturity to muster earlier.

I am indebted to my eldest cousin Ichema Thoidingjam Lakshmipriya Devi and my friend Aribam Shantimo Sharma for their hours of patient help. As the oldest grandchild of Maharaja Churachand, my Ichema was invaluable in advising me on the nuances of courtly speak and manners, and on details of traditional design and ritual. As she learnt Hindu

sacraments and slokas growing up with our grandmother
Maharani Dhanamanjuri, Ichema was also instrumental in the
translation of Vaishnav lyrics and prayers. My indebtedness
to her knows no bounds. For the timeline, cross-checking
with Manipuri and British historical sources, I am immensely
grateful to my cousin, the historian Wangam Somorjit. My
translation of rituals and songs of pre-Vaishnav Manipur and
their words in Aribalon, as old Manipuri is known, would not
have been possible without the help of my friends the archivist
and scholar Chanam Hemchandra, and the noted *pena* lute
balladeer Mayanglambam Mangangsana Meitei.

Farther afield, a bow of deep appreciation to Namita
Gokhale for encouraging me to embark upon this translation;
Manasi Subramaniam, Toonika Guha, Shreya Pandey and
Paloma Dutta, my editors at Penguin Random House India;
and to Nabarun Paul for keeping it all together administratively
and technically. Across the seas, from the other side of the
world in Washington's academe, Professor Bimbisar Irom
helped me plumb Binodini's literary style in the wider context
of world literature in translation. I note his second-generation
assistance with an inward chuckle as he is the son of Professor
I.R. Babu who was credited by my mother in her original
preface for finally getting her to sit down to write her novel.

It is their collective interest, support and expertise that
have made this translation of Binodini's *The Princess and
the Political Agent* possible, but all transgressions, errors and
shortcomings are mine, and mine alone.

L. Somi Roy

FOREWORD

I have wanted to write a book about Sanatombi since 1965. As I was thinking about it, Arambam Samarendra, the grandson of Surchandra's youngest daughter Princess Khomdonsana, showed me some photographs and so on of Sanatombi and Maxwell. Although this greatly inspired me, I could not take it up. As a writer used to short essays and lyrics, I lacked the courage to take up the story of such a large life. But I continued to do my research. I tried twice but failed, and I have been enduring the pain of the failure of my attempts all this time. After a long time one day, when I was talking to Dr I.R. Babu, he said to me, 'Do not be afraid, just write it.' From that day on 23 September 1975, I started to write my book *Boro Saheb Ongbi Sanatombi—The Princess and the Political Agent*.

Most of us take Sanatombi, the native wife of the Big Saheb, as legend. I had heard snippets of stories about her when I was little. I had also heard children sing as they played: 'Sanatombi, you are lost to us, you are lost to us.' I had thought it was a story of long ago but it turned out to be not that far back. Enormous help came from my mother Maharani Dhanamanjuri, the Lady of Ngangbam, when I was building the story of Sanatombi. She saw Sanatombi when was she was about to be taken to the palace: she and Maxwell ('Menjor Meksin') had come riding on horseback with Little Majesty to see her. This was a story she told with great pleasure. Sanatombi gave her a great amount of valuable jewellery. She often came to the palace after Maxwell had left but she never stepped inside. They kept a seat prepared separately for her. I asked my mother what she looked like. She replied, 'She was beautiful, that woman.'

I approached many elders in my attempt to tell this story. The fragments of stories they told me, about many small incidents, were of great help in grasping the face of an enormous life lived in an enormous world. I bow my head to them.

And the book I especially studied was the *Cheitharol Kumbaba*, the court chronicle. Someone had said to me that this was a book of record, and that I would not get much material from it for the story. But for me, if the chronicle had not existed, this book would not have been possible. For instance, the chronicle says briefly: 'On that day the Saheb took his wife Sanatombi and went to Lamangdong to eat fish', and so on… . The Brahmin Baladeb told me, '"Meksin Saheb" had said he would build a house in Lamangdong.' [Binodini links these two disparate sources to construct her chapter on Maxwell's plans to build his retirement home—*Translator*.]

One big question was why, when the British had just newly conquered Manipur and the pain of being subjugated was still raw, did the daughter of Surchandra become the wife of the enemy? I searched for the answer to this question, and it became *The Princess and the Political Agent*. Brought up in privilege found only in fairy tales, Sanatombi faced the censure of her own blood relatives. I have taken up a task well beyond my ability but I have tried to depict a Sanatombi who belonged to a world of alien ways, who had lived during a time of great change in Manipur's history. This book is built on the foundations of history. I have tried to fill in, as I wished, within the foundational frame of unmovable events. I have taken as much liberty as the conventions of writing a novel allows. With dates that were not very far apart, I have moved these episodes around a bit. I have mentioned all the actual historical figures in the book with respect. In doing this, I have had no thought of mentioning them with any disrespect or depicting them wrongly. Only conventions of fiction have given them a different face. This book is not biography, it is not history, and this I trust the readers will grant me.

This book may not have been possible without the help of *Tada* Ningthoukhongjam Khelchandra. What I asked for was little, what he told me was vast. I owe immense gratitude to Tada. After the printing of the book had started, Mr Takhellambam Prafullo showed me two letters written by Maxwell and Sanatombi. I also owe a debt of gratitude to Mr Prafulla.

Elders Who Helped in the Research

Lairikyengbam Gulap Mohori, Sorokhaibam Thambou, Lairikyengbam Tombi, Nongmaithem Thanil, Lourembam Ongbi Ibemhal, Thourani Kumari Achoubi, Thangjam Oja Chaoba, Hijam Ibungohal, Ngangbam Shyamkishore, Pundit Baladeb Sharma, Sanasam Gourahari, Meitram Bira, Akham Surendra, Oja Lokeshwar, Huidrom Ongbi Maharaj Kumari Angousana, Elangbam Ongbi Sanahanbi, Sorokhaibam Ongbi Thamballaka.

Assistance

Pundit Ngariyambam Kulachandra, Dr Chandramani, Asangbam Minaketan, Rajkumar Jhalajit, Rajkumar Sanahal, Syam Sharma, Takhellambam Prafullo, Khumallambam Rasbihari, Arambam Ongbi Jamini.

The author is indebted to them all.

Binodini, 1976

CHAPTER 1

'Mainu,' the ailing woman calls very weakly.

'Your Highness.' Mainu is seated at her feet.

'Is it today that Little Majesty is coming?'

'No, my lady.'

'What happened to today?'

'Today is the Day of Bor. Your royal little cousin will not be able to grace us. It is tomorrow that he is honouring us, along with the doctor.'

'Oh, it's Bor today. ... ... So today is Bor, Mainu.'

'Your Highness.'

The ailing woman closes her eyes. She is very weak from her long illness. She is greatly reduced but still beautiful—even today there are traces of her loveliness of the past. She is in the master bedroom of an elegantly built house covered with tin roofing. The house itself is Meitei but the room cannot really be said to be truly Meitei. The ailing woman is lying on a bed made of brass. Burnished with metal polish, it gleams like gold. There is not a blemish or stain. Near the bed is placed a small table. On it are a smallish clock, some vials of medicine, a measuring glass, and the like. A meticulously woven rattan mat covers the entire floor. On it, a Kashmiri carpet of floral design. Two small chairs

covered in red velvet, ornately decorated contemporary of
the period, and right next to them is placed a large reed stool
of Meitei make. That too is covered with a folded spread
bordered with velvet. The velvet slippers placed in front of
the bed are new, with little sign of wear; they are perhaps
put there as adornment. There are two photographs on the
wall. One, of a woman. A beauty in an embroidered sarong,
wearing a full-sleeved blouse of laced crêpe and wrapped
in a stole with edging of gold. Next to it, a photograph of a
middle-aged foreigner. The frames of the two photographs
are not like from around here. It is not the craftsmanship
of these lands. The two photographs are of the exact same
size. One is of Sovereign Surchandra's daughter, born of
Jasumati, Maid of Satpam—Sanatombi. The other is of
Major Maxwell, Manipur's, conquered Manipur's, first
Political Agent—'Major "Mesin" Saheb'.

Her Highness Sanatombi is ill. The diagnosis of
her ailment is not known. The doctors and healers may
know. People do not talk much about the condition of the
indisposed woman. They go about silently, each to their
duties, about their work.

The moment Her Highness Sanatombi took ill, her younger
cousin Little Majesty had sent down a healer from the
palace to attend to her care. Two servants stay overnight.
Meals are prepared by Mainu. Not just for her meals, Mainu
is everything to Sanatombi. Mainu is lovely and slender,
with a smallish face. One can see she is not a superficial
scab of a person. She comes across as a woman of her
word, a clear-thinking woman. Both servants seem to be
over thirty.

It must have been about nine in the morning.

Mainu calls softly, 'Your Highness.'
'Hm?'
'Shall I bring your breakfast?'
'What shall I eat?'
'Let us have two pieces of toast and some milk.'
'All right. … … … Mainu, a little later… .'

Sanatombi closes her eyes. Mainu looks at her intently. Tears come to Mainu's eyes. She remembers, no, not remember, she sees before her eyes—the veranda at the back of the bungalow. Many flowers from foreign lands border the green lawn before her eyes—red upon red, white upon white, cluster after cluster. She remembers the many occasions when the Saheb had breakfast with the princess. Bearers scurry around briskly, carrying back and forth many dishes from Western lands. The Saheb eats two half-boiled eggs without fail. For Sanatombi, an omelette. Sanatombi can only eat omelette and cannot eat any other preparation of eggs.

The Saheb teases Mainu now and then, 'Mainu, have some. Try, eggs are good for health.'
   The Saheb has learnt Meiteilon pretty well. He could speak it, one can say, but he could never get rid of his accent. Mainu laughs at his inflections; Mainu laughs with embarrassment at his teasing.
   'No, Brahmin, it is not unclean. Mainu, food is food.'
   Mainu runs out in embarrassment without answering.

The beauty of Sanatombi that day was beyond words. She is attired in a limply draping monochrome royal sarong of black and white with a *hijam* design. On top, a housecoat of *muga* silk in robin's egg, worn a little loosely. She wears no stole. Her long hair scatters as it falls. From it a whiff of fragrance from her herbal hair wash the day before, from the *ching'hi* wash Mainu had prepared. Drinking the milk Mainu has handed him, the Saheb asks, 'Mainu, what good is ching'hi?'

'No *pok*, Saheb.'

'Pok?'

'Pok is white hair. If you use it, you won't get it either.'

'No hope. Mine is already grey—whatever remains of it, that is. I have no hair, no pok.' How they laugh. Mainu is very formal with the Saheb, and knowing that, the Saheb tries to break the formality by teasing her. One day he also says, 'Did you see the young man who came to dinner last night, Mainu?'

'No, I did not.'

'The handsome young man, did you not see him, that captain from Assam Rifles?'

'I am afraid I did not see him, Saheb.'

'What a shame! He likes you. He wants to marry you. He wants you.'

'Oh my!' She rushes out, thinking, 'How naughty this man is.'

It was a time when Mainu as well as Sanatombi were very young. Today, the memories sadden Mainu; she feels like crying.

'Mainu,' the call comes again.

'May I bring it now?'

'What?'

'Breakfast.'

'I am not going to eat. ... ... Oh, so today is Bor?'

Today is Bor.

The message had gone out four or five days ago to the homes of the married princesses and their daughters. Who is going to the Bor, who will ride elephants, and who in palanquins? Elephants were sent to the houses of those who wished to ride an elephant, and palanquin bearers to the homes of those who wished to ride in a palanquin. The princesses are setting out on Bor to pray. It is on the road to Hiyangthang. Crowds line the road on either side. Everyone wants to watch whenever the palace puts on a show. What with the beauty of the princesses and the beauty of their ladies-in-waiting and all.

It is during the royal reign of Sovereign Chandrakirti. His royal daughters come to the palace for every festival, noisily, happily. The princesses fill the quarters of the Grand Queen Mother—Princess Tharaksana, Princess Makhaosana, Princess Amusana, Princess Phandengsana, Princess Thadoi, Princess Maipakpi … … … As well as the many princesses and ladies of the lineage of Maharaja Narasingh.

Today is Bor. The princess daughters of the kings go in a procession on the road to Hiyangthang—on elephants, in palanquins.

Earrings swayed on the ears of Princess Amusana.

'Her gold earrings are not even that dangly—she is making them sway on purpose,' says an onlooker at the spectacle.

'Be quiet—they might hear you.'

'Princess Maipakpi is the most beautiful of all to me—how simple she is! She does not even let her ponytail down from her chignon.'

'Oh please. She is not being simple; she is being stylish. … … … Oh my, do you think she heard me; she is looking our way!'

'Auntie, is that the one called Princess Thabalsana? She is fair for sure but she is without an ounce of charm, I tell you.'

'Be quiet; you talk too much. There will be trouble if someone overhears you.'

'Oh my, aren't we allowed to say that?'

They talk among themselves, one to another.

Today is also Bor.

Sanatombi will not see Little Majesty today.

'Did you see the car with the flag back then? Upon the gods, how undignified.'

'Ride a brace of elephants, I say. How times have changed, my dear. How dignified is it for the king to come to Bor in a car?'

'My dear woman, it hurts his tailbone to ride an elephant, they say.'

Yes, Little Majesty will not come today to inquire about his older cousin. He is busy. Word had come that he will visit tomorrow. But Sanatombi believes—He is still a child, so who knows, he might just drop in.

'Mainu, lay out the royal seat in its proper place. Who knows, his Little Majesty may drop by.' She closes her eyes.

'Your royal cousin is not coming today. But I have made Matum the bearer wait for him outside.'

Boom boom boom. ... ... The sound of cannons. It is the sound of cannons being fired at the new palace in Khurai Khundon.

Sanatombi is startled. 'What was that?'

'It is nothing, just the sound of cannons from the royal palace.'

'Kangla ... Sovereign Father! Go call the royal son-in-law, Mainu! Run, tell Uncle Pakasana ... ... Go run. ... ...' raves the delirious woman, agitated.

It seems she thought the foreigners were firing cannons at them.

Sanatombi saw Manipur's last war first-hand. She witnessed as a young child the bitter rivalries of the princes, their quarrels, the entanglements of politics. She had seen it all: the fears, the sorrows, the consultations, the talks.

And there were many internal matters of the palace. She saw the splendid throne her grandfather his lordship Chandrakirti sat on for thirty-six years. But she did not get to live in the palace for very long. She was given in marriage at a young age to a man called Manikchand from the Nongmaithem family. There was a reason for this.

One day the Grand Queen Mother summoned Jasumati, consort of her royal grandson Crown Prince Surchandra and said, 'My dear, keep a close eye on your daughter. She is wilful and is going to be a handful. It is not enough to be kind-hearted. It will not do to be an accommodating and accepting worm of a person. You do not have any male offspring. The astrologers also say your daughter is of strong birth. I want to find a good match for her and get her married. What do you think?'

'The Grand Queen Mother needs only to instruct us. What can your humble servant say? After you inform your royal grandson, I defer to whatever the Divine Majesty and the Grand Queen Mother decide,' replied the meek Lady of Satpam.

Jasumati was a gentle woman. No one in the palace talked about her much. She may have had her disappointments and sorrows but she expressed them to no one. Most people in the palace did not even know of her existence. Her senior sister-wife Premamayi, Lady of Ngangbam, dominated all. Even though Premamayi was not the first wife of Surchandra, she overshadowed all—and so it must be. It was only to be expected that the clever rises above the many. It might be said that Jasumati merely gave birth to her daughter, for Sanatombi spent most of her time with her co-mother the Lady of Ngangbam, and the Grand Queen Mother. She only came home to sleep and her mother barely got to see her at all. She spent her days going from one household in the palace to another. Jasumati worried about her too. She knew her daughter was unruly, strong-willed and driven to win. It would have been better if she had been a boy, she thought to herself. Time and again Sanatombi would cause an uproar and stir up trouble. Even when as a mother she could not bear it any longer she could not beat Sanatombi or discipline her, for the Grand Queen Mother stood as her bulwark. The Grand Queen Mother, Lady of Meisnam, doted excessively on her great-grandchild. And then she says—Watch your daughter closely, when it is she who allows her to run wild . . . —but who could she have said this to? There was no one who could dare to talk back to the Grand Queen Mother, the Lady of Meisnam. So, even though she followed all palace protocol with great care, she suffered defeat at the hands of Sanatombi; she weakened when it came to her. Her great-grandmother favoured the unruly Sanatombi.

One day when Sanatombi had grown up a bit, she said, 'I will play *kang*, Grand Queen Mother.' 'Of course, my grandchild shall play. And who will be the kang teams?' The Grand Queen Mother arranged it all. The court shuffleboard teams were Hijam Leikai and the palace. They gathered only the prettiest girls among them, both the palace and Hijam Leikai. They established many rules—no borrowing of pucks, no throwing of pucks in the air, and suchlike. The shuffleboard court was polished with fresh milk. There was a lot of noisy activity. Sanatombi was going to play her first game of court shuffleboard at the palace. But as the sorry tale unspooled, Sanatombi came to her royal great-grandmother, her face red with fury, and demanded, 'Grand Queen Mother, beat Lukhoi. He has stopped us from playing kang, he says we cannot play.'

A little while later, there was a great hue and cry. 'Sanatombi has bitten Prince Lukhoi! Oh no, what is to be done!'

The matter was this. Prince Lukhoi had barred Sanatombi when she arrived to play at the shuffleboard court. Lukhoi was born to the Lady of Ngangbam, wife of Surchandra. The Lady of Ngangbam was not only clever but she had even produced a male offspring, and one day, sooner or later, Lukhoi could ascend the throne at Kangla. Even though he was a child, Lukhoi was well aware of this. His unthinking caregivers and attendants never failed to remind the child of it, and so he was very headstrong. He and Sanatombi were not that far apart in age.

He had come in while Sanatombi and her friends were noisily busy in the shuffleboard court and said, 'Is it true you all are going to play kang, Royal Elder Sister? You may not play.'

'Why not?'

'Because I am telling you. You cannot.'

'And who are you? Should I stop just because you do not allow it? It is none of your business. I am doing it. What are you going to do about it?'

'You cannot do as you like.'

'And why not?'

'I am Prince Lukhoi.'

'And I am Sanatombi.'

'I am the male offspring—you are female.'

'What attitude, Mr Male Offspring!'

Sanatombi flared up in anger. It was true she was a daughter. A daughter had no claim upon the throne at Kangla. But she did not accept this; she did not accept being told she could not do as she wanted. She did not know that her mother who only had daughters was not considered a blessed woman. It was especially true in the palace. How was she any different from a barren woman? Her birth mother lived choked in secret, her throat constricted, dry. It was not as if Sanatombi had not sometimes heard her mother heave a deep sigh. But she never found out why. The Grand Queen Mother had never once said to her face, 'You are a female; you are of inferior destiny.' She had said, 'Now, there's my great-granddaughter, now that's my great-granddaughter.' But sometimes late at night, her mother Jasumati said to her quietly, 'Sanatombi, you are a daughter, so conduct yourself with that knowledge … … … .' What was it she said? Sanatombi, her thoughts wandering somewhere else, paid her scant heed. Lukhoi not allowing her to play court shuffleboard enraged Sanatombi no end.

Sanatombi said, 'So what if you are a male?'

'I am stopping you from playing kang, that's what,' Lukhoi answered with attitude. He was also just a boy at the time. It was around that age just before youth when boys are at their most obnoxious.

Sanatombi said, 'What is it that you want?'

'Let Hijam Ibemhal play on the palace team.'

'Oh really? The one from Hijam Leikai?'

'Even so.'

'Oh, is that why you are coming and sticking your nose in?'

'Why did you go to Grand Queen Mother without telling me first you were playing kang?'

'Meaning?'

'You have to inform me first—I was going to rehearse my dance here. If you want to play kang here, you have to inform me first.'

'Your dancing goes on in the women dancers' court. Has this male offspring no shame, being in the women dancers' court?'

'Men should be part of the women dancers' court. You cannot play kang, and that is that.' Saying this, he plunked himself down cross-legged in the middle of the shuffleboard court. Smoothened and polished for many days beforehand, the shuffleboard court shone like a mirror. It was not to be stepped upon. Sanatombi could not bear it any longer. She leapt at him and grabbed his hair. The two fought, they could not be pulled apart.

Suddenly Lukhoi yelled, 'She bit me! The witch, the witch!'

Sanatombi went off to tell the Grand Queen Mother. Lukhoi was left crying, yelling 'She-Demon, She-Demon' at her. 'She-Demon' was Sanatombi's hated nickname.

All hurried towards the quarters of the Grand Queen Mother. Sanatombi's mother, the Lady of Satpam, heard and came running. She lashed out at her child and hit her. She struck out at her wildly. Sanatombi did not cry. She stood rock-still. The others separated them. Hearing of this, Sanatombi's nurse came running and put her arms around her child.

Sanatombi said, 'Of course, I beat him up. Can he do as he pleases just because he's a male offspring? I will beat him, I will keep on beating him.'

'Look at the mouth on her.' Her mother tried to hit her again. The Grand Queen Mother tried to separate them. Then Sanatombi went and stood by the Grand Queen Mother, watching. She was very pleased with herself.

Lukhoi's mother, the Lady of Ngangbam, arrived.
Laughing, she said, 'Do not beat her, sister-wife. Why make a big thing of a matter between children?' Saying this, she examined her child's wounds. She did not mean what she said, for she was upset.

'Please do as you see fit, elder sister-wife. I am not going to be able to handle this girl. Look how she has bitten the child on his arm … Here, let Mother take a look.'

The Lady of Ngangbam laughed and said, 'Of course you should beat him, my child. How can he be disrespectful to his older royal sister? Lukhoi, say you are sorry to your older sister. Why did you try to destroy my daughter's kang court? What right does a boy have to do that.' She pretended to blame her son.

'Why should I kowtow when I did no wrong?'
'How he lies and says he did no wrong!'

They went at each other again. The Lady of Ngangbam stopped them, laughing. They made light of the matter but both the Lady of Ngangbam and the Lady of Satpam each knew what the other was thinking.

There were countless incidents and uproars like this because of Sanatombi. The girl-bearing Jasumati conducted herself with great discretion. But male offspring or female did not matter to Sanatombi. She did as she pleased. Controlling her was a major headache for Jasumati.

She lived with palpitations on her daughter's account.

It was a time when the princes of Kangleipak, the sovereign kingdom of Manipur, held complete sway. But there were also restraints that bound them. They could not do completely as they pleased because they were royalty—What will people say? In addition to that, the daughters had to be even more careful. And the all-powerful Lady of Meisnam still lived. But it was not as if at times some did not breach these walls and broke free.

Many princesses grew up under Chandrakirti. They were not all alike, one to another, but they all were always made to remember that they were not like the common people. Sanatombi had grown up among these royal aunts of hers. She was also adored by her aunts who let her do whatever she liked. How was Jasumati to discipline her under these circumstances?

One day a man offered a tribute to the Divine Majesty Chandrakirti of a type of fruit called a Java plum. A seedling he had brought with great difficulty from Nabadwip and planted in his yard had borne fruit this year and he had come running to the king to offer it at his feet. The king sent a few of the fruits to the homes of each of the married princesses. The rest, he called his daughters who were still in the palace and handed it out among them.

'What kind of fruit is it, Sovereign Father?' They looked at it in wonder, but were afraid to eat it. 'Just try it, it won't hurt you,' he said with a laugh. While they hesitated, Sanatombi grabbed one and stuffed it into her mouth. 'Mm nice.' 'Only my granddaughter has guts. Your aunts will amount to nothing.' The princesses laughed together loudly in the royal presence over this incident of eating the Java plum. Her aunt Princess Amusana laughed the most, more than the rest. How pretty she was and what a handful she was. Keeping Amusana in check was indeed a problem.

The Lady of Meisnam said, 'Who are these women laughing in the residence of the king?'
      Word came back promptly. 'Your royal granddaughters.'
      'Go call them.'
      They shuffled in.

No one looked forward to a summons from the Grand Queen Mother. She was no ordinary queen mother, she was the formidable Lady of Meisnam, Queen of Gambhirsingh. She had been his mainstay. Since the Seven Years Devastation, she had seen a great many wars in Manipur. She had been part of disentangling many a knotty political problem. Consolidating the throne of her husband, securing the position of her small child Chandrakirti, and on top of all that, never shying from many a fearsome incident, the Lady of Meisnam had always jumped into the fray. Such was the Lady of Meisnam. Even now, when the reign of her son was firm, she occupied an important place in Kangleipak, the kingdom of Manipur. The Lady of Meisnam held that the palace must maintain a distinctive and different image. It would not do to hold the reins too tight, nor let them too loose. We must be loved, and we must be feared. She reminded her son the king of this constantly.

… … … The princesses were in the flower hall of Lord
Govindaji threading garlands with the Grand Queen Mother.
Their hair was tied down tightly, chinstraps worn, there was
no talking. As they were threading garlands in this manner,
the Grand Queen Mother came upon a leech among the white
blossomed *kuthap* leaves.

She asked, 'Who gathered these flowers?'

The flower gatherers shook with fear.

'Head Priest, put this leech in iron chains immediately
and exile it to Sugnu.'

This absurd command was not aimed at the temple priest,
the punishment was not for the leech—it was aimed at the
attendants who picked the flowers carelessly. This, then, was
the Lady of Meisnam.

… … … Once a poster was put up in the Sana Keithel, the royal market. Women must not wear their clothes loosely; There will be no entering the quarters of the Indian monks to seek their good offices: This is a royal decree of the Divine Majesty. … Who was behind this decree and ordered it? The Lady of Meisnam.

Therefore, when a person such as the Lady of Meisnam summoned, it was never cause for cheer.

Little Sanatombi marched in at the head of the group of cowed princesses. She did not care a whit.

The Grand Queen Mother asked, 'Who was it who screeched and laughed in front of the king?'

There was no answer.

'Who were those who laughed in his royal presence?'

Sanatombi said, 'Aunt Amusana.'

Princess Amusana glared at Sanatombi. If the Lady of Meisnam had not been there, Sanatombi would surely have gotten a hiding.

'Shameless one. Is it proper for a grown maiden to laugh and screech like that, even if he is your father? What would people there have said? Shall I rip the bangs off your forehead by their roots? Never do that again. He may be your father, but he is the king.'

Chandrakirti had several wives—the Queen, the Elder Apambi, the Younger Apambi, the Elder Leimakhubi, the Younger Leimakhubi, and so on … but they were mere shadows under the bright intensity of Queen Mother Kumudini, Lady of Meisnam. The Queen Mother was his pillar of support, and though he was the king of the land and blazed upon the throne, none of his wives had the power to raise their head.

It was not an easy task to navigate among the rivalrous lineage of kings, amidst the frequent wars among the princes. The Lady of Meisnam was a woman who had faced battles, their heat and their flames. It was not that she had not witnessed generosity and decorum among the princes even at the bleakest of times in Manipur, but Manipur was a land that was never completely out of danger. One could never sit back and slacken, thinking that the throne of the land of the Meiteis was free of the barbs of enemies. The Lady of Meisnam regularly reminded her royal son of this.

The lord chieftain of Yaiskul was held in great favour by Chandrakirti. If he did not see him for a bit, he would ask, 'Has not my younger brother been coming?' If he did not attend the royal court for a while, he would dispatch emissaries to his royal homestead and send for him. Those who were close to Chandrakirti began to resent the close friendship between the two men. But they could not say it out loud, it was the favour of the king.

Quietly, they whispered among themselves: 'It is not right for the Divine Majesty to do this. Perhaps he has forgotten who the lord chieftain of Yaiskul is; it is not wise to trust him too much … … … .'

The princes in particular could not bear to see this. Obliquely they hinted and let it be known to the chieftain of Yaiskul—We do not approve of you.

One day, a prince approached the Grand Queen Mother. 'Sovereign Father favours our uncle the chieftain of Yaiskul a little excessively. He should not be trusted too much. Would the Grand Queen Mother please bring the matter up? It is not our place to say so.'

The Lady of Meisnam thought.

'My Chandrakirti is not that shallow a person. There must be something he must be thinking. Fine, I will talk to him one of these days.'

'But even we have come to disapprove of what is going on. He was walking with our Sovereign Father with his arms around his shoulders the other day. This is a breach of decorum, and it is not a good thing to see. He will surely one day climb all over him … … … .'

'Hm, it does look like he is crossing some boundaries to me too. All right, I will think about it.'

It was not that his lordship the chieftain of Yaiskul was not aware that people disapproved of him. He knew that. And so, he stayed away as much as possible but the Divine Majesty always summoned him.

One day he said, 'Your Majesty, please permit your servant to take leave from your royal service for some time.'

'Has anybody been saying anything to my younger cousin?'

'No one has said anything but it seems it is not right to come too frequently to be at your royal service.'

'Tell me, what is the matter.'

'I realize that the royal princes do not trust me,' said the chieftain of Yaiskul emotionally.

'They are all very young and must be being possessive of me. There is no need to take the words of the young to heart,' appeased the king.

The envy and enmity escalated. The princes gathered information on the quiet—Are people meeting at the chieftain of Yaiskul's? Is he hosting them? How many guns do they have? Are they training for battle?

Borachaoba, the chieftain of Yaiskul, knew very well that spies were being kept to monitor him closely. He was furious and he swore he would not set foot in the palace after informing the king. Bowing, he said, 'I swear at your royal feet, I have not done anything against Your Royal Majesty, and I never will. I shall not be coming to the palace from this day on.'

'Has someone said something to you again?'

'There are people who suspect that I am plotting for the throne. I swear upon Lord Govinda, I do not harbour thoughts of harming a single hair on your body. Until Your Majesty dies … … …' He stopped suddenly.

The king pretended not to notice. Laughing, he made light of it. He instructed one of his junior staff, 'My younger brother here and I will lunch together today.'

But the seeds of discord had been sown and could not be undone. Chandrakirti also did not forget the incident when a man called Nobin had attacked his uncle Narasingh and the father of Borachaoba the chieftain of Yaiskul, in front of Lord Brinamchandra. It seems just like yesterday. Whose plot had that been way back? The beloved, the esteemed Lady of Meisnam, mother of Chandrakirti, was the suspect at the time.

The word spread—'The chieftain of Yaiskul wept in the front of His Majesty, and vowed he would never do anything to harm the king.'

But the Grand Queen Mother, Lady of Meisnam, shook her head. She was thinking something.

The chieftain of Yaiskul also shook his head, thinking, 'It is not going to be as simple as before.'

Sanatombi grew up in this vast, splendid, cultivated prison. She was fortunate to have had such a powerful great-grandmother. There was no other grandchild who could climb up and lie on her grandmother's bed but Sanatombi. Sanatombi forced her to tell her stories. So many stories. The Seven Years Devastation, the Burmese War, stories of Cachar ... ... Many were the afternoons when she would fall asleep holding her great-grandmother while listening to these stories. After she had fallen asleep, her royal nurse would carry her on her back to the residence of her father Crown Prince Surchandra.

CHAPTER 2

The reign of Sovereign Chandrakirti, Little Protector of the Hills and Skies, was stable and Manipur scaled new peaks of accomplishment. Standing by the king were his royal father-in-law the Major of Meisnam, Thanggal, Sougaijamba, and other wise and strong noblemen. And towering above them all, the Grand Queen Mother, Lady of Meisnam. But there was no peace within the household. The resentments among brothers born of different mothers, and the many indiscretions and scandals of wayward daughters, though not known to the outside world, festered on many an occasion. Though born in such a milieu, none of this had any effect on Sanatombi. Like a fawn in the morning, she ran around, playing. She wandered into the rooms of her royal aunts. She was everybody's tasty little titbit.

The Angom clan came to pay their respects to the Grand
Queen Mother one day. They entreated the Grand Queen
Mother to grant them the hand of Princess Phandengsana,
daughter of the Lady of Chingsubam, to be their daughter-in-
law, for their son. The Grand Queen Mother said she would
relay their request to the king and let them know of his royal
wishes. But everybody knew that if the Grand Queen Mother
acquiesced, it was as good as the king's word; that it was just
a matter of her staying one step below in protocol. Sanatombi
saw the Angom clan arrive. She was there standing, holding
her nurse's hand. She ran immediately to her royal aunt
Princess Phandengsana.

Panting, she told her aunt, 'Royal Aunt, the Angom were
here. They brought so many, many, many gifts. Grand Queen
Mother has given you to the Angom. Wow! They brought so
much stuff … … … .'

Princess Phandengsana did not answer. Her face clouded
over.

Sanatombi went up to her. 'What's the matter, Royal
Aunt? What is it?'

Her aunt held her and said, 'Sanatombi.'

'What is it, Royal Aunt?'

'I am going to ask you to do something. Can you do it?'

'Yes, I can,' declared Sanatombi without even knowing
what it was.

'Can you go to Lord Govindaji for the evening prayers
with Sovereign Father later today?'

'Yes, of course. I go with him all the time. Sovereign
Grandfather never even scolds me.'

'Tell Grandpapa Khetri, the temple water bearer, then that I want to see him. Ask him to bring a banana leaf offering from Lord Govindaji.'

'Sure, I'll tell him.' She scampered off.

On another day, Princess Phandengsana was found in her room crying.

Sanatombi asked, 'Why are you crying, Royal Aunt?'

Upon hearing the child's words, her aunt broke out in sobs.

Sanatombi, too, began to cry loudly without understanding why. She lifted her aunt's wet bangs and wiped away her tears with her little hand.

Phandengsana said, 'See, I am not crying any more. Here, lift up your face. Sanatombi, can you do one more thing for your aunt?'

'Yes, I can.'

'Do you know who Chancellor Meri is?'

'Yes, the one who is in the *dhop* choir. Of course, I know him really, really well. He said he would teach me to sing, he said he would teach me how to play the *esraj*, he is so handsome, isn't he? Who is more handsome, Chancellor Lamphel or Chancellor Meri?'

'For your middle aunt, it is Chancellor Lamphel, for me, Chancellor Meri,' answered the maiden, laughing.

As Kondumba was among the elephants, so was Chancellor Lamphel among men—so it was said among the royal ladies.

Sanatombi heard them say so. She had remembered that and that was why she had asked.

She said, 'I don't like either of them.'

'I will find the handsomest, the most dignified man for you to marry,' her aunt joked.

'Shut up. How dirty. Why are you saying bad things?'

'I am only saying it because you brought it up. Look here, Sanatombi, what did I tell you before?'

'What?'

'Have you forgotten that I asked you to do something for me?'

'No, I did not forget. So, what is it?'

'You must not let anyone hear anything about it. If Grand Queen Mother hears of it, you and I both are dead.'

'If Grand Queen Mother asks I will not be able to not tell her. I am scared of hiding anything if Grand Queen Mother asks me.'

'She won't know anything, you little fool. Just you don't tell anyone.'

'So, say it then.'

'Go with Sovereign Father to Lord Govindaji like the other day and tell *Ta*'Meri, no, tell Grandpapa the temple water bearer something.'

'I can't do that. That hunchbacked temple water bearer makes fun of me.'

'What did he say to you?'

'He called me Princess Bride of God.'

'You should be happy, silly girl ... ... Bring temple offerings for mother Lady Thokchom—what's wrong with saying just that?'

'If you want, I will bring it for you. No problem.'

'No, children must not touch it. What if it touches your hands or feet? Just do as you are told. I will make you a doll.'

Sanatombi ran off happily.

Chancellor Meri was a son of the Chingakham clan. His real name was Tonjao, and his home, Yaiskul. The king favoured him greatly and called him '*Meri jan*', my heart, and so he came to be known as Meri. He was handsome, well groomed and a man extremely gifted in music. He was one of the many artists that Chandrakirti, well versed in music himself, had sent abroad to study drumming, singing and musical instruments.

Meri became famous as soon as he returned. People envied him. Those favoured by the king were not liked by their peers. But who could touch him—he was the king's own Meri. People were resentful that after being a courtier for not very long he was appointed a chancellor when the king sent him to the head the dancers' council. The teacher who had had this position was dismayed. Actually, Meri was sent there to take charge of only the music. But as he was so right for the job no one could oppose it openly. But Meri was not aware of all this. He hailed from Yaiskul so he should have been alert about the goings-on, but he failed to do so. He was engrossed in the world of music in the new temple that he had just joined. And there was one even bigger failing that he could not overcome. And this was his sin—he had fallen in love with Princess Phandengsana, and Princess Phandengsana loved him back. He had leaped over a divide and crossed a great threshold.

It became the talk of the land. The people who disliked him increased in number. True, they knew he was of the Chingakham clan, but knowing fully well that she was betrothed to the Angom, to knowingly. ... This was insolence, it was the conduct of one who was not brought up in the ways of the court. Just because he was good-looking and favoured by the king, should he be treading on the hem of the king's garment?

Unaware of all this, Sanatombi took messages back and forth from her aunt. One day, she was sitting in Meri's lap and watched the *ras* dance rehearsal. The spring ras dance. Her aunt Princess Phandengsana was the lead dancer. Meri sat behind the singers and played the esraj. Meri said many things to Sanatombi, things that she could not understand.

'Your royal aunt's rhythm is not very good, is it? She would improve if I could coach her just one time ... ...'

One day Sanatombi was stopped when she tried to enter her aunt's room. They told her she was very ill, that Sanatombi could not go in. Sanatombi was angry, she was close to tears—she knew her royal aunt was inside the room. She went angrily to the Grand Queen Mother's residence and lay face down on a small rug. She was waiting for her great-grandmother. After a little while, her great-grandmother arrived. She knew Sanatombi was angry. Something had to be the matter.

She stroked her great-granddaughter gently and said, 'Oh no, it seems the child has fallen asleep. She must not have heard me coming. Is anybody there? Call the royal nurse and have her carried back to her mother.'

'Who's asking you to have them take me back?' Sanatombi was near tears.

'So, tell me who did it?' Her great grand-mother drew the child to her.

'Don't touch me.' She burst into tears.

In this way, the great-grandmother and her great-granddaughter always coddled each other tenderly. People enjoyed watching this little show. After she had stopped crying, Sanatombi said, 'What is the matter with Royal Aunt Phandeng?'

'She is sick.'

'Why?'

'Just an ordinary sickness.'

'If it is an ordinary sickness why didn't they let me go in?'

'Oh, is that why my granddaughter is angry? Which uncouth peasant did not allow my granddaughter in? Why, she was only coming to inquire after her aunt's illness.'

'I did not come to visit my aunt. I was looking for you.'

'Then why didn't you just walk in? Who is going to stop a granddaughter from coming to her great-grandmother? What insolence. Tell me who it was.'

'Grandpapa Lusei.'

'Fine. I will deal with him. I will put lime and turmeric on his head and send him into exile, just watch.' The Grand Queen Mother soothed her great-granddaughter.

She called out, 'Tondonbi.'

'My lady.'

'Listen, you must not accept flowers given by other people, do you hear?'

'Why not, Grand Queen Mother?'

'Her aunt is ill because she accepted flowers given to her by somebody. The healer says an image of her heart has been captured and put on five *leihao* flowers.'

Sanatombi panicked. She was terrified.

One day as the evening prayers were coming to a close, Chancellor Meri said to Sanatombi, 'Your Highness, put out your hand—here, I'll give you something.' Sanatombi put out her little hand. Chancellor Meri gave her two *bera* sweets— bera made by the temple water bearer from Yaiskul. His bera was famous. Then he said, 'Here, look at this too.'

A posy of ginger lilies lay on three trimmed layers of banana leaf. A posy made with a pair of ginger lily buds that had been forced open a day before their flowering.

Sanatombi did not understand. She stood staring at Meri.

Meri hugged her and said, 'Look, this one you must not eat. Give it to your royal aunt. I will bring you bera from Yaiskul again tomorrow.'

Sanatombi had many aunts, but she knew the aunt Meri was asking her to give it to was Princess Phandengsana.

Today she was uneasy. Was her aunt sick because of the posy Meri had asked her to give to her aunt? No, that was a posy, not a leihao flower—the little girl thought to herself.

One or two days after this incident, she went to her great-grandmother's and found that the Grand Queen Mother had summoned all the queens and princesses of the palace and was talking to them.

She told them all to draw closer, and said, 'My granddaughters, my daughters-in-law, never wear flowers unless you pick them yourself. Not even flowers that bloom in the palace.'

Sanatombi said, 'Younger Royal Aunt wears a lot of flowers given by other people. She even grabs flowers off other people's ears and wears them.'

Amusana slapped Sanatombi. 'What a liar this child is.'

The Grand Queen Mother rebuked her, 'She only told what you do. Don't do that to the child.'

She summoned the temple keeper right away and asked, 'Keeper, who plucks the flowers for Lord Govindaji?'

'We have three servants, my lady,' replied the temple keeper, on his knees, his mouth covered. He wondered nervously what she would say next.

'Tell all the bearers, priests, ministers and followers of Lord Govinda that they are not to offer flowers brought by other people.'

'We do not do that from before, my lady.'

'Tell them again. … … … Now, go.'

Word began to spread that Chancellor Meri of the Chingakham clan had cast a spell on Princess Phandengsana the previous Saturday. Severe punishment was meted out. He was made to pray at all the temples. He was taken to the marketplace and paraded around the villages. Then he was tonsured in front of the palace citadel and spreadeagled in the sun upon a wooden frame.

But Princess Phandengsana did not hear of any of this. It was kept away from her. Stern orders were given that whosoever breathed a word of this to Princess Phandengsana would receive punishment far harsher than what Meri had received. Trusted royal women of the palace kept a close watch over her. Princess Phandengsana had entered a prison—for it was indeed a prison.

But the Lady of Thokchom wept secretly for her neighbourhood brother Meri.

It was a little excessive what they had done to Meri this time. People said the punishment given to the king's favoured Meri for falling in love with his daughter was a little too harsh. He could simply have been told to go away, or sent away. Meri himself was surprised—What did I do?

It was his ill fortune that Chandramukhi, daughter of the minister Thokchom, was the youngest wife of the king and was from his neighbourhood. This maid of Yaiskul had called Meri her 'brother' when she was still living at home, now elevated to a queen's birthplace. She was very young, the Lady of Thokchom. Several princesses were even older than her. Even though she was a consort of the king, she could not do as she pleased.

She was the king's youngest consort, but the Grand Queen Mother was still alive and several other heir-bearing consorts preceded her as well. She used to call Meri over and confide in him her many frustrations. She conferred with him. It was also at the royal residence of the Lady of Thokchom that Meri and Princess Phandengsana got to know each other.

Even though Meri was from her neighbourhood, it was really not proper for him to go to the Lady of Thokchom so frequently. He should have been more careful. Meri, who was talented in music, was foolish when it came to these snares. He did not understand what it meant to conduct oneself with humility at the palace, nor gave it much thought. His frequent visits began to be whispered about: 'Why is Meri visiting the Lady of Thokchom so often?'

It was a serious matter. It was a fearsome matter. But Meri had failed to realize this. He was besotted with Princess Phandengsana at the time. He was madly in love. He thought— What is wrong with love, who would be against such a thing!

An influential nobleman who liked him advised discretion, but Meri answered airily, 'But what is the problem, Uncle, as long as I do no wrong.'

'You will find yourself in the wrong, my son. I am telling you this. If this is come to be seen as treading on the king's garment, you will suffer ill fortune. I am telling you this because I am fond of you. When the time comes, you will not be able to say that you have done no wrong.'

'Why would I be in the wrong? Is it wrong to love a woman?'

'The woman you love is no common woman. She is the daughter of the king.'

'What are you saying, that the daughter of the king is not a woman?'

'How stubborn this boy is—don't start with this arrogance of your Yaiskul people. My words will come true tomorrow. If you think you are born of Yaiskul and decide not to listen, there is nothing I can do.'

It was true.

In those days, the courtiers from Yaiskul were disliked by other people. They were mocked as the arrogant, disrespectful people of Yaiskul. People said, 'They think they are doing the palace a favour by being courtiers.'

As Yaiskul folk related at great length, 'Actually, let us just say even the Divine Majesty Chandrakirti asks for his turban to be straightened when he is approaching Yaiskul … … … .'

The people of Yaiskul loved to tell this story no end. They repeated it over and over again to people they did not like. Gifted at embellishment, the people of Yaiskul lengthened the story every time they told it.

The people of Yaiskul said, 'Let us put it this way, even the Divine Majesty Chandrakirti is afraid of coming near Yaiskul. Have you not heard?'

'Yes, yes, we have all heard, man. The story about adjusting his turban, right? Yes, we have heard, we know, now shut up.'

What with being from Yaiskul, favoured by the king, and with his good looks and all, Meri had himself heard that he was disliked. But he was immersed in his music and did not pay it much mind. He was submerged in his music. He was in love with Princess Phandengsana. He thought of nothing else. Impatiently, he ran to the Lady of Thokchom and said, 'Please do something for me, Your Highness.'

'What is the matter?'

'I must see his royal daughter today. I have composed a new song. I have to let Her Highness hear it first … … … and then I will offer it to Lord Govinda. Please set it up for me.'

'You are going much too far. It won't be good for either of us if word gets out. You will die, and I will be sent packing home for sure.'

'I don't know anything about that. I have to let Her Royal Highness hear this song. ... ... I am kowtowing to you and touching your feet, please let me see her. I will never ask you again.'

In this way, Meri pestered the Lady of Thokchom many times beyond count. The Lady of Thokchom was annoyed, but seeing his face and his manner, she could not say no.

Meri emerged from the Lady of Thokchom's. He came across Chancellor Lamphel, standing in his way. He looked at him. He did not like that look. Lamphel asked, 'Where are you coming from? It is getting dark.'

'I had gone to convey a reply to a message the Lady of Thokchom had sent with me to her royal birthplace.'

'Are you telling me the Divine Majesty has not assigned a junior attendant to the Lady of Thokchom to run messages back and forth to her royal birthplace?'

'I do not know anything about that. It is also common practice to convey messages through people of the locality, Chancellor. Is there anything wrong with that?'

'The chancellor should know himself whether there is anything wrong or not. How would I know—nor is it my place to know.' Chancellor Lamphel's answer was barbed.

'If it is not for you to know, then it is better that you do not want to know.' With head held high, Meri brushed by Chancellor Lamphel.

General Thanggal's son Chancellor Lamphel was a prominent figure in the palace. He was a man useful to the king of the land. One day an argument between the two young men at the household security council escalated into a fight. Without considering whether it was appropriate or not, Lamphel said, 'Word of the chancellor loitering in the colonies of the royal ladies has reached the royal ears. It would behove you to proceed with care.'

'What loitering?'

'The Lady of Thokchom is the youngest wife of the Divine Majesty.'

'The Lady of Thokchom also happens to be my neighbourhood sister.'

'Even so, she has become the king's consort.'

'Even so, she is like my younger sister.'

'The chancellor has also driven the royal princess crazy.'

'And what about that is bothering you?'

'The chancellor is blind because you have the king's favour.'

'Is it my fault that His Majesty favours me?'

'Stepping on the hem of the king's garment will be your crime. ... If you wish to know the palace, it would do well to know the court etiquette of the palace.'

'If my love for Princess Phandengsana violates the etiquette of the court, so be it.'

'The palace is not like the neighbourhoods of commoners. It is not the practice in the palace to sit smoking a pipe beside a maiden's loom.'

'Is it the court practice in the palace to be disingenuous? I am not very good at faking it. And the courtier's ways that

say that the princess cannot be loved are not for me. I am also
of the Chingakham clan. Why does not the chancellor also try
his luck? Is Princess Phandengsana the only princess?'

'I am only saying it is not the court etiquette of the palace.'

'And what about with the gods in heaven above?'

'But the palace is not heaven above. It is a matter of court
etiquette. You were prematurely promoted to the rank of
chancellor and do not seem to have had the time to learn the
etiquette of courtiers.'

Meri laughed and replied, 'No, I did not get a chance
to learn the courtiers' ways that say one cannot love. If
someone like the chancellor had shown the way, it might
have been better.'

Their confrontation spiralled. People stepped in and
stopped them.

It was Meri's mistake to earn the enmity of Chancellor
Lamphel. He should not have challenged Lamphel. Meri
had not thought it through—he had been a fool. Chancellor
Lamphel was the scion of an illustrious and powerful family.
His father Thanggal had been in royal service since the reign
of Maharaja Gambhirsingh, Protector of the Hills and Skies.
He himself was also an up-and-coming nobleman.

And what of Meri? He was fortunate to get to know the king
on his own merit. It was not easy for him to rise up the ranks
in the palace. He did not have the power to gather allies in
the palace. Meri was a fool, he was merely a foolish singer of
songs. Coming up against Lamphel was like an egg coming
up against a rock. And it was also said, there was no royal lady
who was not infatuated with Lamphel.

But Meri was saying, 'Why do you tidy others' houses without tidying your own? Is good trumped by those with powerful allies?'

There was another murky stream running in the bowels of the palace. There were many stories, merging and flowing in the palace, that were widely known but not spoken about out loud. These stories had many holes, many exaggerations.

There was a story about Chancellor Lamphel that was whispered from ear to ear. It seems to have taken place before Meri had become a courtier in the palace. Meri heard it too—and so he had no respect for Lamphel and found it quietly amusing that he would instruct him about the etiquette of the palace. What he had heard was that a well-known married royal lady of the palace and Lamphel had fallen in love. Their affair intensified but they seemed to not care—for Lamphel was the son of Thanggal. Unable to tolerate this any longer, the woman's husband came to the palace one day. Upon seeing him enter, the Divine Majesty Chandrakirti sent everyone away and asked, 'What is it, my man?' It was as if the king knew what he was going to be asked. The walls have the ears of the king, as they say. The man said, 'Your Majesty, branches of the imperial sacred fig growing in the royal compound have overgrown—may your servant take care of it?'

'Hm. I have been thinking that too. You may prune the branches that you do not like. But do not chop it all down, he is of use to the land.'

But Meri should not have tussled with Lamphel. He was a man of great venom—a powerful man. Meri lived happily in his dreams of Princess Phandengsana. He was truly taken by surprise by the punishment he received for casting a spell on Princess Phandengsana. He realized when he woke up to reality that he had been a fool—it had been foolish to wrangle with someone who meant nothing to him.

Meri was punished for having loved. The punishment was thus—first his house was turned upside down and then he was taken prisoner. Utom, a son of the Narongbam clan, and Chaoba, a son of the Athokpam clan, were also imprisoned for having carried messages for him. He was spread out in the sun at Minuthong Bridge on Wednesday. At Nongpokthong Gate on Thursday, and on Friday, at his home in Moirangkhom. For having cast a love spell on the princess, Meri was taken to all the holy temple sites and made to pay obeisance. They made a wooden frame and spreadeagled Meri in the sun upon it in front of the palace citadel. Word was sent throughout the land and the public was made to look at Chancellor Meri who had loved, who had loved the daughter of the king. He had first encountered his punishment as he was coming from taking part in a debate at a forum on the finer points of melodic frameworks and modes. He had come out humming a melodic mode—and he had stumbled.

Meri was not seen in the palace any more after this—his name was expunged. There was only one person he was ashamed in front of upon his departure, and that was Chancellor Lamphel. And there were only two people he worried about— What would become of Princess Phandengsana! Would they implicate the Lady of Thokchom?

Sanatombi saw Chancellor Meri when he was spread out in the sun in front of the palace citadel. She held her nurse's hand and was among the onlookers. She could not bear to see Meri—she could not believe that the man in the loincloth

with the shaved head was Meri. She put her arms around her
nurse and hid her face, and said, 'Let's go, mother, I do not
want to see any more, let's go to the Grand Queen Mother.'
She burst into tears when she got to the Grand Queen Mother.
And she said, 'They are killing Ta'Meri ... ...'

She could not believe, she did not believe, that Meri had
cast a spell on her royal aunt Phandengsana. She remembered
many things. Her little mind whirled.

She did not understand why her aunt had hit her one day.

Princess Phandengsana had said, 'Sanatombi, can you go
the dancers' council for me?'

'Why not? I go there all the time. I go to watch Lukhoi
learn to dance.'

Lukhoi was little then and would go to the dancers'
council though he had not started to learn how to dance. He
was just dancing by himself.

Phandengsana said, 'Very well then, please go there for me.'

'For what?'

Phandengsana thought for a bit, and said, 'You know
what, Lukhoi grabbed a ring of mine and ran off with it. Go
see if he is wearing it or not. Just look, and don't say anything.
If his mother hears she will think I am spying on him and get
angry. ... And see if Ta'Meri the chancellor has come. If he is
there, tell him my mother the Lady of Thokchom asks if he is
ill or what. Do not let other people hear you.'

Sanatombi went to the dancers' council and came back.
'Lukhoi is wearing a ring on his hand. He said bad words
when I asked him. I must really beat up this kid good one of
these days. I don't care if Royal Mother gets angry or not. It
was so funny, as if he is dancing and all ... ... How is he
allowed to dance, Royal Aunt ... ... ?'

'Did you ask what I asked you to?

'I asked. I told you he said some bad words. He says it is his.'

'Not that, what about what I told you to ask Ta'Meri?

'I didn't ask that. He was singing. Uncle Paka and all were sitting there too.'

'Go away. This child cannot even do as she is told.' She grabbed at her a little and pulled at her hand.

Sanatombi was upset, but she asked again, 'Shall I go again, Royal Aunt?'

'Don't bother, you fool, you're so careless.'

Sanatombi was left wondering, 'What happened?'

Some time passed. Princess Phandengsana was to be married into the Angom clan. Preparations began. Dowry gifts were arranged, each a hundredfold—one hundred spindles, one hundred spinning wheels. Sanatombi went into her royal aunt's room one day. She was crying—Phandengsana was weeping.

Upon seeing Sanatombi, she said, 'I will kill myself. I will throw myself from the elephant and kill myself ... ...'

Sanatombi's anxiety knew no bounds. She ran to her great-grandmother and said to her, 'Grand Queen Mother, Royal Aunt says she will jump off the elephant and kill herself when she is in the wedding procession.'

'She is just saying so, my child,' she replied, but it made the Lady of Meisnam think.

Then, next, she ran to her grandfather the king and said, 'Sovereign Grandfather, what will Royal Aunt be sent on?'

'On an elephant—on the Beast of Moirang.'

'Can we not send her in a palanquin?'

'Why? We will have to send you in a palanquin for yours. Are you afraid of elephants?'

'No, I am not afraid. Have I not ridden on many?'

'Then why do you ask?'

'I was just asking.'

Sanatombi never forgot her aunt's words. She did not go in the wedding procession that took her aunt after her wedding. She refused to go. Sanatombi could not rest until she heard that her aunt had not thrown herself off the elephant.

CHAPTER 3

It was only four or five days until the Procession of the Crow. Sanatombi and Lukhoi ran around, playing, and hardly spent any time in the colony of their father, the crown prince. The two children wandered around the colonies of the court that were dyeing clothes, putting back together the Swallow's Nest, and was preparing for the Crow. Many people gathered at the residence of the Grand Queen Mother. They were busy sewing, stitching, embroidering. They had started making the complete outfit for their royal grandfather Chandrakirti to wear when he came out to take part in the Crow. All this was great fun for the two children.

The Procession of the Crow was the day after tomorrow. The colour for that year was to be shocking pink. That year, starting with the king, the crown prince, the commander-in-chief, and all the noblemen would all change into upper and lower garments in shocking pink.

The Lady of Ngangbam, queen consort of the crown prince, and all her attendants, had begun to dye pink the sash and sarong that Crown Prince Surchandra would change into in the palace. For five or ten days they had been fetching water from the big river and storing it in large pots. The green lawn of the crown prince's colony was covered with white clothes drying in the sun. They were being bleached white first with vegetable ash before they were dyed, or the colour would not be dazzling bright. The meticulous Premamayi, Lady of Ngangbam, walked around inspecting everything.

The elephants Kondumba and Moirangsa that were to be the mounts of the Divine Majesty arrived. There were also several male elephants to be ridden by the princes. The king would come out riding two elephants yoked together side by side. On either side of him, two princes as the right-hand sword bearer and the left-hand sword bearer. Members of the judiciary and the armoury, bearing the fore spear, aft spear and the spear of Luwang, would guard the king. They had started rebuilding the Swallow's Nest again. The fringe of its embroidered velvet canopy had its peacock feathers replaced. All the halls of the royal court gleamed. Sanatombi and Prince Lukhoi held their nurses' hands and had a great time watching the elephants tethered in front of the palace citadel, as they picked up banana palms with their trunks and smashed them to shreds against their enormous legs before eating them. The mahouts had the children watch as they made a young male elephant get down on his knees and raise his two front legs so that it looked like he was sitting on his haunches. They dropped a half-*sel* coin in front of him. After making the elephant pick up the half-sel coin with its trunk and raise it in a salute, they made it bellow. Startled, the two children grabbed their nurses. This time they had also brought a small baby elephant. The mother and baby elephant were not here to take part in the procession but had simply been brought to be shown to the Divine Majesty. The baby elephant had been born in the stable to the elephant Ngakhaibi. One could not get enough of watching it. The two children watched and laughed helplessly as the baby elephant nodded off drowsily and then as it ran between the legs of its mother.

Lukhoi said, 'You know, I will be riding the elephant tomorrow.'

Sanatombi asked him in surprise, 'Why you?'

'I am saying I am going to be riding the elephant with Sovereign Grandfather tomorrow.'

'You're going to be in the Crow tomorrow?'

'Yes. I am going to be riding in the Swallow's Nest with Sovereign Grandfather.'

'As if they'll let you.'

'Yes, they will. Sovereign Grandfather told me to ride. Father has also said I could. Grand Queen Mother has also agreed. Everyone has agreed.'

'As if I believe you. Are you the king or what?'

'Even so, I am allowed. You are not—you're a girl.'

Sanatombi flared up in anger and ran off to her co-mother the Lady of Ngangbam. The Lady of Ngangbam was very busy at the time. She was folding the slightly damp clothes and making her servants smoothen them with their hands. They would be pressed with the iron later. There were so many clothes today. The pile also included those of the royal younger brother Koireng. His consort had come quite a while before the Crow to wash his clothes. The two sisters consulted each other as they washed the clothes together. They didn't wash them themselves; they were only said to be washing the clothes together but really the two sisters just wanted to chat, and so she came often. The Lady of Ngangbam, consort of the crown prince, and Angangmacha, the consort of Koireng, were real sisters. Because of this relation, the two women felt close to these two princes. Both these maids of Ngangbam were very clever. They visited each other often, consulted with each other frequently and exchanged many bits of news.

This year, the bearer of the sword on the right and the bearer of the sword on the left would be Prince Koireng and Prince Pakasana. These two were an even match. Both had inherited the qualities of the king. Koireng and Paka! Now, this was going to be interesting to watch.

Even though Pakasana and Crown Prince Surchandra were brothers born of the same mother, because of the relationship between these two sisters, Pakasana's consort was not that close to the colony of the crown prince. She kept a distance. Everyone also knew, though it was never shown outwardly, of the rivalry of the two equally powerful and regal princes. It was not talked about openly out of fear of the Divine Majesty. The consort of the crown prince, the Lady of Ngangbam, adept in the ways of the court, sent word to the consort of Prince Pakasana, 'Would my younger sister-in-law like to wash and dye my brother-in-law's garments together with us? His lordship Koireng's clothes will also be dyed here. Since they are going to be the bearer of the right-hand sword and the bearer of the left-hand sword, it would be good to steep their garments together in the same dye. Otherwise it would not look good tomorrow if some are lighter, and some darker … … … .'

Word came back promptly. 'Tell her: Thank you for asking me, my royal elder sister-in-law. I did not know beforehand and so I have already started the dyeing. Would my sister-in-law please come by when you start your dyeing and let us know if we have done it properly? If you are not pleased, we would be happy to do it over—tell her that … … … .'

This message came from the courteous consort of Pakasana.

This was not quite what the Lady of Ngangbam had wanted. She wanted to keep all the brother princes together because her Lukhoi would sit in Kangla one day. That these privileged women would take the high road was to be expected. The Grand Queen Mother called her granddaughter-in-law the Lady of Ngangbam when she was dyeing the Divine Majesty's garments and consulted her, saying, 'Leihao, do take a look at the king's clothes and see if they are all right.'

Even though the Lady of Ngangbam was young, the Grand Queen Mother knew she was a woman of propriety and, moreover, she must be trained. She must see all this, for she was the mother of Lukhoi.

The Lady of Ngangbam was not satisfied with the reply from Pakasana's consort. She felt a pang of regret. She thought, 'I should have called her first. She would surely have heard that my younger sister Angangmacha has started washing the garments at my place.' As she was pondering over this, Sanatombi came and asked, 'Royal Mother, he says, Lukhoi says, he is riding in the Swallow's Nest with Sovereign Grandfather. Is it true?'

'It is true. He is going to be riding in it.'

'I will ride too.'

The Lady of Ngangbam was a little irritated. Sanatombi had appeared just when she was in a bad mood. But she did not show it.

She replied, 'Go ask the Grand Queen Mother.'

Sanatombi ran off at once to her Grand Queen Mother.

'Grand Queen Mother, I will ride in the Swallow's Nest with Sovereign Grandfather. If Lukhoi is riding I will too.'

Her great-grandmother laughed heartily, 'Of course my granddaughter will ride too. Is anybody there?' The king was requested. Let her ride, he said.

But the Procession of the Crow was not for women and children. How can this be? Sanatombi is a girl, contested the noble and the titled.

The Grand Queen Mother said, 'Dress my granddaughter in boy's clothes.' Right away, they prepared a turban and dhoti, and a full-sleeved shirt of velvet. 'This is taboo, it is not done, it is not good,' people said here and there. But the Grand Queen Mother had allowed it—and it was done by the king.

A royal festival with the king, the Procession of the Crow was an important festival of Manipur. People attended from villages and provinces. They stayed overnight to watch. The commander-in-chief was appointed in the morning. He had been hosting feasts at his house since the day before. Noblemen from the four boroughs set out for the palace, sitting stylishly at an angle in their palanquins, hookahs in hand. Adorned with the blue vanda orchids of the Crow, noblemen attired in honorific purple and wearing armbands and bracelets of gold came in a procession towards Kangla Fort.

Blue vanda orchids. Everywhere, the blue vanda orchids of the Crow. Sprays and sprays, the royal palace was awash in the blue of the orchid of the Crow.

This year the Crow would be hunted in the outer polo ground.
The shooters of the Crow would bring the news—news from
the Crow, news for the land.

The administrator of the boroughs prostrated at his feet, and
brought the news to the king:

> Divine Majesty, most Excellent,
> Blessings for the year
> Of goodness and joy.
> A year free of sorrows and cares
> With peace in the land
> For His Eternal Majesty.
> Take in the Crow's tidings
> With calm understanding.

The bearer of these tidings would be bestowed with a cloth
of honour. The king would grant him a share of twinned salt
plates. He will witness displays of sword and spear, and games
of coconut rugby.

The Divine Majesty came out on a two-seat howdah
placed on a brace of elephants. From the western gate. On
either side of him were Koireng and Pakasana on matching
bull elephants, attending upon him as the bearer of the right
sword and the bearer of the left. In front of the king in the
Swallow's Nest were Sanatombi and Prince Lukhoi in turbans
tied with a single twist. The two children chattered happily.
Sanatombi laughed. She found the song of the pena balladeer
trailing the elephants very funny. She found the pena balladeer
very funny.

But Jasumati was not happy. She was not at all pleased that her daughter was riding in the Swallow's Nest in royal attendance today. She knew that this would be the cause of a lot of talk among the populace, and there were many who did not approve of this. Jasumati never liked to cause scandal and incident. She felt annoyed at the Grand Queen Mother. Agreeing to whatever the child wanted created a lot of problems. But how could she confront her with this?

At night as she lay in bed with her daughter, she said to her child, 'Sanatombi, what is Mother going to do with you. Where was that tantrum coming from … … … ? You seem to have forgotten that you are a girl. How can you be the same as Lukhoi? He is a male offspring. He is going to be king.'

'It is because he is a male offspring that I beat him up regularly. If he can ride, why can't I?'

'I am going to come to a lot of grief on your account. How can boys and girls be the same? We are called women with no burial place … … … . Oh dear Lord Vishnu, what have I just said!' She recited the names of the gods and stroked her child's head. She chanted mantras to the four corners of the mosquito net to keep away the spirits. Jasumati wept silently.

Jasumati, mother of an unruly daughter, wept silently. But Sanatombi giggled, remembering the chief of Sekmai with his long mustache bristling stiff with beeswax. She tittered.

Jasumati incanted quietly, 'Lord Govinda, please bless me with a son. I will offer an armband of gold … … … .'

But it was another daughter—the Princess Khomdonsana.

CHAPTER 4

Sanatombi is confused about whose bed she is lying in. It is not the bed of her birth mother Jasumati. The warm body of her Grand Queen Mother who had just been lying next to her is not there any more. It is not in the princesses' chamber of the palace, nor is it the large bed of the residency bungalow. It dawns on her that she is in a room in her small house in Sagolband. She notices someone standing at the foot of the bed—Leiren. The attendant Leiren. He is one of the servants sent by Little Majesty to look after his cousin. He stands silently like a statue, a small black fan in his hand. It has a handle of gold. There are no mosquitos around that bite, nor flying mites, but he waves the fan every now and then. As though in service. For what else is there to do? He needs to hold something, do something, for such is the nature of service. Mainu has gone into the kitchen some time back already to prepare Sanatombi's meal.

Sanatombi looks closely at Leiren and says, 'What did you say your name was?'

'It is Leiren, my lady,' answers Leiren.

'How long have you been with me?'

'About three months, my lady. But I sleep over at the palace.'

She opens her eyes a little later and calls again, 'Leiren.'

'My lady.'

'Where is your home?'

'In Meijrao.'

'Where is Meijrao?'

'It is near Hiyangthang, my lady.'

'Who all do you have?'

'I have my humble wife and three children.'

'Are they all grown?'

'No, my lady. The older daughter is about eight years old.'

'If you say it is near Hiyangthang, will you be going to Bor for a little while?'

'I will, my lady, but, I don't know, I wonder if they will have the proper clothes. It has been about a month since your servant has visited his home.'

'And your elders?'

'Your servant's father died in the Battle of Khongjom. He had gone in with Major Paona. I was quite little at the time. Your servant's mother is also no more. It has been two years … … … .'

So related Leiren.

Sanatombi is silent for a while, then she says, 'Call Mainu.' Mainu comes in from the kitchen. Sanatombi says, 'Mainu, Leiren says he has not gone home in a while. Let him go home today. Give him some money to buy clothes for his children … … … . Leiren, you may stay away for a day or two if you like. … … … So, your father died in the Battle of Khongjom.'

Mainu beckons Leiren out of the room. She says quietly, 'Go later, after Ta'Matum has come. There is no one to stay with

her now. If Her Royal Command asks, just say you will go
after Ta'Matum arrives. And take money from me before
you go.'

Sanatombi drowses off. She is escaping the war along the
banks of the sunken big river. In front of her, her uncle the
crown prince Koireng.

Sanatombi was with the Nongmaithem family at the time. In Wangkhei Leikai, in the house of the royal son-in-law Manikchand. Her marriage was arranged when she was a young girl, after her father the crown prince had ascended the throne and while the Grand Queen Mother was still alive. Her mother Jasumati had worried about keeping her till she was older. Her daughter was impetuous, and so she consulted her elder sister-wife, the Lady of Ngangbam.

She said, 'Royal Elder Sister, there is a very fine young man from the Nongmaithem family. They say he is pretty good. They seem to want to make a marriage proposal for Sanatombi. Shall we ask the Grand Queen Mother?' The two sister-wives conferred with each other. They looked into his antecedents, on his father's side as well as his mother's, whether there had been any divorces, any widows or widowers. His father was no more; he was the son of a widow. There would be trouble if they went in without knowing all of this and when the Grand Queen Mother started her interrogation. His family name was Nongmaithem so there was nothing to be unduly wary about. His looks were the usual masculine. The Lady of Ngangbam was a bit doubtful; there was something that she did not approve but she could not quite put her finger on it if one were to ask her directly.

The two sister-wives approached the Grand Queen Mother together.

'Hm. And what do they say he is like as a person?'

'Everyone says he is worthy, my lady,' replied the Lady of Ngangbam.

'They will all say they are worthy. No one who comes with a proposal for their son will say he is not worthy. Fine, I would

also like to arrange a marriage for my granddaughter before
I die.'

From that day on, Sanatombi ate and slept over at the Grand
Queen Mother's. She loved her great-granddaughter all the
more, the more she thought about her all grown up, going
away to a stranger's house. She looked closely at her great-
granddaughter all the time. She appeared to resemble her
late daughter Tamphasana in her countenance. She dressed
her great-granddaughter with her own hands before she
went to pray at the festivals. She made her wear silk dresses,
ordering them in stripes of deep blue as her complexion was
fair. Sanatombi had had scissors to her hair two or three times
by this time. She would not let anyone near her but the Lady
of Ngangbam, celebrated for her skill in dressing maidens'
hair. She made her trim the bangs to match the shape of
her face, to make her wear the side bangs a little longer. Her
face was made to look a little smaller with fringes that hung
lower in the front. The Grand Queen Mother would sit and
watch Sanatombi's hair being cut. Scarce of daughters, the
Lady of Meisnam wanted her great-granddaughter to be very
beautiful. She began to arrange complete sets of necklaces,
bracelets and earrings of gold, chains of diamond-shaped
nganggoi, a necklace of oval *kondum*, a string of round *bokul*
beads, chains with pointed *kiyang* pendants and chains of
marei pendants. Different kinds of rings—the beehive, navel
of serpent, cluster blossom ring, and so on. The bridal chalices
of bell metal, the silver betel-nut holder, all were arranged.

Sanatombi said, 'Light ones for me, Grand Queen
Mother. I do not want that solid gold kind; light, for easy
wearing, please.'

'Everyone wants a lot of gold, you fool.'

'Not me, not me, my dear lady. Slapping on gold till you droop at the neck.'

So, they were ordered smallish, slender and light. It was very difficult to buy anything for Sanatombi. She was very picky and given to many likes and dislikes. They showed the beads of the necklaces to her first, one by one, to see if she liked them or not. She even asked for the tiny gold circles on the beads to be spaced wide apart and with clear intricacy… … … .

Clothes and jewellery were strewn all over in front of the bed of the Lady Meisnam. Sanatombi was to be going on elephant back to pray on the day of Bor for the first time since she became a maiden. Grandam and great-granddaughter were as excited as can be. They went back and forth—how to dress, what to wear. Sanatombi would wear a traditional striped sarong of black and lotus pink. Studding a velvet blouse of deep lavender with gold had begun. And the stole? With a hand-embroidered border of gold thread. The Grand Queen Mother was not happy. She opened wicker chest after wicker chest. After looking at a great many choices, she finally pulled out a whole roll of crêpe, in a blush of bauhinia pink. The cloth was covered with little embroidered flowers in gold. It was not a cloth woven in this land. It was a gift from the British Viceroy when her son Chandrakirti had gone to the durbar at Jila. The roll had not been opened until now. The Grand Queen Mother carefully kept all the gifts given to her son from foreign lands separately. She did not entrust them to her royal daughters-in-law or to anyone else. She kept them in a separate room under lock and key. The Lady of Meisnam believed that such gifts were not for the use of women and children. They belonged to the country, and should belong to the country, to be looked at, to be displayed. But there were many occasions when the Grand Queen Mother broke rules when it came to Sanatombi. Today, too, she opened the king's treasure chest—for Sanatombi. She took scissors in hand herself and cut the gold embroidered crêpe for her great-granddaughter to wear.

She held up a string of pearls and said with a laugh, 'My granddaughter would look beautiful wearing these.'

'Sure, let me wear them, Grand Queen Mother.'

'This one is forbidden. The Viceroy himself placed this around the neck of your Sovereign Grandfather. One must not touch the property of the king. Using the king's belongings by the unworthy will stem their good fortune.'

She caressed her great-granddaughter and went on with a laugh, 'My great-granddaughter would have been king had she been a boy.'

The Lady of Meisnam was wretched when Sanatombi got married. She was beside herself. But she did not let her great-granddaughter see the tears in her eyes. She did not let other people see her tears.

Today, her Grand Queen Mother is no more, her Sovereign Grandfather has ascended to the heavens. Her Sovereign Father Surchandra has been expelled by his brothers. Today he has sought refuge with the foreigners and is in Calcutta waiting fate's decree.

It is a time of an anxious waiting for the decision of the foreigners: what would become of her uncle Kulachandra, what would the verdict for the land be?

Sanatombi is dreaming. It was not really a dream. Smoke, cannons, sword and spears, cavalry, foreigners … … … .

Sanatombi knew what hardship was, what sadness was, the day her Sovereign Father Surchandra, Embracer of the Hills, Victor in War, was ousted from the throne in Kangla by her uncles. She did not shed tears, strong to the core; she gritted her teeth and endured it.

Only on one day did Sanatombi weep with deep sorrow, and that was the day when her Grand Queen Mother was taken away on the royal bier to her cremation.

Maharaja Surchandra had run away and had sought refuge with Grimwood, the Political Agent of the British Indian Empire. His queens and the consorts of the princes gathered in the residency bungalow one day, having been informed that they could see him. One by one they went in, her royal mother Queen Premamayi, her other mothers, Lukhoi, and so on. When she met her uncle Pakasana who had also fled and sought refuge along with his older brother, she said, 'How is Sovereign Father?'

'You will know when you see him,' Pakasana answered shortly. Sanatombi said, 'If I may, Uncle, I will go in to see Sovereign Father a little later.'

She sat in a room and waited while the others went in. She was deep in thought. Surchandra's family came out one after the other after seeing him. Her younger sisters Ombisana and Khomdonsana came out crying. They were both little girls at this time.

Sanatombi went in to see her father. He had lost a great deal of weight in this short time. She went up to him and kowtowed, touching his feet. Father and daughter remained silent, many things were said inwardly.

Sanatombi said, 'Is it really true as they say that Sovereign Father will be going abroad?'

'Yes, I have to. There is not much point in staying here unless I have a word with the Viceroy. If it is not in my stars to stay in the service of Lord Govinda, I will embark upon a pilgrimage, and I will not return.'

'You cannot do that. Manipur belongs to Sovereign Father. Why do they not know this?'

But who will seek right or wrong when it comes to rivalries
… … … .

'Sanatombi, listen to your father. You are now the eldest of
my children. I won't be able to get your two younger sisters
married. You must look into this. Help your mother. I am
afraid my Lukhoi does not carry much weight.'

'Why should Sovereign Father leave Manipur? Do you
want to give Kangla to other people? Isn't it your right? …
… … I do not trust them, what will they do for us? Let me talk
to them; just let me talk to my uncle Koireng. Why have they
forgotten what Sovereign Grandfather said to us … … … ?'

'Be quiet, Sanatombi—do not speak of such matters
around here.'

'Please call the Political Agent, I will talk to him. … …
… How could they … … … .' Sanatombi was almost in tears.

'Sanatombi, daddy's little princess … … … .' The
monarch's voice trembled.

'I understand, Sovereign Father. I am not Lukhoi,' said
Sanatombi. 'But why did they not tell me first?' she asked
bitterly.

But she knew her calm, kind father had never suspected
anybody. He had been affectionate and friendly towards
all his brothers. But he had not realized that the embers in
the family hearth had flared up during the four years of his
reign and the princes who, while their Sovereign Father
Chandrakirti reigned, had not been able to do so, had now
begun to try to depose their older brother and had risen up
in arms for the throne. He did not have time to think about
it. Prince Borachaoba and Prince Wangkheirakpa were not

enemies to be trifled with. And Surchandra believed that the
British would abide by the treaty of Chatragram and remain
a friend of the throne of Manipur. They would be an ally. But
he had not thought that one's own blood would revolt. The
Political Agent at the time was not his friend, nor was he an
enemy. He had never fraternized closely with the foreigners.
He had kept a distance. Neither did he know that Grimwood
did not consider him a friend because he himself had never
held anything against Grimwood. There was just the one time
though when he had a stern word or two with him—he had had
to. Upon receiving word that the young man Grimwood, who
had come without his wife, had taken a lot of photographs of
Meitei women and were sending them abroad, he had taken a
severe tone and reprimanded him saying that he must stop it
for it was forbidden. He had also called Koireng and said, 'Do
not allow him to do such things', because Surchandra knew
that Koireng and Grimwood were very close.

Soon after, the saheb's wife arrived from Shillong.

Around this time, it became known for certain that the saheb
was a little unhappy with the king because of this incident.
After Sanatombi mentioned that she didn't trust them, the
king recalled this incident and began to suspect him, for had
Grimwood stood by his side, the upheaval over the throne of
Manipur would have been resolved easily. Even though he
was friends with Koireng, he should not have forgotten the
friendly relations with the throne of Manipur. But Surchandra
did not say everything to his daughter—he should not say
everything—for they were in the British agency and Sanatombi
was still a child. What purpose would it serve? It would
only upset the child. But this he had not known, and failed

to remember, that even though she was a child, Sanatombi had been brought up by the Lady of Meisnam, Unifier and Embracer of Peoples. She was wise beyond her years.

Seeing her father silent, Sanatombi once again said, 'If Sovereign Father has really decided to go, I will go too. Allow me to be present at the meeting with the Viceroy. How can Sovereign Father go by yourself? Huh, what business is it of theirs? Why are they meddling … … … ?'

'Why don't you be quiet. … … … My Tombi, if only you had been a boy I would have been happy.'

'I can do it, Sovereign Father—I can talk to them. I will go with you. Let me serve you … … … .'

She remembered the Queen Mother. Sanatombi remembered her Grand Queen Mother. She saw vividly before her eyes—her Grand Queen Mother is riding along the Tongjeimaril Passage, in men's clothes, her jaws girded, taking her small child Chandrakirti with her. Behind her, the soldiers of Narasingh.

But deep inside she felt hurt by her beloved uncle Koireng: What a tragedy; what unhappiness had he harboured. … … … … Why did my uncle keep this all from me?

Sanatombi came back from her meeting with her father, deeply unhappy. She could not sleep all night, her mind whirled. What upset her most was that that her father had no one to turn to—that there was nobody of any worth on the outside who could be said to be on his side. Sanatombi had no one to consult, no one to talk to. At the most there was only the queen, the Lady of Ngangbam. But she was also being closely watched by the enemies—and the enemies were her husband's own younger brothers. So, the king and queen had not been able to meet each other. Even though the shrewd Lady of Ngangbam was not in prison, she was imprisoned by the sharp eyes that surrounded her. Sanatombi bore the pain of her helplessness, of her hopelessness, all by herself. The Nongmaithem family was impervious to matters such as these.

Chaobihal the Brahmin cook had been with the palace since the days of her Sovereign Grandfather. She was still cooking for Sanatombi. She was a friend she could talk to.

Sanatombi said, 'Mother Brahmin, I would like to meet Laikhurasajou the scholar just one time. Where would he be? Could you arrange a meeting with him without letting anybody know?'

Sanatombi met the scholar Laikhurasajou secretly one day. Laikhurasajou was the head scholar since the time of the reign of her father His Majesty Surchandra. Sanatombi said, 'Is there no one in Manipur who loves my Sovereign Father?'

'Why wouldn't there be, Your Highness? The Divine Majesty, Embracer of the Hills and Victor in War, is a king loved by the people, but others have taken control first. There is no one any more who is able to come out openly for your father.'

'I am very unhappy, Grandpa. I am very unhappy about the recent turn of events—I do not believe the people really do not want my Sovereign Father. ... ... And what about grandpa Major Thanggal?'

'Your grandfather Thanggal is the most upset of all, Your Highness. He weeps over what their Sovereign Father's sons are doing to each other but princess, your grandpa Thanggal is a man of sterling quality. He will put Manipur first at the most crucial of times. There will be no question of taking sides with him. We are also all most distraught, Your Highness.'

'And what do you all see as being foretold, Grandpa? Will it not be possible for Sovereign Father to rule again?'

'Your Highness, it has been foretold to your grandfather and the scholars that whoever comes to power will not reign for long. It seems the time of the reign of kings in Manipur is drawing to an end. I am beginning to believe that the forty-year reign of your Sovereign Grandfather Chandrakirti that was foretold consists of the thirty-six years your Sovereign Grandfather ruled together with the four years of your Sovereign Father. Your humble servant Taoriya Hidang firmly believes this.'

Sanatombi was disappointed to hear these words of the head scholar, but she did not lose faith—her Sovereign Father would rule again; he would once again rule over the land of the Meiteis. She then met Tonjao of Moirang in secret. She knew, even though other people did not, that Tonjao of Moirang was a man who loved her father.

She said, 'Ta'Tonjao, do you all no longer really love my Sovereign Father at all?'

'What are you saying, Your Highness. But the situation is dire now. Since Prince Koireng and Major Thanggal are involved.'

'Grandpa Thanggal too!'

'Major Thanggal's exact position is difficult to say right now, Your Highness.'

'I don't know, I don't know what to do. I still have two younger sisters whose marriages need to be arranged. And what can you all do for Sovereign Father at this time? Even though I am the eldest child of Sovereign Father, I am still young. And what would Lukhoi know?'

She hinted to Tonjao of Moirang that she would be giving away her younger sister Ombisana in marriage. She knew Tonjao harboured hopes for her younger half-sister Princess Ombisana.

'But give me news now and then, Ta'Tonjao.'

Tonjao left. She knew then that Tonjao still loved Surchandra. And Tonjao was no ordinary man.

It is better to be quiet and stay low, thought Sanatombi. What could she do, a mere child? She had her Manikchand, but she knew that Manikchand was no Chancellor Lamphel. But she never gave up hope, for who knows, the British government could very well help her Sovereign Father. She constantly thought of Lukhoi: if only he grasped matters a little better. She could not bear to remember her father's helplessness, his defeated face as he went in alone with a handful of people, prepared to seek asylum in a foreign land, and thought—How dare they! They have won. How easily they got away with it! And they are all brothers too!

The outrage at the palace entered a new chapter. Surchandra was now in Calcutta. Kulachandra had become king. But war was inevitable. The British against Kulachandra. But for whom? On behalf of his older brother Surchandra? No, it was not that. Or was it a plan to swallow Manipur whole? It was becoming clear: the brashly confident British would conquer Manipur and bring it under foreign rule. Manipur's final war was not far off. Quinton, the chief commissioner of Assam, arrived carrying orders to capture Prince Koireng alive. Failing to do so, all of a sudden, shots were fired at Koireng's house in the deceitful stealth of night. They failed to capture Koireng—and five white men's heads rolled in front of the leogryphs of Kangla Fort. The heads, severed from their bodies, were interred to Nunggoibi, the War Goddess. War was inevitable—Manipur's final war.

Manikchand was not in Manipur at this time, though he could be back any day now. He had gone to Cachar. He had said that if it worked out he, along with Haodeijam Cheiteino, would go and see her Sovereign Father in Calcutta. She did not believe he would; he would merely say, 'I couldn't make it, I couldn't get any news, it just did not work out.' Sanatombi knew Manikchand was not a man who took an interest in these matters. He was going for business; he had gone to make money. The Nongmaithem family was not one that spent freely. They were not the kind to try to impress people without watching their purse simply because a princess had married into their household. They were a hard-working, frugal family. Manikchand often went to Cachar. He brought back bags and bags of money every time he returned, but their modest lifestyle carried on as before. The extravagant

Sanatombi had difficulty trying to fit in but the thoughtful, far-sighted Manikchand always reminded her—even though she was a princess of Manipur today, her father was no longer the king of Manipur. She must conduct herself accordingly.

The land was restive and people had begun to prepare for war as soon as the shots were fired at Prince Koireng's house, gunfire was exchanged with the British, and after the sahebs had been killed. People started moving their belongings into storage and began sending their women and children away. But the Nongmaithem household could not leave their home because Manikchand had not returned.

It was dusk that day. Someone knocked at the door of the Nongmaithem house. Manikchand's mother, who had been keeping watch over the children and womenfolk, went out to look. She said quietly to Sanatombi, 'It is Crown Prince Koireng.' Sanatombi panicked. She did not know what to do for a moment. She went out and after kowtowing, said, 'Please come inside.' They were silent for a while. They could not quite begin.

Koireng said after he had taken his seat, 'Sanatombi.'

'Your Highness.'

'… … … Sanatombi, Manipur is in a very bad situation now. The British are not going to let it go easily after these incidents. They have made preparations to attack Manipur from three directions. I have received information. … … … Sanatombi, believe your uncle when I say I did not quite want this.'

Sanatombi understood immediately what he wanted to say. He was saying that he had not wanted to depose her father.

She answered, 'Who is this information from?'

'From a trustworthy person.'

'Which trustworthy person? Is there anyone who can still be trusted, Uncle?

Koireng was not pleased with Sanatombi's response, but he said, 'Yes, there is. He is from a foreign land—he is an Indian.'

'What Indian? What is he saying?'

'The government's secret plans, he has been quietly giving information about the government's plans for a long time. That is why I, I mean, we—'

Koireng did not go any further. He wanted to say: Your Sovereign Father will not be able to handle the British. Surchandra will not be able to fend off the British government, skilled at outflanking and taking over lands, once they got a foot in the door. He had appealed to Surchandra quietly many times but he would not listen. He might have, but he had been alienated by his brothers who were born of the same mother. What use would it be to tell Sanatombi about the little sparks of resentment that had now blazed aflame into a conflagration. Sanatombi was smart even though she was young—Koireng did not want to tell her all and go into small, pointless details.

'Who is this Indian? Who is this Indian who loves Manipur so much?'

'I will not say his name. I have given my word. He is a person who came out here to work for the government of the British agency. He does not approve of the land-hungry foreigners. Over in India, they have begun to expel the British. Sanatombi, you do not know this, but the British are greatly hated in the land of the Indians. It is said a relative of my informant is in the armed rebellion and there are also many in flight after the Sepoy Mutiny. So even though he has to work for a living, deep down, he does not approve of them.'

He told her briefly about the Sepoy Mutiny. Many rebels had sought refuge and were hiding in Manipur at this time. Koireng seemed to be quite familiar with them.

'Why has my uncle come here today? How may your servant serve you?'

'I want to move you all to a suitable place. A war with the British is certain. It could be today, it could be tomorrow.' Koireng appeared to be deep in thought.

'Uncle, I am hearing all sorts of things. Is it true?'

'What?'

Sanatombi did not quite want to voice it but she said, 'About all sorts of foreboding signs … … … .'

Sanatombi had heard of many mysterious signs, ominous signs that had been the talk of the land. There were murmurs about what would become of the king of the land. Spirits had been seen in the reservoir of the armoury, the face of Lord Brinamchandra had been turned around, there had been blood at the temple to Lord Ramchandra, and so on … … … . Not only that, at the south-west corner of the shrine to Lord Pakhangba, Ruler of the Gods, his great chariot, emblazoned with his banners and flags, had been seen hurtling down from the heavens only to vanish an arm's length from the ground. The scholars of the king of the land had debated this divine sign from the gods. They had been worried.

'Yes, there have been some signs. But who can stop what is destined to be. … … … All right, go get ready, let us go.'

'Today?'
'Today, right now.'

Manikchand had not returned. It did not look like he would be coming back in the next day or two. But Sanatombi's mother-in-law said, 'Please take Her Highness. She is young and should not be in the midst of a war. We will wait for a few days if we may.' Sanatombi's mother-in-law could rely on her brothers. And so, it was decided thus.

'Sanatombi, I brought horses for you too. Would you still be able to ride a horse?'
'Yes, Uncle.'

All the princesses of Manipur learnt to ride. When the Divine Majesty had gone to the durbar at Jila, he had taken a few of his daughters on horseback but a few of them who did not know how to ride had caused a great inconvenience. Koireng had taught Sanatombi to ride from then on.

Koireng and Sanatombi rode together on their horses along the bed of the big river. Sanatombi was in men's clothes. As they crossed the bridge at Minuthong and approached Khurai, Koireng said, 'Sanatombi, here, hold both horses and stay down in the riverbed for a bit. I need to go bring someone— will you be afraid?'
'No.'

He came back after a little while with a woman, her face and head covered. Sanatombi was surprised but she did not ask anything. There was no time to ask. Koireng put the woman on his horse and rode on ahead. Sanatombi rode behind him. Every now and then he would look back to see if she was keeping up. She was riding right behind him. Koireng laughed and said, 'Now, that's my girl!'

They reached Koirenggei. He must have sent word on ahead for many servants and attendants were waiting for them. Koireng jumped off his horse, and he helped the woman down. Sanatombi also alighted from her horse.

He made the two of them go into a neat little cottage that looked like a bridal house and said to an attendant, 'Balasingh, look after them.'

The little village of Koirenggei was somewhat tucked away and was a convenient place to take refuge from the war. There were also many paddies there that belonged to the crown prince—and so there were many there in service to him. There were also other houses where women and children of the palace were sheltered. They were not all kept in one place for fear that it would attract attention. They were scattered, one or two to a household. The house where Sanatombi and the woman were kept belonged to Balasingh. Balasingh was a tenant farmer of Koireng, and the young woman was his sister's daughter—her name, Tilotama. She must have been around Sanatombi's age. Sanatombi wondered—Has the woman caught the attention of the prince with the roving eye?

Balasingh had already started to prepare a meal for the crown prince and his guests. But no one was really able to eat properly as they worried about what the next day would bring.

Preparations were made for the prince's immediate departure. Sanatombi kowtowed to her uncle and touched his feet.

'Never forget Lord Govinda, Sanatombi. Your uncle will be back.'

Prince Koireng leaped up on his horse. He galloped away with his three servants. Sanatombi was left standing, listening to the sound of hooves fairly into the distance.

Their enemy now was the British government. It was not Koireng, it was not Kulachandra, it was nobody else.

It was after Manipur had come under foreign rule. The day
her uncle Crown Prince Koireng Tikendra Bir Singh was
executed on the Mound of the Eunuchs by the royal market.
Sanatombi saw this vividly before her eyes. It was the last time
she saw her uncle. She leaned on a post and stood stock-still.
She thought, 'My uncle, hanged! Was the Indian who was also
hanged for siding with the crown prince the Indian my uncle
talked about? No, that was Niranjan the subedar. Then who
was it? … … … Uncle, so was this what you meant when you
said you would be back?'

CHAPTER 5

Of all her uncles, Prince Koireng was most similar to Sanatombi. Koireng emerged as an exceptional person from among the ranks of the nine princes born to Chandrakirti. Sanatombi had also felt that there was something about him. She liked everything that her uncle did. Koireng too believed in Sanatombi, and adored her. Even though there were many years between them, the dandyish Koireng always discussed matters with Sanatombi. How a bond of friendship had somehow sprung up between them was hard to say. It was also Koireng who overthrew her Sovereign Father and installed her middle uncle Kulachandra on the throne, and this Sanatombi knew. And this was why she had been hurt by Koireng. She thought—If you had any grievances you should have at least told me. Why did you keep such an important matter hidden!

It seemed like just yesterday. It was during the spring festival. All her uncles were going to be in the palace choir of Lord Govinda. Prince Koireng too. It was morning. Sanatombi went to his residence. Koireng had started to don his clothes, shirt, dhoti and turban of turmeric yellow. How handsome he looked. He saw Sanatombi coming and said, 'Ah, my niece has come. I was also thinking of sending for you. I don't know,

I am never satisfied until you have given your approval. Take a look. Your uncle is not that bad looking, is he now?' he joked.

As she looked out she saw a flame-of-the-forest tree in full scarlet flower. She went out and had a junior servant pick a beautiful bunch of its blossoms and bring it in. She said, 'Shall we put this little bunch of flowers on top? It is all so yellow, I think a touch of red will look nice.'

'Fine, put it on.'

Koireng looked at himself in the mirror. The scarlet of the flame-of-the-forest flower made a striking highlight amidst the yellow.

Towards the end of the royal choir the Divine Majesty called Koireng over and said, 'How beautiful your flame-of-the-forest flower is today, my son.'

'It is Sanatombi's doing, Your Highness.'

'My granddaughter? Let the royal choir all wear a dash of red on their turbans from now on. One may not always get a flame-of-the-forest flower.'

One day as he toured his land, the king saw a young flame-of-the-forest tree flowering scarlet in a field of yellow mustard flowers. He saw it vividly. And he remembered this incident.

Prince Koireng had a secret sorrow deep inside him, a sadness that he did not reveal but yet was glimpsed now and then. Even though she did not know exactly what it was, Sanatombi felt her uncle was hiding something, that he had a pain buried in him. What was it, a sickness? It was a sickness—the sickness of being all alone. He was alone in the midst of so many—he had no one. Most did not know of this sickness in the man who was excessively given to forced laughter and carousing, and they thought of Koireng as a man simply given to bursts of temper. But Sanatombi, for one, suspected—there was something, some other thing she could not put her finger on. Sometimes when he was overcome by his temper, he would pull a horse out from the stables and ride off without any direction. He would whip the horse mercilessly. They would be drenched in sweat, Koireng and the horse, both.

One time he said to Sanatombi, 'I don't know, I don't know what it is. I do not know what comes over me when I am riding—I think, let it die, let me die too.'

Koireng's mother Kouseswari, the Elder Lady of Chongtham, was the fourth wife of Chandrakirti. Her younger sister was also a consort of the king—Lukeswari, the Younger Lady of Chongtham. She was the mother of Kulachandra. The Elder Lady of Chongtham, whom the king had first wanted to bring to the palace, the first one he had loved, never got to be the queen. The queen was the Lady of Angom. She bore him Surchandra, Thambousana, Pakasana and Gopalsana.

The Grand Queen Mother, the Lady of Meisnam, had said, 'A maid from the house of Angom must be the first to be brought to the royal residence.' This was because the Grand Queen Mother owed the Angom clan an enormous debt. She let Chandrakirti know of this in strict confidence. Chandrakirti could not shrug off the orders of his queen mother. Long ago, the father of the Lady of Angom had been of great help to the Grand Queen Mother when she fled to Cachar with her young son, the child-king. He had stood by her in times of danger. The Lady of Meisnam never forgot this. To be in-laws with the Angom was also called for according to tradition. Moreover, she did not want the Lady of Chongtham whom Chandrakirti was in love with as her daughter-in-law. But he ended up marrying both the sisters of Chongtham. The Lady of Meisnam never took to the proud and high-handed sisters of Chongtham, but she never voiced it. The Elder Lady of Chongtham knew this and kept her distance from the Lady of Meisnam. That annoyed the Lady of Meisnam even more. She thought—The insolence!

The Lady of Chongtham, too, had her grievances. She knew very well who it was who had prevented her from being brought to the palace first. She took it as an enormous personal defeat that she was not able to share the throne with the man she loved so much, Chandrakirti. She felt deeply hurt by the king. She bore no anger towards anybody else, it was only the king that she blamed. She seemed to say—You have no spine, you did not elevate me first. ... ... Did I not love you first? In this way, there were times when to all appearances, his intense wife seemed to challenge the Grand Queen Mother. This alarmed the king greatly, and he chided the Lady of Chongtham discreetly. But she replied, 'Your servant lives very meekly in the palace. Who could I challenge?' She let him know obliquely—I have no child. And who would recognize a barren woman in the palace?

Except for the queen, it was customary for the king to call for whichever of his consorts struck his fancy to serve him in the royal residence. None of his consorts lived with him in the royal residence. It was forbidden for the king to live as man and wife in the manner of commoners. They all lived in separate houses built for them. Except for at the queen's residence, the royal bed could not be made in the residences of the consorts. It was therefore customary for the king to call for a consort who came to mind. The only consort who refused to come to the king when summoned in this manner was the difficult Elder Lady of Chongtham. She would avoid it by saying she was not feeling well and so on. Even when she came, it was always only after the king went over and requested her himself. The king knew she was being difficult and petulant, but he never got angry with her. The Elder Lady of Chongtham seemed to say—You have to come, even if you are the king. It made Chandrakirti love her all the more, this woman who loved him and who threw tantrums at him.

This did not sit well with other people. 'The Lady of Chongtham is a bit excessive,' so said the king's closest attendants.

The Grand Queen Mother thought—It is just that it cannot be done but she really ought to be thrown out by the scruff of her neck.

But none spoke out loud, for all knew that the Lady of Chongtham was Chandrakirti's first love, and that he loved her still.

One time, a little late in the day, Chandrakirti came to the residence of the Elder Lady of Chongtham. It had been four or five days since she and the king had been angry with each other. The more intimate attendants knew that the Lady of Chongtham always came out on top whenever they fought like this.

The king walked in and said, laughing, 'So what is it you are saying?'

'What, I am not saying anything.'

'Why didn't you come when I asked you to?'

'Am I the only consort of Your Highness?'

'The one whom I asked for was you. You are the worst of the lot. What you are saying seems to be that I should stop governing the land and stay here pampering you. Why do you give me grief like this time and time again?'

'As if I can. What am I?'

The king laughed out loud, and said, 'You? My wife. You are the one I am most afraid of. I would rather climb Mount Koubru and capture ten elephants than confront you.'

'If I am such a nuisance in the palace, I can just leave.' The Lady of Chongtham got even more angry. The king teased her. He was not angry. The Lady of Chongtham could never treat Chandrakirti like a king when they were alone. She said whatever she liked with no regard for the etiquette of the palace. Her manner was refreshing. To be a commoner for a while amidst his mannered life of strict rules and artifice was a relief for Chandrakirti. The king found it restful to fight with her and forgot the cares of governance for a while. Even though she was simply preposterous, Chandrakirti loved the Elder Lady of Chongtham very much as a woman.

The Divine Majesty settled into the bed and said, 'Come here.'

She pretended not to hear.

'I said come here. Don't be difficult.'

At this time, she had not changed out of her sarong of raw silk after their dinner. Her figure was svelte. She was sharp-eyed, magnetic, refined, and a little different from the others. She was not a beauty beyond compare, but she was bewitching. The raw-silk sarong of maroon was very becoming on her. Her long hair was loose, and she covered her head a little in the king's presence. She sat angrily at a distance on a reed stool.

Chandrakirti sat on the bed and smiled a little.

He said, 'You are really very cheeky.' Saying this, he came over and carried her to the bed. And starting that day, he spent his nights with the Lady of Chongtham for quite a long time. From the next month on, the Lady of Chongtham carried Prince Koireng.

The Grand Queen Mother was not uninformed of this. The Lady of Meisnam was a woman with a thousand eyes and a thousand ears. She stayed silent but she knew that the king was breaking the rules and was secretly sleeping over at the

Lady of Chongtham's. She pretended not to know, but the Lady of Meisnam's dislike for the Lady of Chongtham grew. The Lady of Meisnam was also disappointed with the king. The king seemed to have forgotten that there was a council of nine women called the *pacha* to oversee the rules governing multiple wives and to deal with various matters pertaining only to women. It was a council composed of exceptional, distinguished women—and it was mandatory for the mother of the queen to be on it. But on this occasion the Lady of Meisnam pretended not to know this.

When Prince Koireng had grown up to be a little boy, a tragic incident occurred at the royal palace. And that was, someone had made wax figures of the king and the Grand Queen Mother and hexed a spell on them. There had been a plan to kill them. There was a serious investigation into who was involved in this. People suspected, and the Grand Queen Mother suspected, that this had to be the doing of the mother of Koireng, the Lady of Chongtham. The incident blew up. An attempt to kill the king was no small matter. Chandrakirti was very upset. He said to the Lady of Chongtham, 'Tell me, tell me it wasn't you. ... ...'

'I will not. I will not say a word. Why did you punish people you suspected of aiding me without asking me first, without first finding out the truth?'

Among those punished there were some who were acquainted with the Lady of Chongtham, and some who were not. But was the actual hexing done by the Lady of Chongtham? She was very hurt that the news was spread all over even before it was determined if it was meant to kill, or if it was a love spell. She was stung to anger. There were thirteen who were rounded up in connection with the wax figures. They were Sorokhaibam Tonu, Paona Uchek, Haobam Papu, Thokchao Thambal, a son of Chongtham, Sanamanik the Brahmin, Sabireima, Leichaobi, a Chongtham daughter-in-law of a royal nobleman, the Lady of Potsangbam, the shaman priestess of Moirang, Mother Sano of Wahengbam and the wife of the subedar of Huidrom. Four of them had even already been ordered into banishment to India. But all of them gave conflicting testimonies. They were all testimonials that made it difficult to find out the truth. It was never really determined what the truth was. The Lady

of Chongtham was very wounded by Chandrakirti as he had
gone along with the accusation of a woman with whom he
had borne a son. And this the king should have realized—
such a serious matter, a matter of life and death, could never
have been known to so many. The king should have thought
through on the situation. The Lady of Chongtham would
have been satisfied if he had given some due consideration.
What would she have gotten out of killing the man she loved
so much? It was impossible that it would have made a king of
her Koireng since he had three older brothers before him. She
thought—Why should I plead for my life when so many have
suffered on my account? Let him find out, let him try to arrive
at the truth; he who is able to find out wrongs should also be
able to find out the truth.

She said to the king, 'I will not give any answer, may
the king do as he pleases. The king must seek out right from
wrong.'

'But what about Koireng? Will you not think of Koireng?'
Upon mention of Koireng, the Lady of Chongtham choked up.

'My Koireng! Your Majesty, my Koireng will not go to
waste. I am telling you, he may not be king but my Koireng
will not come to naught.' The Lady of Chongtham wept.

There was a lot of discussion for two or three months after this.
What should be done with the Elder Lady of Chongtham? The
relatives of the thirteen accused asked restively, 'Your Majesty,
what punishment will you give your wife?' Chandrakirti was
at a loss as to what to do. He would have wanted to take the
advice of the Grand Queen Mother but when it came to the
Lady of Chongtham it was a step he could not take. He had to
decide this on his own.

Her distraught younger sister, the Younger Lady of Chongtham, mother of Kulachandra, came running to her older sister and said, 'My royal sister, why are you taking the blame when you did not even do it? If you do not answer, people will think their suspicions were correct. I will go to the Grand Queen Mother.'

'What nonsense. And what about the thirteen people who were punished on my account?'

'If you did not do it, His Majesty will forgive them on his own. Let us appeal to the Divine Majesty.'

'It is that Divine Majesty of yours that I am angry with.'

'What use is it if you challenge him for no good reason. Won't you even think of Koireng? What will he say tomorrow when he grows up? He will have to live with the shame.'

'When he grows up, he will come to understand on his own what the palace is like. He is my son after all. ... ...'

'I don't know what to do, my royal sister. What will you get out of challenging the Divine Majesty?'

'Who says so? I am not challenging the king. I am just saying he is simply not getting it.' Her younger sister went back, defeated. But she wept all night for Prince Koireng and her obstinate older sister.

The Elder Lady of Chongtham was sent back to her maiden home. She had not believed it would come to this. No one had believed it would come to this. It had not occurred to her that the man she loved was a king and that was just her ill fortune. The king had sought to take this difficult woman as his second consort. She had refused, and hung back in a tantrum. The king in anger took her younger sister to the palace and she was left being the fourth wife. Who knows, if it were not for this, if she had not been sent back to her maiden home, if she had told the truth or had asked for forgiveness, she might have sat on the throne beside the man she loved! Who knows, her fortunes might have improved. One day after this, on a tenth day of the lunar months, on a Wednesday, the eldest queen Maharani Manil Loirenkhombi, Lady of Angom, also died.

The name of the Lady of Chongtham was never again mentioned in the palace.

When Jasumati quietly told Sanatombi these stories that had gone from one ear to the next, she said, 'Sanatombi, the palace is a place where people are destroyed quickly if they do not know to conduct themselves according to its ways. ... ... I was so curious that one day my younger sister-wife Angangmacha and I secretly went to see your grandmother the Lady of Chongtham.'

'What did she look like? What did she say?'

'She had great dignity. She looked a bit like your uncle Koireng. She wept a great deal when she saw us. She entrusted your uncle to me and asked, "And how is the Divine Majesty?"'

Angangmacha, the consort of Koireng, and Jasumati were very close. They shared confidences about many discreet matters.

Sanatombi was on edge at Nongmaithem after Prince Koireng was hanged. She saw before her eyes—Koireng, the lonely, motherless child Koireng, the young man Koireng who laughed a bit too loud, who bore a burn inside him. She thought—What a tragedy. And what becomes of my royal grandmother the Lady of Chongtham?

CHAPTER 6

Mainu finishes cooking and comes in to inform Sanatombi.

She calls to her, 'Your Highness, lunch is ready. Let's get ready to eat.'

She opens her eyes. Sanatombi has been crying. Her eyes are still brimming with tears. She looks at Mainu—a distant look, a gaze looking back from a distance.

'Let us get up.'

'I don't have much of an appetite, Mainu.'

'You cannot not eat, even if it's just a little. Your servant Leiren will be bringing water to freshen up.'

'Leiren has not left yet?'

'He will be leaving. He will go home as soon as Ta'Matum arrives—here, let's get up.'

Sanatombi washes up. Mainu changes her into clean clothes. She loosely wears a thin shirt of parrot green made in a foreign land. A soft fine wrap of Indian weave covers her like a throw. The way she lies in that bed of dazzling white makes it hard to tear one's eyes away. She takes a dab of clay from the potted holy basil that Leiren has brought in and places a generous spot upon her forehead. Sanatombi has not worn her marriage sandalwood paste since she became the consort of the Saheb—but she never stopped applying clay to her forehead. The Grand Queen Mother had taught her to do so when she was little; she could not easily stop doing it. She even takes a little of the holy basil clay with her whenever she travels with the Saheb. The black earth on her forehead is very becoming on Sanatombi.

Sanatombi is ready. Mainu arranges her food to bring to her. Leiren's skilled hands winch up her bed so that only her head is raised. The bed had been imported from England back when Sanatombi had become indisposed earlier, for her to lie in when she was unwell. Mainu has laid out her meal. She has already covered the little bedside table with a white cloth. She brings a little bit of rice in a small bowl of bell metal. Three or four serving dishes of silver on a silver tray made in Dacca. Sanatombi looks to Mainu, she looks at the dishes.

'Let us start eating. Here is the finger bowl.'

'Where is Khomdon?'

'The younger princess has gone to the palace. I think she is going to be in the choir singing to the Lady Goddess today.'

The house Sanatombi is in today is the one she built for her younger sister Princess Khomdonsana. Her husband was Ramlal—Meino. Since the man she herself had picked for her younger sister was a prominent police officer from the time of the British, he was also a powerful person during the reign of Little Majesty Churachand. He was a good choice to have entrusted Sanatombi to. In addition to arranging for appropriate servants, Churachand had said to Meino, 'If my younger cousin and you would please let me know what my elder royal cousin is able to eat. ... ... I am afraid it is going to be a bit of an imposition on you.'

Princess Khomdonsana was at her side every day when her sister had her meals, observing what she was able to eat, what she seemed to like. She was inquiring today upon not seeing her younger sister. Princess Khomdonsana had quietly entrusted her to Mainu. 'I won't be around today, sister Mainu. If she asks, please tell her as you think best.'

The Saheb and Sanatombi had brought up Maharaja Churachand from when he was still a boy until the time he was able to take over the reins. They had defended the land in his stead. Churachand knew all about it; he had not forgotten. Maxwell had actually looked after Little Majesty as a father would, closely supervising him so that nothing went wrong. When he was about to be sent to Ajmer for schooling, his royal father and company had strongly urged, 'He is the king, he must go as a king, with servants and attendants, an idol of Lord Vishnu, and balladeers to sing to him in his bedroom.' Maxwell was alarmed. 'The boy will be spoiled.' His father disagreed, and said firmly that he would send only a few necessary personnel. The child wrote letters regularly to the Saheb from school—in Hindi, in English. How pleased the Saheb was: '... ... ... The boy is improving.' Little Majesty did not forget any of this.

He also knows that Sanatombi does not reveal how she has been drained by her sadness, and that she has lost her will to live. Little Majesty strives to make sure that nothing upsets her for any reason whatsoever. As do Meino and Khomdonsana. But Sanatombi is merely amused—Look at what these children think they are doing.

Many memories come to her today. Mainu says, 'You are not eating anything at all today. What am I going to say when the Divine Majesty sends for information later?' 'I have had enough, Mainu.' Saying this, she bursts into sobs. Gathering herself at once, she said, 'Mainu, what is the point in getting better?' Sanatombi is very prone to tears these days. She cries without any warning. She has been ill for quite a long time now. Mainu also turns her face and wipes away her tears.

Sanatombi may be remembering her Grand Queen Mother. Whenever Sanatombi made a fuss about eating, Jasumati would have the Grand Queen Mother informed. There were countless instances when her great-grandmother would come on foot to soothe her fussy great-grandchild: 'Here, let great-grandmother feed you, there's a good girl now.'

The Saheb would feed the ailing Sanatombi with a spoon. 'Please, Sanatombi, just one more. ... ...'

Sanatombi is not being difficult today. She has no one to be difficult with; she simply does not feel like eating.

'Shall we have a little of this grilled fish? Her Royal Highness sent it for you.'

'Royal Mother?'

Yes, her royal mother, the Dowager Queen, had sent it. The Lady of Ngangbam is still alive, Surchandra's queen Premamayi is still alive. Even today she has not stopped thinking of others or looking out for them.

She has finished eating. Tobacco is brought to her. Mainu offers her the hookah embossed with the gold lotuses.

'Where is the banana leaf, Mainu?'

'Oh, I forgot! Leiren, bring a piece of banana leaf.'

Mainu fashions a mouthpiece from the banana leaf and inserts it in place of the gold pipe. The hookah of gold lotuses is tiny. Maxwell had sought out the smallest hookah he could find in Calcutta and brought it. He had said, 'This is better, portable.' The hookah is embossed in gold and is smoked through a gold pipe. At that, too, the Saheb had said, 'Sanatombi, this pipe is terrible. Most unhygienic, it is never cleaned—you wash yourself daily but you have many dirty habits. Very bad—worse than your Hindu unclean pollution business!'

Maxwell looked after himself well and conducted himself very carefully. He never forgot his habits. He always chided Sanatombi for her lack of personal discipline, sleeping when she felt like, eating when she wanted to, skipping meals, and forbade her from doing so. Ever since Maxwell said so, she always smoked using a mouthpiece of banana leaf, and the gold pipe simply hung on the hookah.

She hands the hookah to Mainu and says, 'Little Majesty will come tomorrow for certain, won't he?'

'Yes, he will come tomorrow.'

'Send word for him to come tomorrow without fail. I have many things to discuss with him. ... ... Mainu, I am going to give my temple grove in Vrindavan to Little Majesty.'

'What happened to moving to Vrindavan when you are old? You can even move in before that when you have gotten a little better, and go back and forth. Why not just leave it be?'

'Mainu, I am not going to live in Vrindavan. It is fine to just live here, it is all right to die here.'

'You mustn't say that. Your humble servant is waiting for Your Royal Highness to move to Vrindavan and serve you.'

Sanatombi is silent for a little while. She looks at Mainu. She watches Mainu tidying up the room. Mainu seems to be a little tired of late. She is getting a little older. She is just a couple of years and a bit older than Sanatombi. Most do not know what Mainu is thinking, and what she is saying, not even Sanatombi. Mainu never likes to talk about herself. She never asks anyone for anything, or ventures an opinion. And so, everyone is afraid of Mainu, and none can see her as someone working for another person.

Sanatombi says, 'Mainu, are you still happy staying with me? Sometimes I think to myself, what will I do if you leave me?'

Mainu almost cries, and says, 'If you are going to say things like that to me, I am going to go away. It upsets me greatly, Your Highness, so please don't ever say things like that. What will we come to if a little illness makes you act like this? Your Highness has brought this illness upon herself.'

Sanatombi laughs a little and says, 'Fine, I won't say it. … … … Mainu, you have never once eaten from the Saheb's kitchen. You can rejoin the others if you want to. I will talk to Little Majesty.'

Mainu does not answer. Sanatombi knows the meaning of her silence. Mainu never talks about useless things for very long, but there must be something that she is thinking. It is true that Mainu has never left Sanatombi. Why is that? She never did once eat or drink with the Saheb. She cooks for herself. And there were many times she went hungry when she was not feeling well. When the Saheb learnt of this he had even hired a Brahmin to cook for Mainu. She has not been excommunicated. If she so desires, she can surely rejoin the others. Mainu knows this as well. But not now. She also knows that for all of everyone's efforts, Sanatombi's illness can no longer be stemmed.

She says to Princess Khomdonsana, 'Please write to the Saheb, my lady. Tell him to come soon. The onset of fever this time is not a good one. I don't know, I am very worried.'

Sanatombi has been getting a fever very frequently these days. Even if it ebbs for a day or two and it seems like she might be getting better, it always comes back again. Who knows why, but it has also been quite a long time since there has been news from the Saheb. The letter from three months ago was the last one. But Sanatombi does not bring this up. Mainu knows she thinks of the Saheb often but she does not mention him frequently. She does not know why. Perhaps she is upset with the Saheb for some reason.

She could only ask Little Majesty when he comes, 'Did you get any letter from your brother-in-law?'

'No, I have not received any, Elder Royal Cousin. There have been no letters from him these days for whatever reason. Fine, I will telegraph him. My brother-in-law is very busy. He said he was running around. But letters from there take a long time to arrive, my royal elder sister. I will definitely send him a telegram.'

'It is all right. I was merely asking. It does take some time for news to arrive from England.'

Sanatombi did not want her cousin to be inconvenienced on her account. But it could be her desire for news about the Saheb that has led her to frequently ask Mainu about the king's whereabouts.

'Mainu, I will go to sleep.'
    'Please rest.'
    'What did my royal mother say?
    'Nothing very much, my lady.'
    Sanatombi said to herself, 'What my royal mother endures on our behalf. She has always suffered on my account.'

CHAPTER 7

The war was over. The war between Manipur and the British: the war that brought Manipur's sovereignty to an end. How did that happen? The people and the princes had not believed it would come to this, but the princes of Manipur did not seem to have remembered that a house divided against itself cannot stand. The powerful British did not let it go so easily after the palace guards had cut off the heads of the white men. They attacked from three directions—the Kohima contingent, the Silchar contingent, the Tamu contingent. A man who had come with the Silchar contingent raised the Union Jack at Kangla Fort. He was Major H. St P. Maxwell.

When Jasumati heard that Chief Commissioner J.W. Quinton of Assam was coming because of the upheaval over the throne of Manipur, she came running to Sanatombi and reported, 'Sanatombi, your Sovereign Father will be coming back. They say that he will be coming with the "Comeson Saheb" this time. They say the throne will be given back to him. By the grace of Lord Govinda we will be able to see your father. … … …' It was true, it was indeed believed that Quinton would be bringing Surchandra with him. But the information turned out to be wrong. He was coming to capture Prince Koireng alive. It turned out that he was coming with a plan to annexe Manipur.

The Meitei soldiers fought for a fairly long time. The good and the bad, the weak and the strong, all stepped up—saying, 'I will fight too, I will fight too.' But how were they to know that it would be as a creek against the ocean? How could the backward soldiers of a tiny country stand up to the highly trained soldiers of the British? On top of that, many ignorant people held the Meitei soldiers back. Along with Paona, Yengkhoiba and his lordship the chieftain of Yaiskul, many others died, scattered, or fled.

News came to the palace, one after the other—news of the attacks by the British. Prince Koireng was not well at this time but he had no time to be sick. Even as he commanded the war, the king called the learned to read the signs from the gods. The astrologer said, 'It is but five days until the ill-boding grip of Saturn is released.' After hearing the words of the astrologer, just as the Divine Majesty was about to offer a feast to Lord Govinda, news arrived—the British were advancing upon the palace from three directions. The ladies of the palace and all the women and children were shifted to appropriate havens. All the idols, including that of Lord Govinda, were relocated to the royal priest's. The Divine Majesty Kulachandra, Thanggal, Koireng, his younger brother and company remained in the palace. And the defence was merely a group of sixty soldiers. It was therefore clear that it was futile, but sixty select men lay in wait to fight off the vast army of the British.

The soldiers who came in from the west arrived first, led by Lt Colonel Rennick. They brought with them advanced weapons, but what of the Meiteis? Each man was issued only five rounds, no more was given because the soldiers who had set out to fight had taken a lot of ammunition with them, and the palace was left running low. But Thanggal did not tell that to the soldiers. He said, 'Men, stay sharp; Kangleipak must be saved … … …'

Shots were fired at the northern and western walls. The commanders of the drafted contingents said, 'Men, do not fire wildly at first. Fire one bullet first towards the heavens.'

'Victory to Goddess Durga'—bang bang bang. Sixty rounds were wasted, fired into the sky.

A son of Heingam said, 'Hey, this is not right when so few cartridges are given.'

The British planted their flag at Kangla Fort. The people of the land wept a great deal. Sanatombi also heard the news at her hideaway at Koirenggei. She knew right away that it was impossible for her Sovereign Father to return to rule the golden heart of Manipur. Sanatombi thought to herself—So what becomes of Sovereign Father? And what will befall my uncles? So, it is all over!

She felt a deep regret—If only her Grand Queen Mother were still alive! She would have easily disciplined these errant princes. She would have easily settled it all. … … … If only my uncle Koireng had not kept secrets hidden from me! I might have done something too.

The Grand Queen Mother had said to her one day, 'Sanatombi, your father is a good-natured man but he is not forceful, he does not know how to build allies.'

This was also what had troubled Chandrakirti—that, and his Koireng's combativeness and rebelliousness. Even though

Sanatombi was young, the Grand Queen Mother had confided these internal matters to her. She was confident that she could hear these—Let her hear, she was now the eldest of her father's children. Indeed, the Divine Majesty Chandrakirti had been troubled. He had worried—Who will follow after me, what will happen after me! He knew his Surchandra and Kulachandra would not make strong monarchs. There were only two men who could ensure its future, to fend off the powerful, crafty British government waiting for the right time and an opportunity to swallow Manipur whole, who could defend Manipur, rife with rebellious princes waiting for their chance. One was Prince Koireng, the other was Prince Pakasana. But no, it was forbidden to break with righteousness, Manipur must maintain righteousness.

One day the king saw in a dream a tall ladder that grew taller and taller to touch the heavens. It became one with the sky. Climbing it were his sons, one after the other. Surchandra seemed to be leading them. All of a sudden, as they climbed the ladder, they seemed to start fighting amongst themselves. Each tried to drag the other down. The ladder and all his sons fell towards the earth.

'Oh, dear Lord Vishnu, what have I dreamt!' muttered the king.

The Grand Queen Mother and the king called all the princes together into a room. No one else was allowed to enter.

The Divine Majesty said to them: 'My sons, do not do what is not right. Know that the day righteousness is no more is the day Manipur comes to an end.' Sanatombi heard this story from her Grand Queen Mother.

The Lady of Meisnam knew her son's time was at hand. His illness this time did not augur well. She consulted the scholars, and they said, 'The forty-years' reign that the Divine Majesty was foretold has some time left yet. According to our calculations, we think there are four more years to go.' But the Lady of Meisnam worried. She was his mother, and she worried. She issued strict orders. 'No other people may enter the palace, word must not spread that the king was not well.' The aging Grand Queen Mother, the Lady of Meisnam, did not remain quiet. She worked out all the internal affairs and gave discreet directions—for what if something ill befell Chandrakirti? The king's condition worsened but the Lady of Meisnam did not have time to shed tears, she did not have time to grieve. She called Thanggal and consulted with him, 'So what about it Major, what needs to be done?' Thanggal was her closest friend, one who had been in service of the court since the reign of her husband Gambhirsingh.

'One must be prepared, Queen Mother. Your sovereign son did not heed my advice but there lives one powerful man still whom we should be careful about ... ...' answered Thanggal. The Lady of Meisnam knew of whom he spoke. He was Prince Borachaoba, chieftain of Yaiskul, the son of Maharaja Narasingh. It hearkened back to the time before the accession of her son. It was counsel that Thanggal had given a long way back to Chandrakirti, before his sons rose up in rebellion.

Thanggal had said to Chandrakirti in the past, 'Your Majesty, it would be better to uproot the imperial sacred fig that is growing at Nityaibat Square. It is a tree of great strength.'

'Major, you may not touch my cousin. Do not worry, he will do no harm,' the king had hastily replied.

The king Chandrakirti's fondness for Prince Borachaoba had been the talk of the land. But Chandrakirti never once forgot that even though they were only clan relatives, had it not been for his uncle Lord Narasingh, it would not have been possible for him to sit on the throne of Manipur. It would have been easy for Narasingh to have occupied the throne of Manipur had he wanted to. But Narasingh was a man of true Meitei blood. He never once forgot how during the Seven Years Devastation, his older cousin Gambhirsingh had tried with enormous difficulty to wrest Manipur back from the Burmese. Gambhirsingh had also known that it would not have been possible had not a generous and selfless man like Narasingh been by his side. The monarch Gambhirsingh, the Powerful and Patriotic, had held his younger cousin Narasingh, who had shared great tribulations with him, in fond regard. Before he died, he had held his hand and entrusted the merely two-and-a half-year-old Chandrakirti to his younger cousin. For nine long years, Narasingh had brought up little Chandrakirti without a false thought and ruled the land in his stead. Chandrakirti never forgot this. He could never wrongly take Prince Borachaoba who had grown up with him like a brother in the same house. And this he also knew—that his mother had never known Narasingh's true character. His intensely protective mother sometimes took things to excess. That the attempt to assassinate Narasingh with the swing of a sword was recorded in the court chronicle greatly pained Chandrakirti.

Once he passed away, the Lady of Meisnam and Thanggal completed all the arrangements. Surchandra was installed as king before the royal remains had turned to ash. It was not announced to the public before all the preparations were in place. The Lady of Meisnam had said as the king was taken to the royal cremation ground, 'My king, mother's son, my precious, so you have left your mother today.' But she did not weep for any in the land to see.

Today, the throne that was so deeply loved is occupied by foreigners. What next? The people waited restlessly.

Sanatombi felt restive—she felt a certain emptiness, it seemed as if there was nothing more to think about. She was at her war haven. Elders, women, children, all wept: Manipur was finished, what would become of them? She did not feel like joining them and talking, she preferred to keep to herself. And what with her husband's mother weeping—her Manikchand had not made it back. Sanatombi consoled her, 'He will surely return, mother. The royal son-in-law is not that stupid.'

She was also worried about Manikchand. This trip to Cachar was one she had encouraged. She had strongly urged him to go to Calcutta to see her Sovereign Father but who knows what he would have done, where he had reached? And what use was any news that he would bring now?

People started returning to their shambolic homes after things had calmed down a little. Sanatombi and company were going home too. Now it was clear, the ruler of Manipur was the Political Agent. He now sat firmly in Kangla Fort.

One heard the news, one after the other—Kulachandra was captured, Thanggal had surrendered himself, Koireng had been apprehended from the house of the Dewan of Thokchom. People were left watching from a distance. No one could come to his aid. Word spread—horses and cattle of the Meiteis had been rounded up, the people were starving. … … … For a full month, the golden land of Manipur was like a graveyard. The royal market shut down. The defeated Meiteis were brought in droves. They were made to kneel in rows in front of the sahebs. Several tall white soldiers walked to and fro in front of them. The Meitei who had accompanied the sahebs from Cachar said in Meiteilon, 'Say you are sorry, say it.' One among the lot raised his face and replied, 'Why should I say I am sorry?'

The saheb said in Hindi, 'What did he say?'

The interpreter replied, 'He says he is sorry, Saheb.'

'All right. Let them go. Tell them they must be afraid of us.'

'Go, go along now, go back to your homes,' the Meitei said.

They returned to their homes but found there was no rice to eat, there was no money to buy any. Destitute women and children overcame their fear in their want and came out at night with lit torches. They picked up anything that had been discarded, anything that people could not take with them and had left behind as they fled across Yaralpat. They scattered as soon as they heard the horses of the foreign soldiers. It was a time when foreign soldiers swarmed all over the place.

Sanatombi did not know what to do. She paced back and forth at the Nongmaithem household, nursing a burn she had not known before. Slowly she began to gather news—news of where the Lady of Ngangbam had fled to, of her mother Jasumati, her younger sisters, and of her friends and acquaintances.

She wanted to meet the Lady of Ngangbam just one time. But whom could she go with?

'It would have been good if Manikchand were here,' his mother said to herself constantly. Sanatombi also wanted her husband to come back soon.

The Lady of Ngangbam was all she had now. She was also the only one she could really talk to, and the Lady of Ngangbam would have accurate information. Her younger brother Lukhoi was not that astute.

Oh, what a fool I have been, we missed it by so little— Sanatombi thought to herself all night long.

The Lady of Ngangbam had called her one day and talked with her. Sanatombi was already at Nongmaithem at the time. And the king was her Sovereign Father Surchandra. The Lady of Ngangbam had said, 'Sanatombi, I have a suspicion. I see that your uncles are perhaps dividing into camps. There are some who resent your father—this will not be good for your Sovereign Father. And what with the rivalry between Koireng and Pakasana increasing, I am very worried. What shall we do? It would not do to remain silent.'

'I have not heard anything. All right, we will do as you say.'

'All your uncles are fond of you. Mainly, Koireng must be pacified. I will handle Paka. I have also spoken to my younger sister Angangmacha to calm Koireng down. Why don't you also go and meet your uncle Koireng, and approach him in a roundabout way and see? Do not say anything directly.'

Sanatombi came to Prince Koireng's residence early one evening and asked Angangmacha, Younger Lady of Ngangbam, 'Is Royal Uncle in the residence?'

Koireng came out briskly when he heard Sanatombi had come. 'What is it, my dear, what is the matter?'

He was in the house in a serious meeting with some people at this time. He sent the others away and, after making her sit down properly, asked again, 'What has happened that you have come today, and so late?'

Sanatombi did not know how to talk indirectly.

She forgot what the Lady of Ngangbam had advised her when she saw Koireng and blurted out bluntly, 'Is it true what I am hearing, Royal Uncle?'

'What have you heard?'

'That Royal Uncle has some ill feelings towards Sovereign Father.'

'Who has been saying all sorts of things to my child?'

'It is going around that people are angry with Sovereign Father, including you. Why is that? What's going on?'

Prince Koireng realized it was not possible to keep Sanatombi in the dark. He looked down like an apprehended thief. He knew that Sanatombi trusted him and loved him more than anybody else.

'Whatever your dissatisfaction, please tell me. I will tell Sovereign Father. What have you been doing to each other?'

'It is not quite what you're thinking, Sanatombi.'

'Then what is it?' pursued Sanatombi.

'I know what you are getting at. As Lord Govinda is my witness, I have no gripe with my elder brother the king. But we are outsiders, we are the children of the other wives.'

'Who is saying that?'

'No one, but we are reminded of it very often.'

'But by whom?'

'Who else but your uncles who are the blood brothers of your Sovereign Father? Mainly Paka, he has been very insolent, Sanatombi. ... ... Huh, as if to say my brother is the king. They are the king's younger brothers, and we the sidekicks. We feel very hurt, Sanatombi.'

'Are you saying my Sovereign Father is also of the same mind?'

'Let us stop this talk. It is all right by me, but Jila is young and I cannot control him.'

'Please do not spare the insolent, break them into pieces.'

'One cannot just do that, can one? The ties of blood are not that simple,' Koireng said with a laugh.

Sanatombi realized the matter was not an easy one. It had become serious. And that Koireng's anger was at her father, Surchandra. What could she do? She was but young, and she did not live nearby. How was she to put out the embers that were being fanned. She had also heard of little incidents of resentments here and there on the side, but she had not realized that matters had come so far.

Before he died, the Divine Majesty Chandrakirti had given his youngest son Jila'ngamba a boat to ride in and play. He named him Victor of Jila because he was born after the durbar at Jila. He loved him dearly as he was the youngest. Prince Jila often rode in this boat and played in the royal moat, and would pull it ashore and store it in the armoury when he was done. Jila remembered the boat sometime after his Sovereign Father had died and sent for it, only to be refused by the armoury. He was told, 'We cannot give it, it is the order of His Highness, the Keeper of Horses.'

Prince Jila was stung. He was also embarrassed in front of his servants. He sent his men again: 'I was not planning to ride in the boat, I was only going to keep it in my house from now on.'

The reply came: 'No property of the palace can be given to anybody without informing His Highness Prince Pakasana, the Keeper of Horses.'

'Oh, so now I am no longer of the palace! I have now become anybody!' The truth was that Prince Pakasana was a man who liked rules, and he watched closely over his elder brother Surchandra. He thought playing on boats in the royal moat could pose a danger to the enemy-ridden throne at Kangla, that it could result in strangers infiltrating the land easily. But Prince Jila who was merely seventeen did not understand this.

Instead of ordering it to be kept at the armoury, it might have been better to have called him and explained things to him, but being a half-brother, the misunderstanding came first. There had been no time to find out the truth and umbrage had preceded.

Little resentments began to mount in this manner. Though not obvious on the outside, Surchandra's brothers born of the same mother were on one side—Prince Pakasana, Prince Thambousana, Prince Gopalsana; on the other side were those born of different mothers—Prince Kulachandradhwaja, Prince Koireng, Prince Angousana and Prince Jila'ngamba. The camps fell into place. The seeds of Manipur's destruction were sown from that day on. But Koireng did not reveal all to Sanatombi. He chattered cheerily about other things and escorted her back to the Nongmaithem family himself. Sanatombi thought her work was done and believed that there was nothing to fear, that it was all hearsay. She did not worry any further and went on living her life at Nongmaithem.

One evening at dusk, Manikchand returned quite unexpectedly. Manikchand's mother wept as though he had come back from the dead. She had believed he would never return. No one had thought he would be able to slip in like this in the middle of the war with the foreigners. Manikchand said, 'There are about twenty of us who came back together.

We came after getting a pass from Silchar, it wasn't that much trouble. ... ...' The entire household was overjoyed. Sanatombi was also happy, and they exchanged news about the ones who returned, and those who had stayed back. She asked him if he lost anything, about where he took refuge, and so on.

Manikchand's mother said, 'I don't know what to say, my son, I had not believed you would ever return. It is good that you have come back in one piece. Some of the paddy got confiscated by the sahebs. They left most of it when we said it belonged to Her Highness. Four of your uncle's horses got caught up in the sweep. So many horses were taken away this time.'

'Where do they keep them after taking them away?' asked Manikchand.

'I don't know, people say Indian traders bought them and took them to India. Never go away again from now on, my son. Whether we have enough to eat or not, let us all stay together always as a family from now on.'

After dinner that night Sanatombi said, 'Did you drop in on Sovereign Father?'

'How could I, what with all the news around us. I had thought of going but Ta'Cheiteino and the rest said it would be pointless, they would not allow us to see him even if we did, so we dropped the idea. Then we thought we just had to get back in to Manipur, and hurried back. ... ... The Lady of Ngangbam, and your mother, how are they all?'

'I don't know. It's been a while since I saw them. They say they have come back from their war havens.'

'Then I have to go look for them. And where are the British staying?'

'In Kangla,' answered Sanatombi shortly. She had hoped that Manikchand would bring news of her Sovereign Father. She had heard that some people had gone to see him. They had been allowed to and there had not been much restriction. But Sanatombi let the matter go and did not question Manikchand any further; perhaps it just hadn't worked out that way.

Sanatombi worked very hard those days, it was astonishing. As soon as the sun rose, she jumped into the pond. She dabbed clay on her forehead and went into the kitchen. She got the meals cooked. There was no waiting for her to finish the chores. The Brahmin cook from before the war had stopped coming and Sanatombi had not been able to ask after her.

When it became apparent that war was going to break out, Sanatombi had said one day, 'Mother Brahmin, please do not come any more. It is not good to travel far from home at this time.'

'But who will cook for you?'

'Mother and I will manage. There aren't many of us anyway.'

She sent people to ask after the Brahmin cook at her hideaway one day but she did not ask her to cook again, thinking, 'What is the point?'

Sanatombi lay low. She just worked and worked. Manikchand began to gather news of his friends and relatives—the Lady of Ngangbam, Jasumati, Princess Khomdonsana, and others.

Manikchand said, 'Shall we send some paddy over to Royal Mother?'

'Send some to the mother Brahmin instead.'

Sanatombi said to her mother-in-law, 'Mother, teach me how to weave with fine thread. I am going to weave.' Her mother-in-law was surprised to hear Sanatombi say this, but she was pleased too. She thought to herself, 'My daughter-in-law has come to her senses.' Sanatombi and her mother-in-law wove together. It was not that Sanatombi did not already know how to weave at all. She had taken part a little bit when the Grand Queen Mother hired people to teach the maidens of the palace how to weave. Among the looms set up in a row for the princesses there had been one for her too. But she did not learn to weave properly, having merely wandered about here and there. Her mother-in-law was surprised that Sanatombi wove beautifully, as if she had woven all throughout her life. She had stick-to-it-iveness and her handiwork was neat like those of the clever women of Wangkhei.

One day, Manikchand said, 'The queen, the Lady of Ngangbam, is asking us both to come urgently. There seems to be an important matter she wants to talk to us about.'

'What about?'

'I think it is about Prince Lukhoi. The Lady of Ngangbam has some inside information that they are going to appoint a new king altogether for Manipur.'

'What about Sovereign Father?'

'That is what the queen wishes to talk to us about. It seems the government is no longer thinking about bringing back His Majesty. ... ...'

'Then what is the point? What is there to talk about?
Would the royal son-in-law please go on your own. Please tell
my royal mother I wouldn't know anything about this.'

Manikchand did not bring it up a second time. He went
by himself. He apprised her when he returned but seeing
Sanatombi's manner, he felt apprehensive and did not
elaborate. Who knew how she might answer!

Sanatombi did not seem to want to hear much about the
palace these days. Sanatombi was only twenty-two years old
but she seemed to have matured all of a sudden. How frugal
she was and how carefully she ran the house. Her mother-in-
law was overjoyed.

'If only I could get a grandchild now that she has become
responsible,' said Manikchand's mother.

A child had been miscarried at two or three months.
Sanatombi was taken very ill at that time. Despite a lot of spells
and rituals she never conceived again. Seeing her mother-in-
law's disquiet Sanatombi said one day, 'Since I am not bearing
any children, please find another wife for the royal son-in-
law. … … …'

Her mother-in-law was startled. The thought had indeed
crossed her mind—Did she know that or what! She did not
think that one so young would say such a thing.

Life was calm on the surface but a powerful storm continued
to rage within Sanatombi. Not a day went by when she did
not remember her good-natured Sovereign Father who had
shamefully sought refuge among strangers. She wanted to see
him just one time, but how? She did not get help from her
husband Manikchand. He was a clever man in other ways. He

was a man who conducted himself very carefully and never wanted to put himself at personal risk. And so Sanatombi kept quiet.

What is to be done about Sovereign Father? What shall I do, what to do?—thought Sanatombi all the time. But she felt exhausted, she didn't feel like doing anything, of being able to do anything.

But news filtered in whether she wanted to hear it or not. News of the might and accomplishment of the foreigners. One day, a deep sound of cannons was heard from the direction of Kangla Fort. The earth shook, the windows and doors of the house rattled loudly. It was a fearsome sound. People panicked—What is it now? They began to pack up their belongings, preparing to flee again. But it was nothing, only the sahebs blasting the two enormous leogryphs of brick that stood in front of the palace citadel. Why? And to say that that was nothing?—She saw the two beasts clearly before her eyes. The child Sanatombi had played at their feet. She knew the two beasts very well. They were alive to her. Oh, so the two beasts have been reduced to dust!—Sanatombi was grieved, she was very aggrieved.

News came shortly, news that the British had installed Crown Prince Bhubonsingh's seven-year-old little grandson as the king of Manipur. Notices were posted here and there—'Manipur is ruled by a king.'

But what about Sovereign Father!—thought Sanatombi.

Manikchand gave the news when he came back, 'What a travesty, a child who is not entitled has now been made king … … … Do you agree with this? It is like they have not thought at all about Prince Lukhoi … … … .'

'What of it? He is also the grandson of royal grandfather Narasingh.'

Sanatombi busied herself as a housewife. She mopped and wove and the house was sparkling clean. Not once did she show her unhappiness to members of the household. Manikchand organized the household and sought to establish a good and proper lifestyle.

But she heard the news, one after the other, and she could not hold it in any more. Their only Lukhoi died from smallpox. The government's refugee Surchandra, Ruler and Victor of the Hills, passed away in Calcutta. There was nothing more to think after this.

CHAPTER 8

It is still light when Princess Khomdonsana enters Sanatombi's invalid room. Tall and slim, she is not fair like Sanatombi. There are slight traces of pockmarks on her face. Khomdonsana is setting out to sing in the women's choir for the Festival of the Goddess.

Sanatombi looks hard at her and says, 'Where are you off to all dressed up?'

Khomdonsana is clad in blue of a darkish hue. She wears a chequered stole of raw silk. Her hair is swept up neatly in a chignon that falls in a long ponytail. She wears a marei necklace, a single strand of gold.

'There are two places to sing at today. First, we sing at the palace, then there's another venue, at the house of the palace administrator.'

'But why so early?'

'The teachers say I have to sing a solo passage. I am going to go rehearse it a bit first.'

'Oh, so you can sing solos and all now?'

'Who knows. ... ... Well, I will get going now. You're all right today? All your staff are here. Ta'Matum, sister Mainu, I am off ... ...'

Princess Khomdonsana sashays out. Sanatombi laughs, staring after her—Look at her, all married and all. She had been very little at the time of her Sovereign Father's departure from Manipur. Her mother Jasumati had taken her to her parents' home to bring her up. Her little sister had never known the pleasures of being a princess. Sanatombi loves her all the more as she thinks this.

Matum the attendant runs in.

'The Divine Majesty is here.'

Sanatombi is set all aflutter. She is overjoyed that he was showing up after saying he would not be coming today.

'Matum, call Mainu. Tell her to lay out the royal seat.'

The etiquette-savvy Mainu hurries in and places a white cloth on the red velvet, covering the reed stool that was laid out, and retires, standing off at a little distance.

On this day, Little Majesty does not come in the car they call Italy, nor in the horse carriage, but on horseback with two junior attendants. In his riding outfit. He wears khaki breeches and a bright red high-necked polo shirt of fine wool. Rather than taking the royal seat set out for him, he pulls up the little chair and sits down right next to Sanatombi's bed. Sanatombi's face brightens as if shrouding clouds had parted. She says laughing, 'How nice my little brother looks in red.'

'Do I look like a little shrew making off with a red chilli?' the dusky king answers with a laugh.

'Not at all. You look great whatever you wear.'

'So, what have you had to eat today?'

'Oh, I don't know, Mainu keeps feeding me all kinds of things.'

'Sister Mainu is a gem of a treasure ... ...' Saying this, he looks and smiles at Mainu standing, shrinking in a corner.

'Little Majesty, when I am dead and gone, place your sister Mainu with my little cousin the Lady of Ngangbam.'

Maharaja Chandrachand's queen is also a maid of Ngangbam, a niece of Premamayi, the Lady of Ngangbam.

'Has someone been saying you're going to die?'

'No, but who can tell when we will die. ... ... This current illness, Little Majesty, I do not think I am going to recover from it.'

'What kinds of things are you saying?'

'So, why have you come today when you said you were coming tomorrow?'

'I will come today, and I will come tomorrow too. ... ... Here, my royal sister.' He hands three pieces of paper to Sanatombi, three telegrams.

'Brother-in-law sent these from England. He sent them within a week, but they arrived all together today. I wanted to let you know so badly that I hurried here.'

'What do they say?'

'He seems to be very worried to hear Your Royal Highness is not well. In the last telegram, he asks me to take you to Calcutta for treatment. He wants me to let him know if you get any worse and he also says that he will come.'

'Show me.' Sanatombi reads the telegrams.

Sanatombi smiles a little. It is not really a smile of disbelief—it is a smile of exhaustion. Her lips smile but her two eyes are filled with tears.

Sanatombi holds Little Majesty's hand and is silent for a while as she fights back her tears. Little Majesty does not know what to say. The people standing around them wipe their eyes.

She says, 'Little Majesty, let me say something. I have been wanting to say it for a long time now. The temple grove in Vrindavan that your brother-in-law bought for me, take it. It is better that it belongs to you.'

'Will you not reside there again? It is good to keep a temple grove.'

'I am not going. I will just stay here near all of you.'

Little Majesty understands what Sanatombi wants to say, but he asks no more. He says many things to make her forget, making light of it all, and laughs merrily to try and cheer up his cousin.

'Little Majesty, is there anything very wrong to give me a cremation after I die?'

'There you go again. If you are going to say things like that, I am not going to come any more. Even if you must die, do it after brother-in-law gets back.'

'You are the king, whatever you decree will be accepted. Please cremate me after I die.'

'Yes, yes, but what if I die before you?'

'Do not say that, such things must not be said.'

'Is a king immortal, my royal sister? Come, let us talk about happy things. Mainu, did you get the bread I sent over? Was Her Highness able to eat it? I had my Brahmin cook in the palace bake it. They are really getting very good, my Brahmin cooks.'

Little Majesty knows that Sanatombi was used to their food after having lived with the Saheb for so long. She ate it with pleasure.

'Aren't you getting late, Little Majesty? Go, you will be late for Lord Govinda. And why did you come on horseback? Don't go riding in the dark, late at night. … … … Little Majesty, tell your brother-in-law I shall not be going to Calcutta. … … … It is fine here too. How would Calcutta be any better?'

Ever since Sanatombi took ill, the Saheb would take her to Calcutta or Shillong for medical treatment every so often. Today, too, across the distant seas, he is thinking of taking his Sanatombi to Calcutta for treatment. But today she does not want to go. The zest to live seems to have died in her. Little Majesty also knows that though not seen outwardly, Sanatombi has started to fall apart. The patient had ceased to help in her treatment.

'Sister Mainu, what will she eat tonight?'

'She does not eat at night, Your Majesty.'

'Bring the bread I sent, let us give her that.'

'I'll eat on my own. Go, you will be late. It is not good to be late. They will be waiting to start the dhop choir.'

'I will stay to watch you eat. I will not go to Lord Govinda today,' answered Little Majesty.

'You cannot do that, Little Majesty. You must not take the royal duties of the land lightly. I am all right, go.'

But still, the king cannot leave Sanatombi.

'Little Majesty.'

'Yes, my royal sister.'

'I was thinking. … … …'

'What is it, Royal Sister?'

'I want to offer kirtan hymns for Sovereign Father. I have been seeing Sovereign Father in my dreams very often lately.'

'Your humble servant offers one every year. The kirtan I offer to Lord Govinda every year is for all the kings of all the lineages of Manipur.'

'I know that, but I was thinking I wanted to offer one on my own. Please arrange that. If I can't ask you, who can I ask?'

'Then of course I will.'

Sanatombi had offered a kirtan when the Saheb was around. But it was not at Lord Govinda—it was at the queen's, the Lady of Ngangbam. She had wanted to offer it at Vrindavan but she was not allowed to enter the grove at the Pool of Radha that the Divine Majesty Chandrakirti had built. Unhappy at this, she had talked with the Saheb and had bought a temple grove at Vrindavan. Sanatombi wants to offer the kirtan to Lord Govinda just for her Sovereign Father. Maharaja Churachand decides to arrange it to fulfil his cousin's wish. Sanatombi looks intently at her family cousin. Her two eyes brim with tears. Little Majesty lowers his head.

Sanatombi was the royal granddaughter of His Majesty Gambhirsingh. And Churachand was the royal grandson of His Majesty Narasingh. The two kings had loved each other greatly. They were related by lineage, not blood brothers, but they had joined hands on the battlefield, on the battlefield to save Manipur from the Burmese. What relation could be closer than that powerful alliance forged by Gambhirsingh, unmatched in his prowess with the spear, and Narasingh, unmatched in his prowess with the sword, as they came together as one, to deliver Manipur, a land that had been under the Burmese for seven years. It was a relation forged when together they washed their hand-weapons that had slaughtered the Burmese, in the dark, clear waters of the Chindwin. The river Chindwin was their witness. One said 'my younger brother' and the other murmured 'my lord' in reply. They never dropped the word 'my' whenever they addressed each other. With a strong bond in trust, the true defender of truth Narasingh never once harboured a false thought about his kinsman Gambhirsingh. Manipur never forgot the story of these two men. Everyone still remembers it. This was why Chandrakirti loved the sons of Narasingh. Therefore, years later, it is no great surprise to see the royal grandson of Narasingh treat the royal granddaughter of Gambhirsingh with love.

After a little silence, Little Majesty says, 'From tomorrow onwards, I will come once a day every day to look in on you. Otherwise if brother-in-law hears of it, it will be the end of me.'

'I am fine, Little Majesty. You are the king; it is not right to waste time like that. Your brother-in-law was always angry about wasting time. All right, leave now. I will send word if I am really not feeling well. Never fail in your worship of Lord Govinda, Little Majesty.'

Little Majesty rides off on his horse. Sanatombi listens to him as he gallops away. Her uncle Koireng had also ridden off like this one day; Maxwell had ridden off like this one day too. The sound of the horses fades into the distance. Sanatombi grips the bed that she lies in and sobs. Sanatombi is weeping, and today she takes a pleasure in it.

CHAPTER 9

Manipur was once again a land ruled by a king. The sahebs installed Amusana, also known as Churachand, the great-grandson of Maharaja Narasingh, in the newly constructed palace at Khurai Khundon. Lord Govinda was also moved back in from His refuge during the war. How happy the people of the land were, how many of them wept. They had not believed that the royal family of Manipur would ever return to the throne of Manipur. They had thought that the throne where the Lord of Lords Pakhangba, the Heavenly Serpent King and Leisna, his Meitei queen, had shone for one hundred and thirty-five years would become a playground of the foreigners. They had thought they would never hear the great bell of Lord Govinda ring again. There was great joy when they heard that the child Churachand, the royal great-grandson of the Divine Majesty Maharaja Narasingh the Powerful and Patriotic, was made the king.

But the sacred palace at Kangla had become a footstool of the foreigners. On one hand, the clever British sought to conquer the hearts of the Meiteis but on the other, they razed and renovated Kangla Fort, its shrines that had been there for many centuries, and the palace, in order to display the civilization of the West. Most of the buildings in the Kangla were pulled down. The shrine of Lord Wanggol, the shrine of Goddess Nunggoibi, the shrine of the Elders, the shrine of Lord Lainingthou the Mighty, were all considered unsightly and razed to the ground. And with that, the religion, rituals and beliefs of Manipur, its civilization, were flattened over. From that day on, the distinctive face of the land of the Meiteis began to gradually disappear.

But life slowly returned. The calendar of service rituals to Lord Govinda was resumed without any change. The king was the child Churachand, but the land belonged to Lord Govinda. Slowly the lives of the Meiteis began to continue again. They began to build new residences, temples and offices at the new palace. But the foreign government ignored their pain at not being allowed to return to Kangla: they pretended to be unaware of it.

The mother of Little Majesty, Lalitmanjuri Numitleima, Maid of Moirangthem, and her father, the king of Moirang, tried to conduct themselves with propriety. They went door to door to the princesses of Manipur and the distinguished royal ladies of the royal dynasty and requested them: 'Little Majesty is but a child, so would the royal princesses and ladies lead, instruct and arrange for the uninterrupted worship of Lord Govinda?' Princesses who believed a lost Manipur had come back again came in droves and gathered at the palace. They gave advice for the king, and taught him the ways of the royal court. Some who remembered the age gone by also wept. Though the Maid of Moirangthem, mother of Little Majesty, and her father remained very deferential, there were some new princesses in the new palace who sometimes said hurtful things. The royal grandfather, the king of Moirang, requested

the princesses: 'Would their royal highnesses arrange the new
kunja ras dance to be performed for the first time in the new
palace … … … .' Sanatombi was also among those who were
called up. Sanatombi did not want to go; she was now living
quietly. Ever since her Sovereign Father died, Sanatombi had
lived a quiet life. She did not feel like doing anything. But
her husband Manikchand and her mother-in-law said, 'Go,
why don't you; and if you don't want to be a part of it, don't.
It is not nice not to go when people invite you in a friendly
manner. And on top of that, the worship of Lord Govinda
must not be interrupted. … … …'

So, Sanatombi went one day. The ras rehearsals had already
started. Since it was a dance that everyone pretty much knew
already, it was really more about getting together, so they sat
around, talking. They asked about each other: 'So how have
you been? And where did you flee during the war … … … .'
Forgotten were their sundry dissatisfactions as the fallen
princesses of Manipur once again found a place to gather
and meet.

'And how are you, Sanatombi?' her royal aunts asked
of her.

'Just getting by.'

'Has Manikchand returned?'

'Yes, he is back.'

They all knew Manikchand looked after Sanatombi well
and let her know no want. The well-behaved Manikchand was
always highly commended by her royal aunts. But Sanatombi
brooded. The new palace and the new set-up was like a dream
to her; there seemed to be something not quite right about
it. She sat in a corner watching what the others were doing.

At this point, a sharp-tongued, newly hired court attendant at the palace, a busybody from who knows where, came up to her and said, 'Why are you so quiet, Your Highness? You must want to be the lead dancer since you are still young, but I suppose it is not possible now. It seems Little Majesty's older sister Muktasana is going to lead. Do not be unhappy, Your Highness, it is just the times. I don't know what to say, it's actually quite sad come to think of it.'

Having said this, the busybody pretended to have work and briskly walked away. Sanatombi did not know whether or not she really felt unhappy, but it left her feeling wounded.

She had answered shortly, 'Sister Tathong, I am not here to be in the dance. I merely came because I was asked to.'

Sanatombi felt deeply hurt. She could not easily dismiss the words the insolent woman had hit her with. She remembered her Grand Queen Mother. She had been a part of the worship every time a ras was offered to Lord Govinda ever since she was very little. It was not simply because she was a daughter of the royal household that she was the lead dancer or the second dancer, or played the role of Radha the Divine Consort. Sanatombi danced very well. Her movements were right, her sense of rhythm was faultless. Her Grand Queen Mother had summoned teachers to coach her privately in movement and rhythm. How her great-grandmother laughed happily, as she tilted her head and watched.

She would say, 'My granddaughter is the best of all. Sanatombi, rise on your toes a little when you dance. Do not make a lot of waves, just give a hint of it. … … … Now, that's it, how beautiful, my princess heroine, my heroine.'

Sanatombi smiled as she danced.

'Do not smile, it is not proper. It is not proper to smile when worshipping Lord Govinda.'

'I won't smile tomorrow, all right?'

'You will end up making a habit of it.' So instructed her great-grandmother.

Sanatombi said to herself, 'I do not covet them at all, I do not want to be in their dance at all. Just look at what they think they are doing, I do not envy them at all.' She remembered how she was made to dance the Divine Consort in the maha ras when she was very little. She slept soundly in her nurse's lap. They woke her up just before the disappearance of Krishna when it was nearing the time for the Divine Consort to make her entrance. The dresser had already swirled her hair into a little topknot and finished everything while she was still sleeping. They only had to put the dancer's skirt and peplum on her and shake her out of her drowsiness before they made her go in and join the dancing cowherdesses. She had not forgotten any of it. She remembered it all, and it came back all over again. And to think that I would want to lead in today's dance! What a laugh … … … —thought Sanatombi. She was fairly young at this time and she was furious. Sanatombi quietly crept away while everyone else was noisily occupied. She headed not to her husband's home in Wangkhei, but straight to Janmasthan, the residence of the Dowager Queen, the Lady of Ngangbam. She herself had no idea how she came to head in that direction.

It was getting a little dark that evening. Manikchand had said he would send someone to fetch her. She left without waiting.

On this day, there was no royal parasol over her head, no attendants, as the daughter of Maharaja Surchandra walked by herself towards Yaiskul. She had never walked alone like this before. Even though Manikchand could not send her on a palanquin, or keep palanquin bearers at home as had befitted the princess during the reign of her Sovereign Father, he never let Sanatombi go by herself. He had unfailingly assigned a person to accompany her every time. Today Sanatombi came out unhappily from the new palace all by herself. She was feeling an urgent desire to see the Dowager Queen Premamayi.

The deposed Premamayi still lived; Premamayi, the Conqueror of Leisang, had now moved and was residing at the place called Janmasthan in Yaiskul. She lacked nothing befitting a queen. With servants and attendants, relatives and clan, she still upheld the dignity she had lost. Today she was no longer the queen of the land of the Meiteis but her residence was still the gathering place for the people. The capable Lady of Ngangbam still lived with fortitude. Sanatombi walked quickly to the Dowager Queen's. Over and over again, she revisited the mocking words of the acid-tongued woman.

Suddenly the passers-by scattered frantically to the side of the road. Sanatombi did not know why. She looked about her. All of a sudden there was a sound in the distance. The sound of horses. Sanatombi looked behind her a little uncertainly and stopped for a while. It was a time when foreign soldiers were all over the place, swarming their neighbourhoods, in every corner and byway. No one could tell when and where they would show up. Sometimes a white foreigner would chase down the passers-by and beat them—for not saluting, for not making way. In this manner, they had instilled great fear among the common people and tyrannized them. At the slightest incident, at the merest sound, they panicked and cowered in the canals and riverbeds. Raising their heads to see if they had gone by, they would only come out later from their hiding places. But Sanatombi did not hide because she did not know how to hide, she didn't know she should hide. She stood still, bewildered, in the middle of the road.

There were only two horsemen. It was almost full moon, and a gibbous moon came out from behind Nongmaijing Hill. It was the month of Mera and it was not yet completely dark; there was still some light in the twilight. The two horses came up to her and stopped. It must have been a surprise to come across a woman standing in the middle of the road in this time of great terror. The two horsemen dismounted. Sanatombi saw them—one was a foreigner and the other a Meitei. The Meitei came up to her and asked, 'Who are you?'

Sanatombi did not answer.

He came in a little closer and took a good look and said, 'Your Highness, what are you doing? Where are you going without any attendants?'

Sanatombi knew this man very well. He was the man they called Ta'Pheijao, the man who used to look after the horses of her horse-loving royal uncle Prince Pakasana. Pheijao went up to the man he had come with and said something quietly. The foreigner saluted Sanatombi. He was Maxwell. Major Maxwell, the first Political Agent of colonized Manipur—the man the Meiteis called 'Menjor Mesin'.

Sanatombi stood there looking. She did not know what to do. She was a little relieved that Pheijao was there.

Pheijao said, 'What is going on, Your Highness? Aren't you afraid to be walking without anyone?'

'Ta'Pheijao, I am going to my royal mother's on an urgent matter. I am not afraid. It is still early.'

But the two men kept standing there. It seemed they could not simply take leave of Sanatombi. The Saheb said something in Hindi to Pheijao. This was not the first time Sanatombi was seeing the Saheb. She knew Maxwell very well. It was just that it was evening and she could not quite make him out. The Saheb also knew Sanatombi.

Pheijao said, 'Your servant the Saheb says he will drop you off.'

'It is not necessary.'

She quickened her pace. The two men came along leading their horses. Pheijao said a word or two to Sanatombi every now and then. But Maxwell did not say anything. He followed them leading his horse behind him.

Sanatombi turned to him and said, 'Saheb, I can manage. I can go on my own.'

The Saheb bowed his head again and said, 'Your Highness, sit on horse. I will walk.'

After a year and a half in Manipur, Maxwell had picked up passable Manipuri.

Pheijao said, 'Your Highness, please mount my horse, your servant will attend to you on foot.'

Sanatombi walked on ahead without saying anything. She did not ride. The two walked behind at a little distance. As they approached the gate of Kangla Fort after crossing Sanjenthong Bridge, the Saheb said to Pheijao in Hindi, 'Pheijao, I asked Bamacharan to come see me about an urgent matter. He must be waiting for me. Tell him to wait for me for a bit. You go on into Kangla. I will escort the princess.'

'Your servant has to drop off here to deliver an important message. Please permit your servant the Saheb to attend to you.'

'What nonsense,' Sanatombi replied.

It was not that she was afraid of the Saheb. Sanatombi had met many sahebs like him. The Grimwoods had occasionally invited over Manipuri princes and princesses to the homestead at Konthoujam. She had had the chance to meet foreigners at close quarters as her royal uncles Pakasana and Koireng had also occasionally taken her along. Sometimes she and the memsaheb had boated together in the little pond in front of the bungalow. Various other sahebs had also come by. Sanatombi was among the princesses when the princes Koireng and Pakasana shrewdly introduced their nieces and daughters to Grimwood and his memsaheb in order to keep friendly relations with the foreigners. She was not that afraid of foreigners but she felt uncomfortable going with this man, because a few months earlier there had been an occasion when she had spoken harshly to this Saheb. Today was the second time she was meeting him.

Pheijao translated the Saheb's words, 'Your servant Saheb says he will attend to you. But I am afraid I can't go any farther. Please do not have any misgivings. … … …'

Having said this, he mounted his horse and went galloping into Kangla Fort.

They walked silently. Sanatombi in front, the tall Saheb leading his tall horse behind.

Walking in silence must have felt awkward, for Maxwell said after a great deal of thought, 'Princess, are you angry with me?'

'About what?'

'When we met that day, you were anger with me … … … angry … . I sent you a message, I will send word.'

Sanatombi knew what he was talking about. It was about the other day.

'I will send word,' he said again.

'It is all right even if you don't.'

'So, you're stopped being angry?'

'What on earth is this man going on about? Why should I be angry? No, I am not angry. Just keep walking.'

'Don't be angry with me.'

'No, I am not angry, all right?' Sanatombi burst out laughing. His words had amused her greatly.

After they had walked a while, he said again, 'Tired? Are you tired? Sit on horse.'

'No, I'm not tired. We are almost there.'

'Afraid of horse?'

Sanatombi laughed again and said, 'No, I am not afraid.'

'Sit on horse. Can I take you?'

'Let's just walk. If you are tired, you can mount.'

The Saheb did not know the meaning of the word for 'mount'. He thought she meant 'ride'. Without a thought, he grabbed Sanatombi and swung her easily up on the horse. Then he leapt on it as well and they rode off at a clip.

Maxwell knew where the Dowager Queen lived. Even though the foreigners at the time instilled fear in the people, their leaders like Maxwell who came to rule the land tried very hard not to anger the wounded royal family. Maxwell was not a common soldier, and so he came to see the queen every now and then; he tried to maintain relations with her. So, without a word he brought the horse to a halt near the queen's gate. Seeing that he was about to take her in after putting her down, Sanatombi said, 'You can go now.'

But Maxwell stood there still.

Sanatombi said, 'Go back now, you hear? It is all right. Go, go. ...'

The forty-something Maxwell said 'good night' and rode off on his horse.

Sanatombi did not look back. She ran in towards the Dowager Queen's residence.

She said to the first servant she met, 'Ta'Modhu, go call sister Amuchaobi. I am Sanatombi.'

Amuchaobi came running briskly and said, 'What are you doing, my lady, what is the matter? What are you doing here in the dark?'

'Forget it, bring a washcloth from my royal mother. I stepped on something, let me just go bathe.' Saying this, she jumped into the large pond of the residence with a splash and bathed.

The Dowager Queen was worried beyond words. She said, 'What are you coming and doing here? Why didn't you just let me know? Has someone done something to my child?'

'It is nothing, Royal Mother. I had gone to the palace as I was asked to come and take part in the dance. I just wanted to see Royal Mother so I came.'

The Lady of Ngangbam did not believe her. She knew she was keeping something from her, but she said, 'Oh, I thought something had happened. You really are always up to one strange thing or another. If you wanted to come you could have come in the morning. Is anybody there? Go take a message to the Nongmaithem household and tell them that my daughter is here with me and I will send her back.'

Sanatombi was drying her hair in front of the full-length mirror. She laughed and said, 'If I want to come and see my royal mother, why should I have to wait till the morning?'

But Sanatombi did not tell the Dowager Queen what she had come to say. She also did not tell her how the Saheb had brought her here. The queen knew Sanatombi's temperament and said nothing more but she knew there had to be some matter she had come about; it was not a simple visit.

Meanwhile, Maxwell galloped into Kangla Fort. Pheijao was waiting at the royal gate. He handed him the reins and asked, 'Has Bamacharan come?'

'Yes, sir.'

He strode inside quickly and said to the waiting Bamacharan, 'Sorry to keep you waiting. Bamacharan, will you please come tomorrow morning between nine and ten?'

'Yes, sir. May I bring a few more files?'

'Oh yes.' And saying this he went inside his room.

He washed up and went out through the eastern door and strolled along the bank of the big river. Moonlight beat down on the glistening current of the slowly flowing waters. Maxwell stood quietly on the riverbank and thought, 'What a beautiful country.'

The Lady of Ngangbam was the most ill-starred of all the queens of Manipur. Her husband was chased away by his brothers, her children Prince Lukhoi and Princess Tamphasana died before their time. If she had had the chance she could have employed her skills and courage to be a celebrated queen of Manipur like Linthoi'ngambi or the Lady of Meisnam. Having known the Lady of Meisnam, she had taken part in the intricate nuances of politics but it was her bad luck. She had to live today, watching as others took the throne and foreigners ruled the land. But because she was born blessed with superior qualities she could not stay down for long, she could not stay quiet even if she wanted to. She heard that after the foreigners had taken possession of Manipur and she had settled down, at the row of residences of the princes enclosed by the Kangla and now where the British platoon was situated, many cows were being slaughtered and eaten by the white men.

Aggrieved, the religious Brahmins came to the queen and petitioned, 'Royal Dowager Queen, please do not let them to do this at least. It is better that we your humble servants were shot rather than live hearing that cows are being killed inside the Kangla. We will go in and kill ourselves. Please tell us what your royal command is.'

The Lady of Ngangbam laughed and said, 'Who am I today? Who will listen to me in this land where my lord does not rule any more. The child-king will not be able to do anything. But let me see, if your holy personages will calm down and wait a little.'

She sent a message without any delay. She sent for Bamacharan Mukherjee.

Bamacharan was a clerk who had been kept at one time by the king of Manipur. Keeping an Indian like him was necessary because they needed a person to communicate with the sahebs since they did not know their language. Princes of the day like Prince Pakasana and others had learnt English but it was not adequate to conduct business. Today the Bengali Bamacharan was not only a clerk to the sahebs but he had become an influential man among them. When the Lady of Ngangbam thought of him, one of her staff said, 'Should we still trust him, Royal Dowager Queen? What good will he still do for Manipur?'

True, he was suspect. Although he was once a man who had enjoyed the prosperity of Manipur, Bamacharan had turned witness for the sahebs at the trial of Koireng Tikendrajit. People had despised this ungrateful man.

But the queen said, 'One must not be angry with people like them. They are outsiders, they come looking to fill their stomachs. Chaoba, there are many people like these. Is there any lack of people whose faces turn with the times? Did you not see this during the reign of your sovereign lord? I will call him and talk to him a bit, and if it does not work I will talk to the Saheb.'

Bamacharan kowtowed to the queen as before and waited for her word. He felt discomfited.

The queen called, 'Mister Clerk Bamacharan.'

'My lady, at your command.'

'Mister Clerk, I have heard that a lot of cows are shot and eaten inside the Kangla. Do not let them do this, it is not good. Nothing good will come of this.'

'It must be the work of rowdy white soldiers, my lady. Your servant Maxwell is not a person to do something like this.'

'Even if he does not do it himself, he is the head. He must put a stop to this. What kind of a leader is he if he cannot control his men under him.'

'Your servant will inform him immediately.'

'Mister Clerk, it is not a good thing to do as you please and hurt the sentiments of the people just because you are the rulers of the land. Why didn't you tell him; you know everything. Have you forgotten the ways and customs of the Meiteis?'

Bamacharan lowered his head. As he was about to take his leave, he requested, 'Will the Dowager Queen please tell Maxwell as well? He will come himself and kowtow to you. Please also tell him of any other dissatisfactions. Manipur is still a land ruled by the king. It is only a matter of Maxwell looking after the land for him as he is still a child. Please call and meet with him.'

'We will talk about that later.'

In this way, the queen met with Maxwell on occasion. The queen's brothers and Bamacharan interpreted for the queen and let the Saheb know whatever she had to say. They also stopped shooting cows openly but most people never knew that even at this time, the fallen queen of Surchandra had not stopped thinking of her people, nor stopped thinking of Manipur.

But the Lady of Ngangbam had nothing much that she wanted any more; she had no more desire for power and station. For whom and why would she desire that? When it came down to it, all she had left as her own were her three step-daughters from her co-wives. She spent her days with her defeat at the hands of others buried deep in her heart.

It also slowly came to light that Maxwell, the man who first hoisted the foreigners' flag in Manipur, seemed to have had a little of their interests at heart. If Manipur were to be kept as a land ruled by a king, the question of 'Who would it be?' arose. At that time Maxwell had submitted to his superiors that if a king were to be installed, Prince Lukhoi, the son of Surchandra, would be the right choice according to custom, and appointing him would best serve all interests ... ... These communications that went on within the government reached the queen's ears one day, and that was why she had wanted to see Manikchand and consult with her eldest daughter, Sanatombi. The Lady of Ngangbam was aware that the throne of Manipur went to the lineage of Maharaja Narasingh because Maxwell's recommendation was rejected by the Viceroy. But she never brought up this matter with anybody. And so, while the queen did not think of Maxwell as their enemy, she called him up on occasion and let him know indirectly: 'Do not do as you please, for subjugation is not on the outside, it is inside.' Even though she talked about many things indirectly, she let the powerful British know clearly what she wanted them to know. She also reminded them that the kings of Manipur had come to their aid in the past. She also let it drop as in a casual conversation, 'When the Ngamei tribes had surrounded you and were about to kill the foreigners' women and children at Kohima during the reign of Chandrakirti, who was it who arrived in time to help them? Who was the man who personally came to save them? It was my husband, Crown Prince Surchandra. But you abandoned such a man. You did not come to the help of my husband, a man who was not given to honeyed talk. … … …'

Maxwell also took the queen's counsel first when it came to matters of tradition. He too knew that the Lady of Ngangbam was no ordinary person, that she was a capable queen of Manipur. Maxwell wanted to win the hearts of the Meiteis and so he took the queen very seriously. He was aware that even though the fallen queen of king Surchandra was no longer on the throne, she still occupied an important position. It would not do to take this lightly. And Surchandra was not a king who was expelled from the land because he was not loved.

But even though she received respect from the sahebs, the Lady of Ngangbam never again attended the festivities and events of the land. She would not be able to bear people pointing to her as a fallen queen. And so, she thought—I will lie low. But her suffering people never stopped gathering in droves at her place.

One day Sanatombi was fishing with the nets in the pond at
the queen's residence. Her aunts sat around their sister-in-law
Premamayi. How happy they all were meeting and talking at
the house of the Lady of Ngangbam that day. It was after they
had eaten that Premamayi, having gathered them all together,
said it had been long since she had had a meal with her
younger sisters. Sanatombi also came from the Nongmaithem
household to join the lunch for the princesses. She went off
while the others were talking, and having caught two fishes
when she pulled up the fishing nets that a house servant had
cast in the pond of the residence, she stayed on fishing for fun.
She was not with the others as they sat around.

There was one important reason the queen, the Lady of
Ngangbam, had called her sisters-in-law today. The queen
had heard that there were some among the princesses who
were not faring well. Some had fallen destitute during the
turmoil and chaos of the war and had even been reduced to
adding water chestnuts to their rice for their meals. They were
living in great hardship—like the proverbial proud python
that starves itself to death. The Lady of Ngangbam was very
distressed when she heard this and wondered—What to
do? During the thirty-six years of his reign, the monarch
Chandrakirti was absorbed in the law and order of the land
and in developing his kingdom. And so, he did not have time
to set up his daughters and women for the future. It was not
just his children, he did not have time to think of anyone
individually. He was not able to think of personal matters
while he was dealing with the responsibilities of Manipur as
a whole. In addition, it was a time when the Anglo-Manipuri
relations that had been established since the time of Maharaja

Bhagyachandra had become much stronger. He always attended to these ties very closely. He maintained relations with the shrewd foreigners very carefully. He had to face many a big groundswell and raise Manipur to a higher level, and so he did not think about small matters. On top of that, he did not think he would die so soon.

In those days, all the princesses were found sons from good families and lineages of accomplishment to marry. They did not look much into the man's own capability and personal accomplishments because, with the merger of their destiny with that of the royal family, it followed that those would be taken care of. The daughters of Chandrakirti were all married to sons from families of good breeding but they were not all men who were worthy individuals. The Lady of Ngangbam was truly agitated when she heard of the distressed princesses of Manipur. With their father no longer as the king, and the shape they were in, what was to be done? Nor did she have the resources to help and set them all up herself.

She first called upon the clever ones among her staff of old and consulted with them about what she could do. The queen summoned various people and sought their advice, and Bamacharan was one among them. She thought that even though Bamacharan was an outsider, and was no longer under her patronage, there was no harm in soliciting his thoughts. On top of that, Surchandra had died as a friend of the foreign government. If one were to think about it, they ought to listen to the queen of Surchandra and do accordingly. She hinted as much to Bamacharan. She said, 'Mister Clerk, my lord Surchandra was never an enemy of the foreigners' government—this much you will agree with. And the throne of Manipur belongs to the Divine Majesty, and this all has happened because of ill fortune. This too you ought to agree with. The Divine Majesty died while on the throne—and I am his queen. … … …'

'It is true, Royal Dowager Queen, it is all true. It was fated to turn out this way. Oh Lord, it is all Your will!' Bamacharan wiped away his tears. And then he added, 'I am just a servant, and even now I am a servant of the palace. What advice could I give? But what you say is all true, I understand it all. I will convey this matter to your servant Maxwell and then I will bring word back to you.'

He kowtowed and left. After discussing the matter with the Saheb he brought back word: 'Maxwell says the queen may say anything to him but he has the Chief Commissioner above him, and the Viceroy. But he will listen to what the queen has to say and he will help as much as possible, and so on … … … . He will come if the queen asks him to.'

The queen listened to this message and thought about it. This matter was not one she should be involved in openly, and thinking it would be better if each of them said so individually, she had called her royal sisters-in-law and princesses to join her in a meal to discuss it.

When she called in her royal in-laws and brought the matter up, there could be no further discussion. The princesses called their father's name out loud and started to weep volubly. 'Sovereign Father, are we now to beg from other people … …

… .' The Lady of Ngangbam waited for them to calm down. Then she said, 'My sisters, there is no use in crying now. Let us discuss carefully what to do. If the ladies will listen to what I am thinking and then consult with the royal sons-in-law, for you should not do simply as I say.'

The solution was to develop paddy lands for the princesses, but to develop the paddy fields they would need the permission of the foreigners. And so, she said, 'Your Highnesses may not be aware, but we now cannot develop or sell paddies without the orders of the Saheb. You must know that Little Majesty and the king of Moirang rule in name only. They cannot do anything. Now you know, don't you, that Manipur exists only in name. … … … Even if the word of Little Majesty were to hold sway, that time is yet to come. He is just a small child now, and so I think there is no harm in requesting the Saheb if we are to keep our paddy fields.'

'We cannot do that, it is better that we die.'

'We can't just do that, can we? If you think about it, it isn't really begging, it is about pointing it out. It is a matter of letting them know that they should not interfere in our interests. Who is going to respect princesses who are starving? Will the princesses think about this carefully? I myself do not see a problem.'

They began to discuss seriously what was to be done. The queen did not want to call the Saheb to her residence for a talk. Since they were in power, it was not desirable to leave the request of the princesses in black and white in writing in case they were turned down. And so, after a great deal of discussion, they decided that they would first write to

Maxwell saying that they would like to meet with him. The Lady of Ngangbam remembered Sanatombi when they were discussing this matter.

'And where is Sanatombi?'

'She is fishing in the residence pond.'

'Oh, how daft that girl is. Go call her. Tell her to come and listen to this.'

Sanatombi came in with her sarong half wet.

'Go change your clothes first, Sanatombi. Come listen to what we are talking about.'

After Sanatombi came back after changing her clothes, the Lady of Ngangbam went over what they had been talking about all over again.

Sanatombi did not answer. Her face reddened. Neither did she cry like her aunts.

'What do you think about this?' asked the Lady of Ngangbam.

Sanatombi did not answer.

'What are you thinking?'

'I do not agree. I'd rather sell vegetables than ask them.'

After convincing Sanatombi with great difficulty, they decided that some of them would go and meet the Saheb. They would say directly, 'Do not stop us from developing paddy fields in our own country.' But it would not do to start a confrontation, it would be best to smoothen things over as much as possible. Only a few sensible princesses among them would go, and Sanatombi, the royal daughter of Surchandra, would be among them.

After the rest of them had left, the Lady of Ngangbam held Sanatombi back and continued, 'Sanatombi, it is stupidity to be courageous at the wrong time. Man cannot live by courage alone. It must be expressed at the right time. And this you may not know, Mesin Saheb seems unlikely to do much wrong. They say he recommended that your younger brother Lukhoi should be made king. It was just our bad luck.'

'Who said so?'

'Your Ta'Tonjao reported to me. It is surely correct.'

They all knew Tonjao of Moirang was a man who was still loyal to them. As a soldier of Kulachandra, Tonjao of Moirang had met the foreign soldiers in battle. Kulachandra was defeated, and he was on the run. Kulachandra and his retinue, along with about two hundred men, fled towards the Nongpok Chasat. The idea was to reach Yunnan but they did not know the way.

Tonjao of Moirang said, 'I know the way, I will lead.' He left three days ahead with a Burmese man, carrying 3000 rupees tied in a bundle of royal cloth. When Subedar Tonjao of Moirang arrived at the rendezvous spot he and the king had agreed upon, the king was not there. Kulachandra failed to reach Yunnan and had turned back. Tonjao's beloved Surchandra was alive at the time.

The Lady of Ngangbam told Sanatombi these stories. At last Sanatombi said, 'All right, I will also go—but I find this excruciating, my royal mother.'

CHAPTER 10

One morning before lunch, three palanquins with parasols and attendants emerged in a procession from the residence of Maharani Premamayi and headed north. Princess Phandengsana and Princess Amusana, daughters of Maharaja Chandrakirti, rode in two of the three palanquins, and in the last one rode Princess Sanatombi, daughter of Surchandra. Her two royal aunts wore long-sleeved tops of velvet, fine stoles draped over with flannel shawls. The younger Sanatombi was also properly attired and turned out. It would not have done to dress inappropriately. She wrapped herself in a striped sarong the colour of mustard blossoms. She put on a white half-sleeved shirt with embroidered lace borders of the kind that was worn in Calcutta by women of the progressive Brahmo Samaj families of the day. She only pulled on a red Kashmiri shawl over it. The shawl had a fine border of gold. Trade between Manipur and other parts of India had begun during the reign of the Divine Majesty Chandrakirti. Many fine imports had begun to be used. Residents of the palace especially used fineries imported from outside Manipur a great deal. Her husband Manikchand, who was fond of going abroad and was a skilful trader, often brought back these beautiful things. During this time, Manipur had an agent permanently stationed in Calcutta to facilitate this trade with the outside world. He was Chancellor Gulapsingh. As Manikchand was close friends with Gulapsingh, the former always stayed with him whenever he visited Calcutta. Manikchand had seen this kind of fancy blouse worn by the Indian women of the Brahmo Samaj at some point and had one made for Sanatombi to wear. Sanatombi had never worn this blouse before as she had never found an occasion all this time. She had taken the shirt out on this day and wore it for the meeting with the Saheb. It was very becoming on Sanatombi. She tied her long hair in a reverse chignon with its lush tail raised to fan up like a black mynah cock. But Sanatombi went gloomily on her palanquin. She gripped the balustrades of her palanquin.

With parasols over their heads, the princesses of sovereign Manipur crossed the royal gate of Kangla Fort. They were met warmly by the Saheb's men who were waiting for them. This was the first time since the outbreak of the war that the princesses were entering Kangla. Who knew what her royal aunts were feeling but Sanatombi was immediately struck by the absence of the two tall leogryphs that had been blown up by cannons. The two beasts that she loved so dearly were not there today. Not a fragment of them was to be found. Everything had been swept away—They had destroyed them! From then on Sanatombi began feeling unhappy. Had it not been the royal command of Dowager Queen Premamayi, she would have turned back from the gate. But no, her aunts were present and she was merely accompanying them.

The Saheb himself came out on foot to receive them. He bowed his head respectfully to them and proceeded to lead the way. Sanatombi tried not to look to her left or to her right.

She was afraid to look, for who knew what else she might see that would pointlessly inflame her again. Bamacharan and Tonjao of Moirang were waiting where preparations had been made for their reception.

Bamacharan said, 'Please come in, princesses.' Tonjao of Moirang did not say a word. He was there because the queen had instructed him to be present. There were also a few people who knew the tongues of other lands. There would not be too much difficulty in their talking with each other.

Except for seeing him from a distance, her two aunts had never met the Saheb at close quarters until this day. They had not been among those taken to the sahebs' place by Koireng as they were all either married or were fully grown maidens at the time. Sanatombi had been taken along as she was still somewhat a young girl. What with not knowing the language, and seeing the Saheb for the first time, the princesses felt very uneasy. But Sanatombi looked hard at Maxwell. Flustered as to what to call him or say, Princess Amusana blurted out, 'Daddy sir.'

They sat in silence for a while.
     Maxwell first noticed Sanatombi's calm face—her fair face framed by her black hair, her delicate eyes. The two clear, sharp eyes were looking at him. The blue eyes of the dignified Saheb could not meet these eyes for long. He diverted his gaze but when he returned his eyes upon her he saw once more—Sanatombi was still looking at him. The look was not that of a friend.

The matter was simply this—You must not stop the princesses of the sovereign king from tilling new paddy fields, you must not tax these lands, and so on. The discussion was mostly in Hindi and English. Even though Maxwell had begun to learn Meiteilon he did not know it well enough to express himself properly on important matters. He still had difficulty in comprehending. After listening to everything, he had the interpreters let the princesses know—He will look into it. But he cannot proceed until he had informed his superiors. 'I will let you know later, I will try my very best. ... ...'

While Maxwell was talking in English, Sanatombi said impatiently to Bamacharan, 'What is he saying, Mister Clerk?'

Bamacharan translated into Meiteilon.

Sanatombi said, 'Mister Clerk, the matter of creating paddies is of small importance. Ask him why he has confiscated the paddy fields belonging to Sovereign Grandfather and Sovereign Father. Tell him to till new paddy fields for the new king. He cannot take the possessions of our fathers and forefathers. Tell him we do not agree.'

Maxwell listened to Sanatombi's words and though he did not understand fully, he got a general grasp and could tell that she had a problem. He smiled a little. The words from this young woman, these words of anger that spilled rapidly from her delicate lips were unfamiliar to him. After listening to her words, he turned to Sanatombi and said, 'Princess, I will let you know later.'

'Ask him, Mister Clerk, how much later?'

Maxwell said, 'As soon as possible. I will surely get news back to you. I am afraid I cannot take action without hearing from my superiors. Please indulge me and please wait a little.'

Sanatombi listened to these words and then she said, 'Why did you blow up the beasts of Kangla? Did you also take orders from there to do that? What use was it to you to destroy the two beasts?'

The Saheb could not understand her as she had spoken these words too rapidly. He did catch her say Kangla. He asked Bamacharan, 'What did she say?'

Bamacharan hesitated about telling the Saheb what Sanatombi had just come out with. The others were also somewhat alarmed. They did not think that Sanatombi should have brought up this unrelated matter when they had come to talk about paddy lands. They were apprehensive about what else the uninhibited Sanatombi might bring up next.

Seeing Bamacharan's hesitation, Maxwell asked again, 'Tell me what she said? Why is she angry?'

Bamacharan let him know briefly that Sanatombi was expressing her unhappiness at finding the 'Dragon Gate' gone.

There could be no more discussion after the matter of the destruction of the Kangla leogryphs had been brought up. That ended it there for the day. They left Maxwell saying over and over: 'I will do as best I can … … … Thank you for your visit. … … …'

Maxwell saw them to the palace door and saluted them. And the three princesses came back on their palanquins in silence. They did not talk, they did not know what to talk about.

Sanatombi said, 'Your servant may please go home now.'

'What, let us go to the Dowager Queen and give her the news. She will be waiting.'

'I will come later please.' Saying this, she stepped off the palanquin, kowtowed to her royal aunts, then got back on to the palanquin and headed off towards the Nongmaithem house.

Sanatombi could not forget the two leogryphs. She could not forget how they were there, she could not bear how they were not there—So, it was him, so it was this Saheb. Is this the man who is said to have written to recommend Lukhoi? Why did he blow up the beasts? Was it unavoidable? Was he ordered to? Lukhoi—her younger brother Lukhoi, the only son among the daughters—was very spoilt, very misbehaved, but today he was no more. How they had fought, how they had played near the enormous beasts—How would it have been if Lukhoi had been alive! The line of my Sovereign Father is now ended … … … . Sanatombi's eyes filled with tears as she went on her palanquin—What use is it now to be angry? I should not have spoken so angrily … … … .

No one in her husband's household had thought Sanatombi would return so quickly since it had been decided that she would lunch at the Dowager Queen's after meeting the Saheb. They were surprised when Sanatombi came in on her palanquin. Manikchand and the rest had already eaten.

Her mother-in-law came out running and said, 'My goodness, hasn't the princess had lunch?'

'No, I didn't have lunch, mother. Please send Tembi, I would like to bathe.'

After she had entered the house, her husband Manikchand asked about the meeting with the Saheb. Sanatombi answered with terse replies. But she did not mention how she had brought up the destruction of the leogryphs. She also did not feel like talking about this much. She thought it had been a waste of time to have gone at all. She had only come back with a feeling of sorrow. She had seen Kangla Fort today after a long time. Kangla! Their Kangla, which now belonged to others.

Manikchand listened to her and said, 'All right, I will talk to Haodeijam Cheiteino. If necessary, we will send a separate letter to the Viceroy on behalf of you three daughters of the sovereign monarch. They should really be thinking about you even more.'

Sanatombi did not answer. She did not pay attention to what Manikchand said. Their meeting with the Saheb today made no sense to her. She felt a great shame—I wish we had never gone, she thought over and over again. Her former cook had been waiting for her on this day. She went in to make lunch for Sanatombi. Manikchand changed his clothes and went out; it looked like he was going to meet Cheiteino.

Sanatombi crawled into bed at this untimely hour, waiting for her lunch. Her servant Tembi was folding her clothes that she had worn earlier. Sanatombi watched Tembi as she worked. Her long-serving Tembi. She was much older than Sanatombi but no one called the simple Tembi older sister or aunt. Everyone's servant, Tembi. Sanatombi watched her and smiled a little. She looked at her fondly.

This Tembi was the child of a slave at the time of Surchandra when he was the crown prince. When the queen, the Lady of

Ngangbam, was still the crown princess she had married off Tembi with a proper trousseau into a well-to-do household in a village. But Tembi came back before long, saying she would not stay there any longer. One asked her, but all she did was cry and there was no understanding her. They called the husband's family and asked them, and they too said, 'We have no idea, she just cries and cries.' Saying, 'All right, since she does not agree, let her stay here,' the Lady of Ngangbam talked nicely to the husband's family and sent them away. A year after that, when the Lady of Ngangbam released her slaves, Tembi refused to go with her father and mother. She remained in the residence of the crown prince.

One day, a few years later. On a morning dark with a winter fog, some men from the armoury brought into the crown prince's residence a young boy found wandering carrying a bundle. He was brought in because when asked, he had replied, 'My sister lives in the residence of the crown prince.' He turned out to be correct: the young boy was discovered to be Tembi's younger brother who had been taken away by his father and mother when he was little. When they opened the bundle, they found about ten measures of assorted rice, two serving dishes that had been missing for a long time, and a coconut that had been brought as an offering to the crown prince. Upon inquiry, it turned out that Tembi had set aside some of the rice that was cleaned for the meals of the crown prince and had smuggled them out to her younger brother along with the rest of the items. When people tried to beat and scold him the Lady of Ngangbam gave him back his things and let him go. But what of Tembi? She was beside herself.

Sanatombi was a young maiden at the time. She called Tembi to her and said, 'Tembi, prepare my herbal wash … Tembi, go wash my clothes. … … …' Using her in this way, Sanatombi shielded Tembi. She had worshipped Sanatombi from that day on. She came with Sanatombi to the Nongmaithem household on the day of her wedding and she had stayed on. The well-to-do Nongmaithem family had several slaves, but when the Saheb put an end to slavery after the British had taken over Manipur, the household set them all free. How the slaves who had lived as part of the family wept when they left. They all parted with love in their hearts, but they all left as free beings. Tembi was not a servant even though she was the child of a slave. She had given herself over to Sanatombi of her own free will. She did not know how to take back her heart that she had given away. All she knew was Sanatombi; for her there was no room to think of anyone else. Tembi lived happily, she lived with Sanatombi.

After the cook had finished preparing lunch, she came to tell Sanatombi that her meal was ready. But at that late hour, it was just a matter of sitting in front of her plate for Sanatombi could hardly swallow a thing. She would have gone entirely without eating if the cook had not especially cooked for her. Though the cook did not work for the Nongmaithem family, she never stopped coming now and then. She cooked for them not because she had nothing to eat at home, but because she loved Sanatombi. And on top of that, her daughter Mainu and Sanatombi were very close friends. As Mainu's father the Brahmin was a chef in the royal household, the cook's family had long been connected with the palace. Her daughter was a little older than Sanatombi so Mainu would come to spend time with her, and her mother was in the service of the Lady of Ngangbam as a favoured lady-in-waiting. There were times when mother and daughter would eat and stay overnight. Even after Mainu's father left his service as the palace chef on account of his having taken a divorcee as his mistress, Mainu and her mother did not sever their ties with the palace.

Now Mainu was also a married woman at a distant place. In Thoubal, where her father lived with his second wife. The two stopped seeing each other often after she got married. It was just the occasional 'How is Mainu?' to get news of her. Sanatombi knew Mainu did not live happily in her husband's family. The reason why Mainu did not visit her family home in Imphal was not because she was so happy that she forgot to. It was because she harboured a bitterness at her family. She harboured a bitterness against all; she was bitter at life itself. But for hearing news of her now and then, Sanatombi did not see Mainu frequently. Sanatombi had thought she would visit her in Thoubal one of these days even if Mainu did not come to visit, but she only just thought about doing so and never got around to it.

She talked with the cook after lunch. She asked, 'And how is Mainu, Mother Cook? Is she expecting any children?'

'No, Your Highness. The reason I came today was also to talk about something but they said you had gone to meet the Saheb. If I had gone back you would have gone without eating at all.'

'So, what brings you here, Mother Cook? What is the matter?'

'Your Highness, your servant Mainu has come back home saying she will not live with her husband any more. This has been going on for a while. You know all about it, but this time she has refused, she says she will not go back. What shall I do, Princess, I am having a terrible time. What with her being a Brahmin woman, what decent man will marry a divorcee? Can you please talk to her? What has happened has happened. How can it look good if a woman has funerals in two homes?'

'Is she still unable to forget Ta'Khema?'

'I don't know, I don't know anything. I don't know what to say about her. I asked her before I gave her away in marriage; I got her consent before I had married her off. Now she says, "I won't stay there, if you ask me to go back I will kill myself." I don't know, I am totally at a loss,' so related Mainu's mother the Brahmin.

Sanatombi knew Mainu and Khema were deeply in love. But they never got married. For Khema was a Meitei. So that could never be—but then how can love be stopped either?

Khema was a son of the Sanasam family in the neighbourhood. An only child, he was very spoiled. The neatly groomed and pampered Khema wandered around with a flute tucked into his waistband. Wearing a sarong of mustard yellow and flashing his white teeth in a smile, Khema came by when Mainu was working on a sarong and sat by her embroidery stool. He came and stood by the paddy pounder in the moonlight. He came and played his flute, he chatted with her. Sometimes he clumsily joined in pounding the paddy. They could never go without seeing each other, but it never went beyond that; they only loved each other madly. Mainu's father and mother were still together then. No one saw much wrong in Khema coming to their house as he was a boy from the neighbourhood. Who would stop him from coming and going as he pleased?

Ever since Mainu had her hair groomed as a maiden, there had been an astonishing stream of marriage proposals. What with her father being a chef in the palace, and her beauty and industriousness, they ran out of seats to put out for people who came seeking her hand in marriage, nor could they eat all the food that was brought for her as gifts. But Mainu refused them all. Many young swains came to court her, but seeing her lack of interest they all slowly retreated. As she said no to one and all, her parents thought that she might as well live at home a little longer. But an unfortunate incident happened around this time. Her father could not go to the palace any more after he took a divorcee as a wife, and he himself left to go live with this second wife.

Mainu's mother said, 'Even if Your Holiness has taken a divorcee as a wife, please look out for your children. It is not right to besmirch the children as well. Please go and live there, and we will keep our distance here.'

But it was only a matter of time before the household was turned upside down. It was at this time that her mother failed to realize that Mainu and Khema had fallen in love. During her pain when her husband took another wife, Mainu's mother forgot that she should look after her daughter. Meanwhile, Khema and Mainu wandered together plucking flowers in the month of Mera, they went pranking together during the spring festival, they climbed Baruni Hill together—and they loved each other.

Khema said, 'Mainu, I am a Meitei. Will it end with us not belonging together?'

Mainu said, 'I cannot think of anybody else. I will never get married.'

'Mainu, do you think you can bear being exiled to Haojangban with me?'

A little later, Mainu said to Khema, 'Ta'Khema, will you be able to disappear into Haojangban in exile together?'

It could not remain hidden any longer. The skies were rent asunder. Mainu's family as well as Khema's family were both alarmed. 'All is lost,' they said. In those days, those who violated the boundaries of marriage norms received severe punishment. Mainu's older brothers intimidated Khema, humiliated him, and sought ways to keep them apart. Mainu stopped eating, and took to her bed and remained under the mosquito net. But Khema climbed a nearby tree and played his flute late into the night. How Mainu wept and wept upon hearing him … … … . Meanwhile, Mainu's sisters-in-law kept her under a close watch.

It was summer. It was towards the end of the month of Kalen, entering the month of Inga. Suddenly a great illness spread through Imphal. People trembled in fear. Many died during the course of a single day; members of a family fell ill one after the other. They waited for the sick to die from this disease that had no cure. Smoke from funeral pyres darkened the skies. There were times when two or three people were cremated together. But the Meiteis did not let a single corpse go without a cremation. People were so terrified of the hairy spirit called *de-ul*, which stood only a forearm tall, that they shut themselves into their homes before sundown and remained quaking indoors, looking after the ones who were taken sick. No one walked outside and grass grew over the roads. None could inquire after one another, all they could do was hide. Courageous young men from the neighbourhood girded their loins and went from house to house looking for the dead and cremated them. Khema was one of them, and the pampered young man emerged as the bravest of them all at this time. He tirelessly took part in the cremations of many dead people on the riverbank. People looked up at the skies anxiously, waiting for the rains to fall.

The rain clouds gathered, the rains came down. Slowly the scourge lightened up on its own. The ones who survived, survived; the ones who perished, perished.

After things got better people began to ask, people began to think about the others—who had perished and who had survived? By good fortune, there were no casualties in Mainu's family. Mainu began to wonder how her Ta'Khema was, and what became of his family. She was too embarrassed to ask openly. The two families had very bad relations on account of the two of them. Mainu wondered what to do.

One day, she threw her shyness to the wind and asked her sister-in-law, 'Sister-in-law, what news have you heard of the Sanasam family? I hope they had no casualties?' Her sister-in-law did not answer. She pretended not to hear. Embarrassed, Mainu went no further.

A day or two later, she asked again, 'Sister-in-law, who in our neighbourhood has suffered losses?'

Her sister-in-law did not answer. Mainu looked hard at her. Suddenly she cried out, 'Mainu, my dearest, your Ta'Khema is no more.'

Mainu did not cry. She stood stock-still— … … … So, all was for this then, so it was for this that I loved you. What am I to do, what am I to do, she lamented inwardly. Mainu could withstand the sickness, bear the pangs of love, but how could she bear the pain of this, how could she go on living? She retreated under her mosquito net. She stopped eating, she stopped drinking. She was so wounded she did not say a word to anyone.

Her sisters-in-law said to one and all, 'Mainu is not keeping well.'

Hearing of this, Sanatombi came one day from Nongmaithem to ask about Mainu. Sanatombi had gotten married much earlier than Mainu.

'Mainu, your princess has come. Open your eyes, dear,' her sister-in-law said, through her breaking tears.

Mainu opened her eyes. She burst out in sobs upon seeing Sanatombi and said, 'Your Highness, why didn't I die too? I am lost … … … . Please give me your blessings to die … … … .'

Sanatombi did not know what to say to comfort Mainu. She held Mainu's hand and sat in silence.

'Your Highness, you are a princess. You will not have known the face of love. Ta'Khema suffered great humiliation on my account. … … … It is all right if we are not together, but why did he have to die?'

It was true what Mainu said. It was true Sanatombi had never known the face of love. She had not endured the pangs of love, she never had a chance to love. But she had seen how one person loves another—Princess Phandengsana and Meri, Mainu and Khema. Even though she had not felt it herself, she knew of what they called love.

From that day on, Mainu and Sanatombi drew even closer. And Mainu never again left Sanatombi.

Mainu got married within that year. To a very wealthy, somewhat older, childless man in Thoubal. Mainu did not make a fuss. Whether to one man or to another, it was all the same to Mainu. But she said, 'I just want it to be known that I got married. I will accept any man you give me. But I will not stay with whoever I marry.'

They thought she would come around once the fires for Khema had died down but Sanatombi knew that for Mainu there could be no man she could ever think of but her Ta'Khema. She was not surprised to hear that Mainu had returned, and she did not think of persuading her otherwise, for the love that Mainu had for Khema was a deep love. Who could have known what the future had held for them?

Sanatombi said to her mother the cook, 'Please do not say anything more to Mainu, Mother Cook. Let her do what she wants. She is yet young, it may be just a matter of her meeting someone she likes and getting married. Please do not say anything to her any more but send her to me now and then instead. I will try to see if I can bring her around slowly.'

After this Mainu came to Sanatombi's often and ate with her and slept over, and it was all one could say that she did not actually live there. She also found it restful to come to Sanatombi's. They talked about many things.

One day Sanatombi confided to Mainu about the time the Saheb had taken her on horseback. Mainu asked, 'What did he look like, Your Highness? Is he handsome?'

'Oh, I don't know. He is older for sure.'

'They say this Saheb beats people a lot, but he seems to have been quite nice to Your Highness.'

'Oh, those are the white soldiers. He does not beat people.'

'I am scared of him anyway.'

CHAPTER 11

Little Majesty Churachand took Sanatombi abroad for medical treatment. After leaving Sanatombi in Calcutta he went to Dehra Dun, and in the middle of it he returned to Manipur as well. He also took her to other places like Puri. Maxwell had sent a large cheque for Sanatombi's treatment. After having travelled around for about three months, Sanatombi came back feeling somewhat better. She could get around the house and get out on the porch as before. She was able to visit the palace sometimes when the king sent a car for her. It had been a very good thing that the king had taken Sanatombi abroad this time. Maxwell had asked the king seriously to take her out now and then.

'She is headstrong. Please try to convince her,' he wrote in his letter.

That morning, Mainu had washed Sanatombi's hair with fragrant herbs and seated her in an armchair on the small front porch. She combed out her long hair to dry. Her hair had thinned a bit but it was still springy and good to look at.

Sanatombi was feeling better and was therefore looking good, her original colour had come back. Little Majesty would come to pick her up today. He had come in the evening the day before and had said, 'Royal Sister, the soldiers of the platoon and my men will be playing polo. There will be a group of sahebs from Shillong who will also come to watch. My royal sister must come. I will send a car tomorrow.'

'I feel embarrassed, Little Majesty.'

'Who are you embarrassed in front of?'

'It is only that I am not at my most presentable. All right, if you say so. I will come.'

'And you must dress up your servant, your sister the Lady of Ngangbam, a little bit too.'

Sanatombi looked happy that day. She was going to be in society after a long time and on top of that she would be dressing up the queen.

'Mainu, bring me my jewellery box.'

Mainu brought out a beautiful ivory box that was inlaid with flowers. Sanatombi looked at her jewels one by one. She put away the rest, setting aside a foreign-made necklace studded with precious stones, and a pair of emerald bracelets. Maxwell had brought them back from Burma for Sanatombi.

'Mainu, I am going to leave these two to my younger sister the Lady of Ngangbam. What will I do with them now,' said Sanatombi.

'Oh, Your Highness, Not Guilty is here,' said Mainu looking towards the gate.

Yes, it was Not Guilty. Not Guilty, the peon from the palace office. Not Guilty kowtowed to Sanatombi and wiped away tears from his eyes.

'Where are you coming from, Not Guilty?'

'Your servant was coming here. It has been a long time. Your Royal Highness seems better now. You are looking very good.'

'Where are you these days?'

'I am still at the palace office. One only calls it the palace office, for one day they send me to one place, then I am sent to another place. You have no idea what's going on, Your Highness. The other time I was asked to go and stay with the queen.'

'And how is the Lady of Ngangbam?'

'All right, I suppose she is all right, but these maidens of Ngangbam are all a bit too clever by half.'

'The Dowager Queen is also a Lady of Ngangbam. If she hears that, you are done for.'

'But of course, why would Your Highness tell on me. I am just saying so since we are all but one family. And what news of the Saheb?'

'The Saheb also was ill, he says. We get news from him.'

'What a dear our Saheb is. There will be no other saheb like him.'

Sanatombi smiled.

'And my lady Mainu is well?' he asked, turning to Mainu.

'Of course, you don't notice people like us now that you are in the palace office.'

'No, no, it is nothing like that. ... ... Oh, something has come over me remembering the Saheb.' Not Guilty held his head and sat down. He said, 'I was really very sad one day. A little bit before the Saheb left I brought his tea and entered his office. The way the Saheb was at his desk with his head bowed! How the Saheb wept that day. That was the very first time I saw the Saheb cry. When I said, "Saheb, I have brought your tea," he said with his eyes and face all red, "Not Guilty, Sanatombi does not do as I say, Sanatombi does not love me." Oh, how sad I was. That dear old man, how badly he was treated.'

Sanatombi smiled as she listened to Not Guilty's story. It was Not Guilty's conviction that the Saheb was treated very badly by Sanatombi. He continued, 'If only the two of you had a child. That would be the tops. He would be a princess's child and could not be the king but how could he have amounted to nothing? The two of you ganged up and did not agree when I said at the time that we should pray to the gods and spirits for a child. He did not believe in it because he speaks another language. But you also went along with anything the other said then.'

Mainu and Sanatombi burst out laughing. One day Not Guilty had brought a witch doctor from who knows where to cast spells for the birth of a child. It would have been all right if only they had come, but Maxwell had been taken aback when Not Guilty had stormed in with all sorts of things, mats and whatnot, that he had bought with his own money, and the witch doctor, wearing his magic herbs, to pray to the stars. Finally, he called Not Guilty aside and gave five rupees for the witch doctor and had him sent away. Sanatombi was quite embarrassed as it really looked like she had set the whole thing up.

After chatting a little, Not Guilty got up to leave and said, 'I am taking my leave, my lady Mainu. I will come now and then to be of service. Your Highness, when you write to the

Saheb please say that Not Guilty asks about him. Please tell him that his servant Not Guilty remembers him night and day, that I offer holy basil leaves for him. How lovable he was. Under which sun and stars shall we see him again? I have not forgotten anything. I was given a new lease of life by the Saheb.'

Not Guilty left talking and wiping at his eyes. As soon as he crossed the gate Mainu doubled up with laughter. Sanatombi also smiled a little.

'Oh, my goodness, how he came in his orderly's uniform and all ... ...' Mainu laughed as she remembered.

It was when Maxwell and Sanatombi had moved into the brick residency at the Konthoujam homestead. This was a house that the Saheb had newly constructed after the British ruled and after the thatched house that Grimwood had lived in had been set on fire by the Meiteis. Maxwell fixed it up a lot. He planted new trees, and flowers, smoothened it all out. An officer brought in droves of convicts to work on the residency.

Mainu had come running in and said to Sanatombi, 'Your Highness, Not Guilty is among the convicts.'

'Who is Not Guilty?'

'The one who was at royal uncle Koireng's.'

'Why him?'

'I don't know, I went out to gather wild herbs for the hair wash and there he was among the convicts. I was taken by surprise. I would not have known it was him had he not called out to me. He called me first: "My lady Mainu, aren't you making any tea, how I would love to have some!" Why is he in prison?'

'Call Ta'Chonjon.'

Chonjon was an old peon of the Saheb.

'Ta'Chonjon, what is the Saheb doing now?'

'He is working on some papers, my lady.'

'There is a man known to me among the convicts—ask him if I can call him and talk to him.'

The Saheb said it would be all right and so Chonjon brought Not Guilty with him into the bungalow. Not Guilty was embarrassed when he saw Sanatombi. It seemed to be mainly on account of his uniform. Sanatombi found out that Not Guilty had been behind bars for about three months because

Not Guilty had found some bullets when he was wandering around with his friends. It would have been fine if he had stayed quiet after picking them up. But Not Guilty had taken the bullets around, showing them off to one and all. When word got around, he was hauled up before the Junior Saheb one day.

The Junior Saheb asked, 'Where are these bullets from?'

Thinking it might be to his advantage, Not Guilty answered, 'We have a lot of these Martini rifle bullets.'

'Who are you?'

Not Guilty thought he would scare the Junior Saheb and answered, 'I am Not Guilty, servant of Crown Prince Koireng.'

They proceeded to interrogate him closely. But what misfortune, for it would have been better if he had simply told the truth. Not Guilty did not give consistent answers to any of the questions asked of him. In the middle of such an important investigation, Not Guilty looked up at the face of the Saheb. As he looked at his red face, his blue eyes and big nose, he burst out laughing. After that there were no more questions, he was marched straight off to jail. Not Guilty wept and said, 'Your Highness, I did nothing wrong. As Lord Govinda is my witness, I truly merely found the bullets.'

Sanatombi heard these words and said, 'That son-of-a, how dare that saheb do as he pleases.'

Sanatombi went in to have a word with Maxwell. She came out and said, 'Not Guilty, you may go now. You have been released. The Saheb has written to the Junior Saheb, he has also written to the jailer.'

Not Guilty prostrated himself in front of Sanatombi and went out weeping.

Mainu came to Sanatombi in the evening and said, 'Your Highness, Not Guilty was released way back. He is refusing to leave. He went to the jail for a while, and then he came back with his things. He has been sitting with me all this time. He says he will meet Your Highness and then he will leave if he must. Shall I call him in?'

Not Guilty came in. He kowtowed to Sanatombi again and said, 'Your servant cannot leave the Saheb and Your Highness. I will not go home. Please do not abandon your servant.' Sanatombi talked with Maxwell. From that day on Not Guilty stayed by Maxwell's side. Mainu could not forget how he got his uniform the next morning, with white clay marks upon his face, wearing a brass nameplate, Not Guilty gave his first salute to Sanatombi as her peon. She had laughed remembering that. The meddlesome, work-shirking new peon much beloved by the Saheb was called 'Boss Not Guilty' by all in the residency. But he cared not a whit. His real name was Tomei.

The royal sons of Chandrakirti, notably Prince Pakasana and Prince Koireng, selected only well-built, tall, strapping men to be on their staff. They did not keep men who were not fit to be in the army. Among Koireng's men was Yengkokpam Kongyangba from Mayangimphal. He was a champion wrestler. Kongyangba was with Koireng at the time when the rivalry between Pakasana and Koireng was building up during the reign of Surchandra. One day Tomei, his wife's younger brother who was about twenty years old, came to him and said, 'Brother-in-law, please take me in to be with Prince Koireng.'

His brother-in-law looked hard at him and said, 'Get out of here, a guy like you cannot be in the employ of the palace.'

'What's wrong with me?'

'How can a puny guy not taller than a hand like you fit in? Didn't you say you were going to learn the pena, and what's happened with that?'

'Who the hell becomes a pena balladeer, people will only look down on you. Would you please arrange for me to stay in the palace?'

'Go away I said. You will only be a nuisance, go home and go to the fields and join the farmers, you idiot. You're not getting any taller as it is.'

'What are you saying? Short people cannot be employed in the palace? There are many short people who go to the royal court.'

'I am telling you, no. I am saying you cannot. I cannot back you,' his brother-in-law replied.

Tomei refused to leave. He kept standing there. After a while he said, 'There is one job in the palace I would like very much, and this one is also all right for short people.'

'And what job is that?'

'I want to join the dancers' council.'

'You? Get out of here, I am not listening to this any more. The dancers' council takes in boys between the ages of twelve and sixteen. They have to be good-looking, and have good singing voices. You are none of that.'

'Just how bad looking am I? As for my voice, didn't I study the pena? The age thing should be all right, I am so short, we can fudge it here and there.'

Kongyangba's annoyance knew no bounds. He didn't like
Tomei much. He could never do anything properly. Even
though Tomei was his brother-in-law, Kongyangba did
not want to bring in a wastrel like him into the palace. He
thought it would only discredit him. As his brother-in-law
would not take him seriously Tomei went away, close to tears.
Kongyangba was also unhappy but there was no choice, one
could not do something that would bring disgrace.

About a month later, Tomei came all dressed up. His brother-
in-law asked, 'Where are you coming from?'
     'Brother-in-law, I am now attending the dancers' council.
The teachers have shown me favour, there is no need for you to
try on my behalf any more.' And saying this, he strutted away.
     'Oh well, do a good job then,' was all his brother-in-law
could say. But he did not like the sound of this. He thought,
'How long is he going to last anyway?'

Kongyangba's doubts were borne out. One day after Tomei
had been attending the dancers' council for about three or
four months, he was arrested for stealing sweet limes from
Prince Koireng's estate. Kongyangba's shame knew no
bounds. Although he had grown up in a village, Kongyangba
always conducted himself with great honour. All this time
he had been in service to Prince Koireng, he had never even
picked up a stray stick of firewood. He lived with great dignity
even if he lived under the roof of another. What his brother-
in-law Tomei had done today made him almost die of shame.

The dandy Prince Koireng loved flowers and fruits and kept
his orchards and gardens beautifully. The orchard behind

the house, a flower garden in front. He even got seedlings of foreign flowers and fruits from the residency and had them planted. Koireng loved his orchards. For all the enormous number of lemons and sweet limes on the trees, no one was allowed to touch them until they ripened fully on the branch and were about to drop. Nobody was allowed to pluck them until they had been offered to Lord Govinda. When one spoke of orchards, Prince Koireng's were held up for their beauty.

For about a month now, the keeper of the orchard had been seeing signs of someone picking fruit from the orchard and eating them. He had been hiding in wait at night but had failed to nab the culprit. He would sometimes come across salt and chillies and rinds of sweet limes on the ground. It was clear that someone was taking salt and chillies into the orchard to eat. That person turned out to be Tomei. Tomei was seized and brought to Koireng by the orchard keeper. Koireng knew Tomei's brother-in-law was Kongyangba and so he sent for him.

Upon hearing of this matter, Kongyangba leapt at him to strike him without even asking anything. Tomei only survived because Koireng stopped Kongyangba. Koireng asked him for an explanation.

Tomei shook in fear as he answered, 'Your Highness, I am not guilty at all.'

'He says he is not guilty even though he has been stealing. I will kill you. Please hand him over to your servant, my lord. I will take care of him,' Kongyangba said in fury.

'Wait. Why did you steal my fruit?'

'Your servant did not steal. I just wanted to eat some. The kids at the dancers' council said, "Tomei, your brother-in-law is there, why don't you bring some lemons and sweet limes from His Highness"—and so I plucked some for them. Your servant is not guilty.'

'Why couldn't you ask and then pick them, you thief?'

'I did not steal, I am telling you. Is picking because I wanted to eat some called stealing?'

'Just listen to him! He is even turning around and challenging me. Didn't I tell you never to come around here?'

'What council is he in?' asked Koireng.

'I am ashamed to even say this. At first, he came asking to be in your service, Your Highness. I had chased him away. Later, I do not know who he went and talked to.'

'Oh that, that was Teacher Keipha,' Tomei interrupted helpfully.

'Shut up you … … … . He showed up saying he was attending the dancers' council. I had told him not to come fooling around in our colony. I have no idea when he slipped in to steal. I never saw him coming.'

'You didn't want me to come at all so I came when you were not here, didn't I? Did I also not prepare the tobacco pipe for His Highness?' Tomei said in his defence.

Koireng said, 'Well, it seems he is not guilty ever. Call him Not Guilty. Not Guilty, you may stay here.'

He went in after saying this. Fingers itching, Kongyangba managed to box Tomei's ears.

There was no colony that Not Guilty did not get into or wander in. He went into them all. People also liked him. He did not attend the dancers' council properly. When he did go, he would prepare tobacco pipes for the teachers, or fool around, but no one considered the transgressions of Not Guilty to be transgressions. But Not Guilty had one big and powerful enemy. Who would look at him with hatred like Tapta the Sprite—his brother-in-law Kongyangba. Tomei said to one and all, 'That big stupid lunk even thinks of challenging me. He has no idea whom he is up against. If I were to yank my sister away from him he would crumple to the floor.'

But Kongyangba's troubles when it came to Not Guilty did not end there. In those days, the stables of Prince Koireng and Prince Pakasana were filled with horses. The two horse-loving princes owned the choicest steeds. They kept horses only of the best pedigrees and true colours.

One day Prince Pakasana's servant scrubbed and brushed a copper polo pony of the highest quality and left it to dry on the bank of the big river. He was only gone for a little while to relieve himself by the river, and the pony was missing when he came back. Then he came across Not Guilty leading the horse, and brought him into the presence of Prince Pakasana. There was also a copper pony that belonged to Prince Koireng and Not Guilty had fetched this horse thinking it was that pony. How he was beaten that day. When he said he was a servant of Koireng he was even branded on his thigh with hot branding irons. Actually, it had not been that long ago when there was a huge dust-up between the servants of Pakasana and the servants of Koireng about a theft of horses. Starting with the alleged theft, and for hiding a pony that belonged to Koireng, two servants of Pakasana were beaten mercilessly by Koireng. In this way, whether at the dove fight, or at the polo ground, there were often incidents of fierce fighting, not just between the masters, but between their servants as well.

In the middle of these fights, Pakasana had thought it was deliberate when they came across Not Guilty leading away his horse. That was why Not Guilty was treated very badly. Hearing the news, Koireng himself came on foot and after speaking somewhat harshly to Pakasana brought Not Guilty away. From that day on Not Guilty had given over his life to His Highness Lord Koireng.

Today his brother-in-law was no more, his Lord Koireng was no more. Kongyangba died when the foreigners fired at the house of Crown Prince Koireng. That day his hated brother-in-law shook Not Guilty hard to wake him up: 'Tomei, get up, the sahebs are firing at us.' Not Guilty hid, bleary-eyed. After a while he came out crawling on his belly, thinking he would at least try to get to the palace, when he came across Kongyangba leaning against the brick wall. Not Guilty said, 'Why are you sleeping now of all times?' He prodded him and his brother-in-law's dead body fell to the ground. How he wept, crying, 'Brother-in-law, brother-in-law.' This daft fellow, this garrulous Not Guilty, took many secrets of Koireng to his grave. He hated the sahebs but Not Guilty loved Maxwell. Sanatombi knew this. As he had been to his prince, he was beholden to Maxwell for the rest of his life for releasing him. He remembered it even today.

The Saheb also always said, 'He is a well-meaning person.'

CHAPTER 12

It had been about two months since the princesses had gone to meet Maxwell but there was no news from the Saheb. Even if she wanted to know, the Dowager Queen, the Lady of Ngangbam, remained silent. She exhibited little of her desire to know anything about it. The Lady of Ngangbam steered the conversation away even if her younger sisters brought up the subject. She was also a little chagrined by their lack of interest. Sanatombi came every now and then but she never once mentioned this matter. Neither did she reveal how the Saheb had brought her on horseback about a month after the meeting. The queen especially did not wish to bring up the matter of the paddy fields with her because Sanatombi had not liked the idea of going to meet the Saheb in the first place. Moreover, the queen had heard about how she had spoken out of turn.

One day, Manikchand really did bring a letter written by the three princesses to be submitted to the Viceroy. It was a letter written in consultation with Haodeijam Cheiteino. Not only was Haodeijam Cheiteino celebrated as a writer but he was a well-connected man, a man of repute. This man, who had been richly rewarded by the Grand Queen Mother, the Lady of Meisnam, for writing the three books, *Victory over the Chinese*, *Victory over Tripura* and *Khamba and Thoibi*, was a very close friend of Manikchand. Manikchand took his counsel very seriously. But when her signing the petition was brought up, Sanatombi said, 'Let us wait a little. It won't look very nice for us to do this on our own. Let us also consult the Dowager Queen.'

Truth be told, Sanatombi did not want to send the letter at all. Manikchand thought she had a point and put the letter away, saying, 'Very well. I am taking a trip to India. I will go to Vrindavan this time and so I may be away for a longer time— there are some other people who will be going too.'

Manikchand going abroad was nothing new to Sanatombi. She would stay back at home weaving and working around the house when he was gone. Sanatombi also felt it was a time to remain quiet. But not a day passed when she did not remember her Sovereign Father. She could never forget her father who had died in an ambiguous manner in an alien land. She remembered him while they talked about the paddy fields. She remembered him all the time; she felt like crying all the time.

As he had assured Sanatombi, Maxwell did not stay idle. He wrote to his superiors that the request of the princesses was a reasonable one. It was simply that he had not heard back. Moreover, he was very busy. He was very caught up in securing the position of the new king Churachand, calming the unrest that was still among the people and with building and developing projects. He also had to go to Shillong and a few other lands in the middle of all this. So, he did not remember the matter of the paddy fields. One day, about a month after his last meeting with Sanatombi, a letter arrived from the Viceroy, asking for details on the matter. As soon this paper arrived, Bamacharan Mukherjee said, 'Perhaps it would be right to write a letter to the queen and let her know? It would be good if we got the necessary details from the queen.'

Maxwell however said, 'Bamacharan, where does Princess Sanatombi live?'

'In Wangkhei Leikai, sir. In her husband's house.'

Maxwell also asked one day, 'Bamacharan, the two "sphinxes" of Kangla, which king built those?'

'Some say during the time of Maharaja Narasingh, others say that they were there ages before him … … … .'

'Do you know in which year?'

'I do not know precisely, but it would be there in the court chronicle.'

'The *Cheitharol Kumbaba*, correct?'

'That is correct, sir.'

'They have stopped writing it?'

'Yes, they have.'

'Get them to write it again. And when you have some time read it out to me. If possible, let us translate it into English.'

'I would not be able to do it on my own without the help of the Meitei scholars.'

'Who is there? Let them take part.'

Taoriya Hidang and the Fortuneteller of Sarang were summoned and Maxwell had them start writing the court chronicle again.

He could not forget how Sanatombi had confronted him in anger about the blowing up of the leogryphs of Kangla Fort. When the idea came up, Maxwell had not agreed to the destruction of the two ancestral beasts on whose mouths the Meiteis had smeared the blood of the slain sahebs in worship. They had seen in this the fulfilment of the powerful prophecy that white heads would roll in front of the beasts one day. The proposal had seemed to him to be a childish gesture of taking it out on them. And the Meiteis were not that stupid a race. They would not be browbeaten with bluster. The matter was discussed at great length but his word did not hold sway at the time—he had had to go along. 'What is to be gained by blowing up the two beasts?' He had used these very words to vigorously oppose Captain Allen and Lieutenant Casegreen, but it was a time when the tension from recent events had not subsided yet. Sanatombi had asked the very same question that he had asked: 'What use was to you to destroy them?' He had been surprised to hear it; it was as if he heard his own voice from her mouth. It woke him up once again. He said to Bamacharan, 'Do not tell anyone yet about the arrival of the paper, I will think on it.'

Manikchand left for Vrindavan. He also took many people along with him, saying he would be back in time for the spring festival. He would surely bring back with him a lot of goods— one-stringed fiddles, Brinam shawls of Jaipur print, lanterns, and the like. Manikchand went trading and Sanatombi took up weaving seriously. Her mother-in-law ran around setting it up for her. She had not thought Sanatombi would be so diligent, or that she would learn so quickly. Mainu came often, and what with her husband being away, Sanatombi relaxed a great deal when she came. Mainu would bring her work with her when she came. She would place her embroidery tripod of brass at the foot of Sanatombi's loom and work on a children's striped sarong. Sanatombi began to get used to her new life.

One day when Mainu and Sanatombi were taking a break and chatting in the weaving shed, Pheijao the Saheb's groom entered.

'What a surprise, Ta'Pheijao! Where are you coming from? Come, come right in. Long time since we've seen you.' Sanatombi received him warmly.

When Mainu started to lay out a seat for him, Pheijao said, 'Forget the seat, my lady Mainu. Your Highness, your servant the Saheb is here. He says he would like to see you.'

'What saheb?'

'The Political Agent, Mesin Saheb.'

'Oh? Why him?'

'He seems to wish to say something.'

'Where is he?'

'He is at the gate. Perhaps your ladyship might come out for a bit.'

'Go on ahead, I am coming.' Saying this, she changed into presentable clothes and came out with Mainu to where the Saheb was.

They found Maxwell standing there. He saluted Sanatombi.

He said to Sanatombi, 'Your Highness, I come to give news.'

'What news?'

'The Viceroy's letter has come. He has permitted the princesses' use of the paddy fields. See.' He brought out the letter from his pocket.

'But I can't even read. I said, I cannot read.'

'Sorry,' he said and put the paper away. Then, not knowing what next to say, he remained standing silently.

Sanatombi finally said, 'Go inform the Dowager Queen first.'

Maxwell did not understand the words for 'Dowager Queen' and 'inform'. He only knew some simple words. He looked at Pheijao. Pheijao translated into Hindi for him.

Maxwell said, 'I will say to you first. I want.'

'What's the point of telling me? What would I know? Ta'Pheijao, tell him to inform the Dowager Queen first.'

After one or two more words, Maxwell went back. He saluted Sanatombi again before he left.

'So that's the Saheb. That one doesn't look like he would beat people. And how did he know where to find the house?'

'Well, Ta'Pheijao was with him, wasn't he?' answered Sanatombi.

As for her mother-in-law, she was left saying it was unfortunate Manikchand was not around so they could understand each other.

After getting back to Kangla Fort, Maxwell called Maisna Mitlao and said in Hindi, 'Mitlao, how is the road repair work coming along?'

Maxwell had made preparations to fix the main roads of Imphal as soon as the monsoon was over. The roads of Manipur used to be in terrible condition after the rains. Maxwell thought it necessary to repair the roads and bridges.

Mitlao answered, 'We are working very hard on it.'

'In which direction?'

'We have begun work on Uripok and Sagolband. After that we will start on Wangkhei and Yaiskul.'

'The road in Wangkhei leading to the new palace is in very poor shape.'

'That road has always been in bad condition.'

'Take up Wangkhei and Yaiskul very soon. The approach roads to the palace should be good. Assign more workers. I will also come to see the roads.'

Repairs on the roads of Wangkhei and Yaiskul began without further delay. Maxwell came now and then to inspect. He would drop in on Sanatombi to give her news or gather information every time he came. He never stepped in past the gate. He would send Pheijao in to tell Sanatombi that he had come. He would always say a word or two and leave. Sanatombi also began getting used to talking with him. She became used to talking so he could understand her.

One day as the conversation veered towards Maxwell's visits, her mother-in-law said, 'Your Highness, I wonder if our older brother's horse that was caught in the round-up has been sold off? Do you think you might ask the Big Saheb? There would be nothing to it if he wanted to give it back. My brother is still weeping over that horse.'

'There are a lot of people whose horses were also rounded up. It would not be proper to broach that subject now.'

'How about giving him the letter now, the one that Manikchand wrote separately on behalf of Your Highnesses?

The Saheb is intimidated by Your Highness,' said her simple mother-in-law.

'Mother, it would be better to wait till the royal son-in-law got back.'

And on yet another day her mother-in-law said, 'It is not right to make such an important person stand at the gate. Would it be a problem for him to sit in the front courtyard?'

'He won't come in, Mother. I also do not think there would be anything wrong since he is actually not coming inside the house,' said Sanatombi.

'As for the gate, there is the holy water from the Ganga that Manikchand brought. We could just sprinkle some of that ... ... What is the problem, let him come in as far as the courtyard at least,' mother and daughter-in-law conferred.

Sanatombi called Maxwell in the next time he came. He entered very hesitantly. He asked Pheijao constantly, 'They won't mind? If they do not like it, I will not go in, Pheijao. Tell the princess.'

Sanatombi assured them it was quite all right and so Maxwell came in as far as the courtyard. Sometimes he came with Pheijao, at other times by himself, and he would ask after Sanatombi. Sanatombi enjoyed talking with him a great deal, and corrected his Meiteilon when he spoke. When she found something funny, she would burst out laughing. Since Sanatombi was young, Maxwell began to call her by her name.

Sanatombi said one day, 'Mesin Saheb, why did you put a stop to the Lai Haraoba? They say you forbade it.'

'Lai?'

'Yes. Don't you know the Lai Haraoba?' Sanatombi let him know it was like Christmas.

'Oh, I see. All right, I will take care of it. It is good you remind me, thank you.'

Maxwell went back and called Tonjao and asked him about the Lai Haraoba in great detail. One day on a Wednesday his lordship the king of Moirang started the festival again. He had notices put up that every prayer and ritual was to be performed without any change in the name of Little Majesty.

One time Sanatombi washed her hair with fragrant herbs late in the day. Her hair loose about her, she came out towards the pond that was at the edge of the compound. Her mother-in-law had gone to fetch yarn as they had finished a weave on the loom. Mainu had also not come that day. Sanatombi felt empty on the days that Mainu did not come. She felt very empty. One could not talk with Tembi. The reservoir in the Nongmaithem household was obscured by the front gazebo and so it could not be seen from the house. It was a pool that was kept very neat and clean. It even had steps leading down to it. As Sanatombi walked towards it she saw Maxwell was standing looking towards the pond. She did not know what he was doing.

Sanatombi called out happily, 'Mesin, what are you doing? You didn't even tell me you were coming.'

Maxwell turned to her and smiled.

'Where are you coming from?'

'There.'

'Who's going to understand if you just say "there". Where were you?'

'Sanatombi.'

'Yes?'

'Do you eat the pond?'

Sanatombi laughed out loud, 'Say, "Do you drink the pond water?"'

'Yes, do you drink the water?'

'Where else would we drink from if not from the pond? We don't have a river, do we?'

'It is bad, do not eat.'

What bothered Maxwell most was not being able to express all that he wanted to say, and not being able to understand all that Sanatombi was saying. He thought, 'How difficult Meiteilon is!'

But Sanatombi could now understand what he was saying. She had gotten used to the way he spoke. She was getting used to him.

Not too long after this, he sent Chonjon over one day to teach Sanatombi how to boil drinking water. There was nothing in Manipur that terrified the sahebs more than cholera. Not long after they had taken possession of Manipur, their soldiers had been mowed down by cholera. One saheb was also among the casualties. Maxwell's alarm knew no bounds when he heard that Sanatombi drank water from the pond. He said to Chonjon over and over again, 'Tell Sanatombi, tell her not to forget to boil water.' Hearing this her mother-in-law laughed and said, 'He is just like our Manikchand, my son is also very fussy. How nice it would have been if he were here.'

Sometimes Maxwell would not come for five or ten days. He would go abroad. Sanatombi would say to herself, 'Whatever has happened to Mesin? He has stopped coming.'

Mainu said, 'I don't know what's happened to him. ... ... Your Highness, I am thinking something.'

'What are you thinking?'

'This Saheb, I don't know, there is something about him.'

'So, what is it?'

'I don't know, Your Highness. He must be crazy about you ... He comes around much too often.'

'What nonsense. He is just dropping by.'

'I am not at all comfortable with this. He's got a strange look in his eye.'

'You're just being mean, that's all.'

'… … … Let him be crazy about you, just you don't get involved, Your Highness. You don't speak the same tongue nor are you friends … … … .'

As she was saying this they heard the sound of Maxwell's horse. Sanatombi heard it first. She said, 'Mesin is here.' When Maxwell saw that Mainu and Sanatombi were by the gate, he got off his horse and said happily, 'I went to the hills. Your hills are very beautiful. I like. I bring for you.' Saying this, he took off the tribal shawl of red cotton he was wearing and threw it over Sanatombi. He was different that day. He looked very happy. He babbled a lot of things in his language like a young man. They could not understand what he was saying. Then, saying he would come again, he galloped away.

'What's the matter with him? Has he gone mad or what? You will have to bathe again now.'

'Why, did he touch me?'

'What's the matter with you, did he not put that cloth on you just now?'

'Oh.'

'Really, this Saheb is going to cross a lot of boundaries, Your Highness. It is better if we don't let him in … … … Your husband is not here either. Who knows what he will say when he comes to hear?'

Sanatombi did not answer. She woke up to the realization upon hearing Mainu's words—It was true, Manikchand was not around now. But she always kept thinking that Maxwell would come, she always thought she heard him riding his horse in.

On another day, Maxwell had a long conversation with her. She had asked, 'Mesin, do you know my Sovereign Father, my father Surchandra?'

'No, but I have seen his picture.'

'Let me ask you something. People say my father Surchandra was kept in jail, is it true? They say he was kept surrounded by white soldiers, is that true?'

'Who told you that?'

'Did you see it? Do you know?'

'No, I do not know.'

Sanatombi asked him about other things too. Maxwell did not want to talk about these matters but she cornered him. Maxwell could not escape her questioning. Even though he could not understand all of Sanatombi's questions, he knew Sanatombi had many frustrations. This fallen princess harboured a profound grief. Maxwell and Sanatombi had a deep conversation that day. Mainu did not approve of this. When he was about to leave, Sanatombi said, 'Wait, one more thing. They say you killed Koireng. That you sat in judgment, is it true?' Maxwell's face reddened. He gave an evasive answer and left. But he left unhappily. Sanatombi, too, was left unhappy.

Maxwell did not come for quite a long time. Sanatombi wondered if he was angry. It was not right to have spoken to him so harshly.

One day around evening, after a long time, Maxwell showed up as if nothing had happened, and said, 'Sanatombi, your road is finished. Let us go look, I will take you.' Without giving it a thought, Sanatombi followed him out, leaving Mainu watching, disturbed. Sanatombi came back after a fairly long time after looking at the road but she said nothing to Mainu. Mainu also waited for her to tell her about it for quite some time, but there was not a word. Tears came to Mainu's eyes. She felt hurt. When Sanatombi bathed and went in that day, she could not hide anything from Mainu. It was fairly late at night but without any fear or hesitation Mainu went home without even saying goodbye. She wept a great deal when she got home—for Sanatombi.

Sanatombi cried secretly that night too, but Mainu never knew that. What Maxwell had said as they were coming back from looking at the road was, 'Sanatombi, I know about your father Surchandra. He did not stay in jail. I am sorry. I am sorry for you all. A woman can reign in England. If Manipur had this custom I would have recommended you. Do not take me wrong. This was plain bad luck. If you want to know who sat in judgment over Koireng I will tell you. They were Lt Colonel St John Forcourt Mitchel, Major Richard Kerly Ridgeway and C.A.W. Davis. It was done by a tribunal of these three. It was my bad luck. It was my bad luck that the day Koireng died, I was the one who bore witness to his death. I am your enemy, but I am not a greedy enemy. ... ... Believe me.'

Maxwell said all this slowly so that Sanatombi could understand. He had recited it slowly, remembering it like homework he had memorized well. He had struggled to express himself but Sanatombi could understand what he was saying. The two of them had this talk standing at the gate. Maxwell had felt happy. He had felt a relief after opening up to Sanatombi. He had felt lighter.

Sanatombi had said to Maxwell after she listened to his words, 'Mesin, we had nobody in those days.' And saying this she had burst into tears. 'Don't cry,' and saying this Maxwell stroked Sanatombi's head. Then he had left on his horse. He did not gallop away. He had wanted to comfort Sanatombi more. And so, he left. He left slowly upon his horse.

Maxwell felt wretched ever since the other day when Sanatombi had asked if it was true what they said about him killing Koireng. He had felt the direct blow of the words of this young woman from this singular mountain-land. He, too, had many dissatisfactions. He did not even feel up to doing his work properly. Koireng had been killed. His crime—starting a war against the British Empire. None of the three men in the court set up to judge him were men of law. Ordinary soldiers had sat judgment upon him as if he were a common soldier. But no court had been appointed to look into the firing of shots late at night at the house of the crown prince of an independent land, into how many people died that day. Kulachandradhwaja had shouted out, 'What are you going to do—the two young girls who were beheaded and thrown into the fire, their hair tied together, those whose hands were cut off, whose houses were burnt down … … … What are you going to be doing about them?' It had not been an honourable battle of men against men, this underhanded war of murder and oppression was not honourable for any civilized people. The world had cried out: 'What are you doing? Civilized England, give an answer.'

The hapless Maxwell had been used as an instrument when imperial Britain tried to cover it up. He was ordered: 'You must do this, but do it carefully.' His late assignment of an earlier incident whose threads were now lost, whose footprints had been erased, was his duty to fulfil. He had to look for it with his eyes closed. He had stood up for his country as an obedient servant. He had answered the harsh questions posed by the world: 'There had been casualties in the crossfire … … … .' But it was his hands that had strangled justice. Lord

Lansdowne, the patriotic Viceroy of India, had said, 'Bravo Maxwell!' Had Sanatombi known of all these things? Had she suffered the blows that he was feeling a hundredfold? Did he disgust her? When they had first met at Kangla Fort and she had spoken harshly to him he thought of Sanatombi as a sharp and bright spark. Her second strike was even more dangerous. And so, he did not come for a long time. But he could not forget that spark for even a single day, and he felt it unceasingly upon his person. He had found these last few days hard to endure. He had thought, 'Shall I say it or shall I not?' He decided to say it; she of all, at least, should know: 'I may be your enemy but I am not that kind of cowardly man who cannot say he is sorry.'

Even though he could not say it openly, he wanted to cry out into the emptiness, 'We wronged you. We, the mighty and advanced, have wronged you, weak and small Manipur.'

He felt a relief that day at having clumsily confessed this regret buried deep inside him to this maiden of his enemies; he felt light as if he had put down a burden. But he did not tell her everything because he did not know how to say everything. He did not know if Sanatombi had understood the little that he had said. He only felt the pleasure of having made a clean breast of it.

His horse walked slowly. Maxwell headed home slowly, thinking. He saw before his eyes the wounded woman he had left weeping behind. He could not quite remember, but he had seen one day, somewhere—a butterfly caught in a large web. It flapped its wings as it tried to escape the web. In a far corner of the web a hideous spider waited for its chance to grab it. Maxwell had seen this sight one day. He was repulsed by it. He slowly disentangled the butterfly and set it free. Maxwell did not know why he saw this incident before his eyes today and all of a sudden, he feared for Sanatombi.

Sanatombi also felt lighter that day. She felt a pleasure in exorcising a burn that she had nursed inside her for a long time. She wanted to weep over it at leisure but her thoughts raced in all directions all night through. Today she remembered her Sovereign Father very much. Now that Manipur had become a conquered land she too heard the loose talk of the people—that fellow Surchandra had lost the country by siding too much with his birth brothers, the problem was that he had not been very smart, and so on. Sanatombi could not bear to hear these words—and she wanted to tell someone about her grief. Today, having revealed her inner thoughts to a foreigner, her enemy, she felt relieved and rested. She had wanted to say many other things too but she also did not know how to say it all so that Maxwell could understand.

Even when Sanatombi was but a child her father had discussed many sensitive matters with her. She thought—Who knows my Sovereign Father like I know him? She remembered today too, how she talked to him one day having heard from the Lady of Ngangbam that there was disquiet within the family. But her good-natured father had laughed and said easily, 'I don't know what these kids will come to. They are acting spoilt with me. They are getting a little too much though. I will have to spank Koireng and Paka. What do they think they are they up to, they are no longer children after all.'

But Sanatombi knew her father would never be able to control his younger brothers, he was merely saying so as an older brother. But it was a lie to say that her father took sides, he never took anybody's side. There had been times when he had sided with his younger half-brothers like Koireng, but no one seemed to have accounted for that seriously. It was like when one is chastised for mismeasuring the rice for a feast but is not commended when the measure turns out to be just right. It was a quicksand one sunk into further with every move. The rivalry between Koireng and Pakasana was personal, and even if Surchandra had not taken sides, it would have blown up one day. On top of that, courtiers adept at whispering campaigns had further confused the princes a great deal. They made them see white as black, and black as white. It was inevitable that the weakling Surchandra would face public censure in the middle of this all. But who would look into this matter in depth—nobody did. He may have been the older brother, but he was the king. Thinking of all of this Sanatombi felt like crying.

Her father had said to her the last time they met, 'I would have been so happy if only you had been a boy.' Maxwell had also said, 'If a woman could be king I would have fought for you.'

She drifted off to sleep towards daybreak, thinking all this. But in a few days the Lady of Ngangbam summoned Sanatombi and said, 'Sanatombi, do not let Mesin, the Political Agent, come to your house often. I am hearing all sorts of things.' Sanatombi did not answer back but she was angry, and then she thought—Has Mesin stopped coming out of embarrassment? What would he be thinking of me? ... ... Oh well, I will stop thinking about him, I am done, that's it.' And thinking this, tears almost came to her eyes.

CHAPTER 13

Tonjao of Moirang would come to consult with Sanatombi every now and then about paddy fields, and about other matters. He was now married to Sanatombi's younger half-sister Ombisana. Tonjao of Moirang was an older man and had two wives at home, but when the young Ombisana was given to him in marriage, no one questioned his eligibility because Tonjao was a man who had stood by them. He was wealthy beyond count. With house and estate, stables, storehouses and so on, he lacked nothing. A man who liked beautiful things, Tonjao even festooned the eaves of the four corners of his mansion with bunches of peacock feathers. Tonjao lived well. The weakened household of Surchandra was fortunate to have someone like him as a son-in-law. The Lady of Ngangbam was also a little relieved to have a man who could stand up for them as if their affairs were his own. He visited Sanatombi now and then, he gave her news. He used to tell her what they were thinking on the sahebs' side, what was going on. She was also the only among Surchandra's children that he could consult. Tonjao enjoyed talking with Sanatombi very much.

Tonjao was now Sanatombi's younger brother-in-law but she could not easily change her mode of address. She called him Ta'Tonjao as before. Sanatombi said, 'As far as the paddies are concerned it is fine if they give it, it is fine if they don't. It was just a matter of bringing it to their attention. What does it really matter?'

'But one has to plan for some contingencies, Your Highness. And the Saheb is very fond of Your Highness so it would be not inappropriate to remind him at some point. You can just mention it by the by. The Saheb is not some thoughtless white soldier. The sahebs are also aware that the foreign government has done a great injustice to the Divine Sovereign. The Political Agent Saheb also knows this.'

'Who said so? Did he say that to you?'

'I did not hear directly from the Saheb himself but I heard it from a reliable source.'

Tonjao told Sanatombi that the Saheb had said so to Bamacharan at some point. Tonjao had another gift, and that was he was good with languages. He who spoke Burmese like his mother tongue also spoke Bangla very well, and so Bamacharan enjoyed talking with him very much. He relayed various bits of discreet information. He had heard from Bamacharan who had pieced together the information from what he gleaned piecemeal from the Saheb at different times. He had said, 'If it was the British policy to recognize Kulachandra as the king after expelling Koireng, then it would not have hurt either to keep Surchandra on as the king after Koireng had been banished. That in fact would have been better, and it would have looked better as well. Kulachandra would never have delivered Koireng who had stood by him, nor would it have been proper to ask him to do so. But Surchandra might have agreed because the force behind this revolt was Koireng, not Kulachandra. It stood to reason that he would not have extended himself to save Koireng.'

And this also he said, 'The British had acted too precipitately; they had exercised their power wrongly. It was a shameful incident.'

Sanatombi listened closely to these words. She questioned the points she wanted to know about in detail. At last she said, 'Ta'Tonjao, let me ask you one thing. According to the Dowager Queen, Mesin Saheb wrote to the Viceroy on behalf of our Lukhoi. Is that true?'

'It is true, Your Highness.'

'Why did he do that, did he know our Lukhoi?'

'These sahebs are not to be taken lightly. They come after researching everything about Manipur, every single one of them. Whether it is because it is the right thing to do, or whether it would be in accordance with the treaty between Manipur and the foreigners from the time of the royal reign of your great-great-grandfather Bhagyachandra, the foreigners should have supported your Sovereign Father. If a king were to be appointed according to royal descent, the Divine Majesty's descendant should have been the rightful king. It seems that Maxwell had felt this way.'

Tonjao continued to relate many confidential matters to Sanatombi, inside information that most were not privy to. He said that back when Chandrakirti had strong and friendly relations with the British, he had written to them that after his death they should recognize his oldest son Surchandra as the king of Manipur. Even though Manipur had a custom of younger brothers being the king in turn, and even if Chandrakirti wished to follow it, the British had advised that it would be better if Surchandra would be king as they had seen many destructive complications that came from this

practice. So, if it came to appointing a king for the subjugated
Manipur, it was natural that they would wish to apply customs
that they themselves believed in. And that was why Maxwell
wrote to the higher-ups to recommend that Lukhoi be made
king … … … . So Tonjao related to her. Sanatombi did not
know of these internal matters in such detail and the only one
who knew it was the queen, the Lady of Ngangbam. Tonjao
said, 'It was a watertight case that after the Divine Majesty's
death, his progeny should be king. It was just only because we
had no allies and Your Highnesses were all daughters. Even if
Prince Lukhoi is no more, it would have been good had there
been even just two male offspring.'

'One more thing. I have wanted to ask you for a long
time. When Sovereign Father died in Calcutta, how did that
happen?'

'I am not following you.'

'I mean, did he die from an illness, or—'

'What are you saying? What have you heard?'

'Nothing, just that I have a suspicion,' said Sanatombi.
Her young face clouded with these weighty thoughts.

Sanatombi shared her suspicions with Tonjao of Moirang. The
two of them discussed it. The younger brothers of Surchandra
rose up in arms against him. All of a sudden someone climbed
the brick walls of Kangla Fort and fired at it. When Surchandra
came out towards Sanjenthong Bridge after hearing gunshots
from the directions of the palace, he ran into his younger
brother Pakasana who had come running with his soldiers.
No one could tell which soldiers were whose in the pitch-dark
night. The battle could not proceed. Even though Surchandra
sought refuge in the bungalow of Political Agent Grimwood,

he said he would be going on a pilgrimage—but he went to stay in Calcutta instead. Sanatombi had known why her father had left for Calcutta. Tonjao and she dissected her father's actions from every angle, analysed them in great detail. Had her father who spoke no English been deceived? Or was it true that they did not want her father? Even if one thought of Surchandra as an unfit king, Kulachandra was no more able a king than her father. Kulachandra did not even want the throne: when it began to get ugly among his brothers he had fled and stayed away, saying he could not bear to see it. He held his older brother Surchandra in very high regard, and even thought of him as his own Sovereign Father.

Tonjao said all this was useless to think about, just water under the bridge, but not long after Kulachandra was defeated by the foreigners and after a completely different child was announced as king, when news arrived that the king called Surchandra Ruler and Victor of the Hills had died, Sanatombi was filled with suspicion. Being his daughter, she had staunchly refused to accept it. She had said this to no one, but today she revealed her thoughts to Tonjao. This was a matter she could never forget. Her suspicions only mounted. A month after this incident, a group of people coming back from Vrindavan also reported to Sanatombi that they had visited Calcutta on their way to pay their respects to the Divine Majesty. How they had wept when they saw the state they found their king in. They look leave of Surchandra Ruler and Victor of the Hills and left him very calm and composed. That very day in Calcutta, they heard the news of his death. They attended the funeral of the Divine Majesty at the grove at the Pool of Radha in Vrindavan. And that raised Sanatombi's suspicions all the more—What was that about? Who witnessed it, who knew of it? What illness did he die of? Who from our side knew of it? Was he silenced …? Sanatombi mulled it over and over. She thought about it when she lay down, she thought of it when she walked, she thought about it when she sat for a long time on the steps down to the pond as she went to bathe. She wept quietly. Her father had cherished her immensely, had loved her greatly. 'Sanaton, Tombi, daddy's little girl … … …' he would say.

It would have been good if she could have had at least one person she could have talked to about it. Her husband Manikchand did not pay much heed to these intrigues; he did not want to be bothered by matters uselessly. But she had wondered—Did they kill my father? Koireng had been killed, Kulachandra had been chased away, so killing Surchandra would have been expeditious. No one would be around then to criticize them. And this she also heard: that her Sovereign Father had lived with a queen called Swarnamayee. So, who was she? How could she get to the truth? She was but a young girl.

She said, 'Ta'Tonjao, I suppose we can't find out how exactly Sovereign Father died now, can we? I really want to know, I will never be happy until I know it. I'll ask Mesin Saheb, do you think it would be all right?'

'Don't bother asking him, Your Highness. These sahebs are very tight-lipped. He will not tell you. And also, do not trust these interpreters too much. … … … It is all in the past. It is so because Lord Govinda did not favour us, or how would the foreigners' flag fly over Kangla? Don't think about it too much, it will only affect your health. I have been noticing you have been looking a little peaked these days.'

Sanatombi was a little embarrassed. In truth, she had not been very regular with her sleep and meals lately. She knew she had lost a bit of weight.

Seeing that Tonjao was about to start talking again about paddies and salt wells, Sanatombi diverted him and said, 'Forget the rest, Ta'Tonjao, whatever happened to the palace horses? And what became of all the horses that they had rounded up?'

Sanatombi knew the horse-loving Tonjao did not care if he went without eating for five days as long as he could talk about horses. He did not just love horses, he loved them with a deep knowledge. Even in Tripura and India people talked about 'The Black Steed of Tonjao of Moirang'. Black as a beetle and as shiny as a mirror, Tonjao even kept his black pony shaded under a canopy. People came in droves to look at 'The Black Steed of Tonjao of Moirang'. The horse-loving noblemen of Manipur all kept a great many horses. A man who could not ride a horse was not deemed to be a man. The Meiteis studied their horses avidly and in great depth. They even knew which colours embodied a good temperament, a spirited temperament, a bad temperament, and which were timid, unruly and so on.

Tonjao of Moirang very happily talked to Sanatombi about horses and their colours—the white *sanabi*, *karu* the black, the off-white *mora*, tamarind bay, the tamarind seed black-kneed bay, the black-maned bay classified as tamarind pulp, the black-legged *khongdei* brown, copper, *kona* brown, the spotted blue vanda orchid, the cotton boll of pure white, raw silk beige, the golden *natrang* with its white mane, the pale-eyed *songu*, burnt mora with dark tail tips, speckled sparrow-egg brown, and so on ... ...

'The white speckled sanabi cannot be ridden by commoners but only by the king, Your Highness,' he continued.

Once they started talking about horses, the conversation went on. Tonjao forgot about the sahebs. People like Tonjao who knew deeply about horses were a rarity in those days. Tonjao, who frequently associated with the Burmese, studied the differences between the Manipuri pony and the Burmese pony. He took pedigrees that could be interbred and tested them out.

Sanatombi continued to ask, 'Is it true that the sahebs have auctioned off all the horses of the palace?'

'Oh, those were only the horses that are weak or had met with some problems in battle. The sahebs are also very fond of horses. They have kept all the good horses very carefully, Your Highness. I am also looking after the Political Agent's black horse at my home.'

'Is Uncle Paka's crazy tamarind still around?'

'Yes, it is, Your Highness.'

'And are they still playing polo?'

'Yes, they are in the inner polo ground. The Saheb said we should play borough polo tournaments and so they have started again. Sometimes they even allow some *chere kare* games.'

'By chere kare you mean when two boroughs pair up as a team?'

'Your Highness.'

'Does Mesin also play?'

'Your servant Mesin Saheb is also very fond of polo. But it is just saying so really, for how can we see anyone play the level of polo of your royal uncles these days.'

Tonjao of Moirang's visit left Sanatombi feeling restless. She also felt good. She could not get back properly to her weaving or household chores. Prince Koireng and Prince Pakasana would play on the borough teams in the outer polo ground. The game of polo was played even before the time of the ancestral deity Pakhangba, the Heavenly Python Serpent. The game had its rules modified in the seventeenth century by Khagemba, Vanquisher of the Chinese. Pakasana played by these rules. Koireng made the play beautiful, a pleasure for the eyes to behold. The princes were as beautiful as a picture upon the green grass. Short-sleeved shirts of velvet, dhoti and turbans of rose pink. They rode before the wind on their ponies, matching polo mallet to polo mallet. Ahead of them, the polo ball struck true, skimming like a swallow upon the green grass. Their supporters did not blink, their hearts thudded in their chests. Manipur's polo was beautiful, it was very beautiful, it was enthralling. Princesses and noblewomen carried in delicacies, piled high as hills. How manly were the men of Manipur mounted on their steeds.

Sanatombi wanted to talk more about this with somebody. But there was no Mainu around today. Looking back, she remembered she had not come back since she left angrily the other day. Sanatombi looked about her—her maidservant Tembi was folding her clothes. Her stocky, fit Tembi did not worry about anything at all, she kept folding the clothes with pleasure. One could not talk with her but one could tease her. Sanatombi looked at the simple Tembi with her shiny cheeks, and she smiled a little.

One day Mainu teased Tembi and said, 'Tembi, has no man courted you?'

'No courting,' said Tembi.

'What's the matter, you are pretty good-looking. No one has courted you at all?' Mainu played the fool and asked her.

'No courting,' replied Tembi.

'What's wrong with these horrid Manipuri men?' Mainu had joked.

She thought of sending Tembi for Mainu but she was also angry—I am also not going to call her until she comes back on her own … … … Oh, now Mesin will never come again, he must have felt embarrassed … … … .

Sanatombi felt empty. Manikchand had been away for quite a long time now. 'Oh, when would he return?'

CHAPTER 14

Manikchand returned in time for the spring festival. He brought with him a great many things from Vrindavan. People came in droves to look and buy the things that had been brought from abroad. The Nongmaithem courtyard was filled with people.

Manikchand said to Sanatombi, 'Would Your Highness like to pick out a Jaipur stole for herself?'

'It is quite all right, I have so many,' replied Sanatombi.

After Manikchand had been back for about ten days, he came back home late one day and said, 'Why did you bring the Saheb into our house? Who do you think I am? Is this house a place where the Saheb can take his outings? Why has he been coming so often to my house?'

Sanatombi was taken aback that Manikchand was already angry when he came home. She did not answer right away, but she said, 'He came to give news about the paddies.'

'Why would he come so often just to give news about the paddies?'

Sanatombi did not know what to answer. Manikchand was right. He would not have come frequently just to give information about the paddies. It had indeed been a few too many times.

'Why have you made him so disrespectful? Can he do just as he pleases? You have made this happen.'

'What the royal son-in-law is thinking is mistaken.'

'How am I mistaken? Why were you walking around with him in the evening?'

'We were looking at the new road.'

'Why would you go look at roads with a man in the evening? Does he not know you are a woman with a husband? This household is where men go in and out it seems.'

Sanatombi was stung. Even though she was a princess and had been brought up pampered and spoilt, Sanatombi had known no man other than Manikchand. She had accepted Manikchand as her husband according to custom. She had not done Manikchand any wrong. Sanatombi lost her temper. Anger mounted between the two of them.

Annoyed, Manikchand finally said, 'Princesses behaving arrogantly like when we were under the king cannot happen any more. And we men of the Nongmaithem are not milquetoast. The man who married your aunt Thadoisana was also a Nongmaithem clansman. She acted arrogantly as a princess and got her back shredded.'

It was true. It had been a scandal in the land. Princess Thadoisana, the daughter of Chandrakirti, had been beaten by the Nongmaithem man until her back was ripped, for coming home late from the palace. The Nongmaithem son-in-law had been severely punished by the king for beating his daughter. Manikchand reminded Sanatombi of this incident.

Manikchand continued, 'Your father is no longer the king. Even if you are a princess you are the daughter of a deposed king. Do not do as you please, it will not be good for you.'

'You have no right to talk about my Sovereign Father.'

'And you have no right to bring men over to my house.'

'I did not bring over any men.'

'Other people have eyes and ears too. I am telling you to stop it.'

A deposed king! These words truly stung her. Manikchand should not have said this. The deposition of her father was the thing that had wounded Sanatombi the most deeply. That Manikchand had never brought back news of her father even though she had asked him every time he went abroad had always filled Sanatombi with pain. She looked at Manikchand as he changed out of his clothes and walked about the house.

She looked hard at him. For the first time in her life she felt that Manikchand had never loved her, that he had never made her heart race. Manikchand suddenly became distant to Sanatombi.

Their troubles began from that day on. The house was disturbed. Manikchand got new information every day. Every time he heard something new he could not wait to come home to fight over it. The people in the household found it unbearable. The Dowager Queen, the Lady of Ngangbam sent word, 'I hear Manikchand is back. Would the couple come over for lunch?' But Manikchand responded, 'I am not free.'

Sanatombi was miserable now, she was truly unhappy. She thought all sorts of things, every which way. She could neither eat nor drink. She always stayed in bed; she began to lose weight. And she saw Maxwell's calm, cool eyes of blue.

His quiet manner of speaking. Mainu also stopped coming, having heard of the trouble in the household, though she sent her mother and got news frequently. She wanted to come very much but she never did. Sanatombi had no one to talk to. She was all alone. Sometimes she thought she heard Maxwell come riding his horse—What now, what would she do! But it was only that she imagined he was riding in.

The dishonoured Manikchand came home late every day. He did not talk as before. He did not try to make up with Sanatombi, and Sanatombi too did not try to appease him. An unbridgeable gulf seemed to separate the two. And Sanatombi wondered—Why have I stayed here in this house for so long? What should I do now, where should I go? There was no place to go. What would the Saheb think when he heard of this? What wrong had he done? Did he really love her? Did she love him? He had said one day, "Sanatombi, I am happy you exist"—what did he mean by that?

Why am I happy when he comes? Now what am I to do?

… … … She reviewed her life up till then. She could not wrap her head around it. She was afraid. She was afraid of Manikchand. She could not reflect on her life. She wondered—Then what shall I do? Shall I leave? Where to? If only Grand Queen Mother were around I would have gone to her. The Dowager Queen, the Lady of Ngangbam; her birth mother Jasumati … no.

She secretly endured the fire that consumed her. Sanatombi fell ill.

Word got around as the illness bore on and people from her family started visiting her. The Lady of Ngangbam came one day and said to Manikchand, 'My dear man, why didn't you come to me first? If there is anything you want to say you can say it right out to me. ... ... These royal women have terrible temperaments, and are impossible to deal with. ... ... I would take her with me for a day or two to look after her but what can I do, I am but a woman in reduced circumstances.' The Lady of Ngangbam knew what Sanatombi's ailment was. She had heard secretly from Mainu's mother the Brahmin that the trouble began when Manikchand had referred to the demoted king and the matter of Maxwell's visits, and so she also hinted at her displeasure. After staying a while, the Lady of Ngangbam left, but she was also worried. She left worrying.

As Sanatombi continued to take to her bed, the members of the household began to suspect—Had there been spells and black magic involved? There was something strange going on.

The witch doctor that the Dowager Queen sent made his preparations. He called out to gather her soul and spirits. But Sanatombi did not recover, nor did she show signs of recovering. She kept thinking of her Sovereign Father: how they had ganged up on him and deposed him, how they killed him. Her good-natured father who never did anyone wrong. He had said, '"Sanaton", my dear, how you wander about all the time. Can you not stay at home with Daddy just a little bit? Let us all three sleep together tonight, you, Lukhoi and me.'

The three of them slept together. Surchandra was not yet king at the time, he was still the crown prince. The two of them held their father's cool body. They fought over him. They said, 'Turn towards me, no, turn towards me.' How they fought, how they cried.

'All right then, I will carry one and the other can ride on my back.' Saying this, he hoisted Lukhoi upon his back and carried Sanatombi in his arms.

How the people in the crown prince's colony laughed as they watched this little spectacle.

My father, a deposed king. She saw Kangla before her eyes. No one had ever treated her badly. No one had ever slapped her on her back. She remembered the Grand Queen Mother—Isn't this all your fault, isn't it, isn't it, Grand Queen Mother, wasn't it you, didn't I marry him because you told me to?

She got up and came out in the evening. She headed north. She saw her Grand Queen Mother in her mind's eye. She would confront her Grand Queen Mother today. She walked right on, her eyes looking straight ahead. She was weak, she was very weak, but she walked on. When she got to Sanjenthong Bridge she groped once for a handhold and she almost collapsed. When she got to Kangla Fort, Sanatombi went right in, into her childhood home. The guards did not stop her but were left looking at her. But she did not see anybody; she saw only her Grand Queen Mother—She will answer me today, let me see what she says for herself when I confront her … … … .

Sanatombi did not head to the ancient mansion. She did not go to the crown prince's colony where her father had lived. She headed straight for the residence of her Grand Queen Mother, to the home of her dearly beloved great-grandmother. There were guards there too. The Meitei guard was left murmuring, 'Your Highness.' She sat down on the tall steps of the large adobe porch of the mansion, lit brightly by petromax lamps, of her Grand Queen Mother.

When Sanatombi came to, the first things she saw were the large, heavy girders carved with flowers. Yes, this was the room of her Grand Queen Mother, but this bed was not her Grand Queen Mother's large bed of *khousa* wood. The person sitting beside her was not her Grand Queen Mother either. It was the man who was involved in the scandal with her—it was Maxwell. She looked at him in surprise. Sanatombi did not understand, she did not know, that the foreigner Maxwell lived in her Grand Queen Mother's residence now. She truly had not known.

Sanatombi raised herself. She did not know what she was going to do. She kept looking at Maxwell. He drew up to her and said, 'Please relax,' but Sanatombi's body shook, she was covered in a clammy sweat. She collapsed into Maxwell. Maxwell held her and said, 'My goodness, she has a fever.'

Sanatombi sobbed into Maxwell's breast. She let go of her tears with pleasure. Maxwell gently lowered her back into the bed. He sat by her and said, 'What is the matter? What happened? Manikchand is angry that I came? Manikchand beat you because of me?'

Maxwell had been very distressed to learn that wife-beating was a practice in Manipur. He truly was very upset to learn that women who could not hit back were being beaten. He was worried for Sanatombi because he also knew that Manikchand and Sanatombi were fighting on his account. The Dowager Queen, the Lady of Ngangbam, had called Tonjao and said, 'Tonjao, Manikchand and Sanatombi are having some trouble. Tell Mesin Saheb not to go to Sanatombi's … … … Tell him to think on it.'

Maxwell had been deeply embarrassed when he heard this, but he could not forget Sanatombi even for a single day.

And today Sanatombi was lying in his bed, looking at him with her two black eyes. But her look said—I am not angry with you.

Maxwell asked her fondly, 'You hungry?' Sanatombi nodded—Yes, she was hungry. Sanatombi was really hungry; it had been a long time since she had had food or drink properly. Maxwell called his peon and said in Hindi, 'Tell the bearer to bring milk.'

But even so, the Meitei peon stood there with his sacred clay marks on his face, looking at the Saheb.

'What are you looking at? Tell bearer to bring milk.'

'Yes, sir.' He kept standing there.

'What is it, what are you saying? Princess is tired. Go tell him to bring milk.'

'Saheb, she won't drink it.'

'Why not?'

'Meiteis do not eat of saheb kitchens.'

'Do as I say, won't eat even if dying?'

The peon scurried off in fear. Taking the milk from the bearer, Maxwell held Sanatombi up and made her drink it. Seeing Sanatombi drink the milk from the Saheb's hands without any hesitation at all, the Meitei peon was astonished beyond words. He stood there.

Sanatombi was resting. Her eyes closed. She was resting happily in Maxwell's bed. Maxwell turned down the glass lamp and left, closing the door softly behind him. He called for the more sensible Chonjon and said, 'Princess Sanatombi is ill, she is here with me.' Chonjon looked at the Saheb in surprise. Maxwell went on, 'Princess Sanatombi, she came by herself. She fainted on my porch. You go to the queen and tell her. ... Chonjon, take the horse carriage. If possible, please ask her to come for a little bit.'

The Dowager Queen arrived. She came in the horse carriage with Chonjon and just one other person. She brushed past Maxwell pacing the courtyard without even a glance and went straight in. She touched her forehead as she entered the mansion that had been the dwelling of the queen, the Lady of Meisnam, and went inside. She closed the door and mother and daughter talked for a long time. No one was allowed to enter. But Maxwell still paced the large courtyard of the mansion, sometimes with quick steps, sometimes with slow, sometimes he stood still. Finally, the Lady of Ngangbam called the Saheb in, saying to Chonjon who was sitting on the porch, 'Chonjon, tell Mesin Saheb to come in.'

The queen said, 'Saheb, I am taking my child with me. She is very ill. If possible, please do not mention this matter to anybody; instruct your people too. Let us go ... ... What did you say, Sanatombi?'

Sanatombi did not say a word but kept looking at the Dowager Queen. She did not get up either. Maxwell looked down. He did not know what to say, he did not know what to do.

The queen said, 'That is out of the question, Sanatombi. I know everything, but even so, no. I am telling you, no. Saheb, this woman is a daughter of a king, she is a woman with a husband, there must not be any scandal. There cannot be any scandal with you. Let's go, get up, Sanatombi.'

The queen, the Lady of Ngangbam, put her daughter in the horse carriage and took her away. Chonjon the peon also

went with her. Maxwell did not even remember to salute the
queen. He quietly went inside his room and closed the door.
He came out late at night and ate some soup.

After they reached her residence, Chonjon said quietly to
the queen as he was leaving, 'Royal Dowager Queen, please
call some wise and skilled men and have her looked at. Your
servant has some suspicions.'

'What is it?'

'Your servant the Saheb associates with all sorts of people.
He keeps the company of a lot of shamans and witch doctors.
I have seen Serei the Tribal go in every now and then. I have a
feeling that perhaps some spell may have been cast.'

'Hm.' The Lady of Ngangbam had only this to say. She
went no further.

Maxwell was an unfortunate man. It was his misfortune
to have come to Manipur. It was his misfortune to have met
Sanatombi. It was his misfortune that he had been curious
about the similarities between African witchcraft and the
spells and spirits in Manipur. The Meiteis believed that he had
ensnared the princess of Manipur. Though they did not say
right out that he had ensnared Her Highness, they were very
angry with him. They hated him. If it had been during the
reign of the king, the fate of Chingakham Meri would have
befallen him for driving the princess crazy. So said the people.

Even though they had survived this incident, they could
not stop the rumours. Sanatombi went mad and ran into
Maxwell's house; she was apprehended on the way by the Lady
of Ngangbam; she had spent a night at Maxwell's. The gossip
flew. But the Meiteis strongly believed that she had gone in

because she had gone mad. Sanatombi on her part refused to go back to Manikchand. And Manikchand would not accept her either for he did not want to take back a woman who had been linked in scandal with the Saheb.

The queen thought hard; she had to think. This incident was not a simple matter. She said to her daughter, 'You shameless woman, do you want your name to be recorded besmirched in the royal chronicle?'

She did not stay quiet. She called Chancellor Gulapsingh who had been stationed in Calcutta to keep relations between the British government and Manipur, and had a serious discussion. Sometime later Gulapsingh left Manipur, saying he was going to Vrindavan, but he sidetracked to Calcutta. He consulted with his network of Indian friends and sent word to reach the ears of an influential person in the British government. It was imperative that Maxwell was transferred from Manipur.

The Lady of Ngangbam kept Sanatombi with her and told people she was undergoing medical treatment but she never stopped trying to send Sanatombi back to Manikchand. She sent Tonjao to relay to Manikchand—Why didn't he come to her first if he had any misgivings? Why did he keep her daughter without giving her any food? If he had any problems he should have said so. What kind of a person was he to believe anything that people told him … … … and so on. But Manikchand replied, 'Let me think about it.'

The Lady of Ngangbam went about calmly as though nothing had happened—but Sanatombi's unfortunate mother Jasumati wept. 'All is lost, your mother is lost, Sanatombi!'

CHAPTER 15

And what of Maxwell! Sanatombi suddenly felt closer to him after this incident. Among the many important affairs that he had to think about, his thoughts of Sanatombi became the most important and weighty of them all. But he felt uncomfortable about inquiring any further; he would come across as a crazy fool if he did so. He attended to his work seriously. He called Bamacharan and set up a tour programme. He decided he would traverse all the hills and villages of Manipur on foot. He began to pour his heart into his tasks of building and developing. He took up his work: he went to every household and counted their members, he determined taxation rates for paddy lands, and put a stop to influence peddling. He made progress. He was very busy, he busied himself. Sometimes he would select a tall Manipuri pony and join in a game of polo. At times, he would make the Kabui tribals dance. He let people engage in wrestling hockey. All these festivities he did in the name of Little Majesty. When he invited the noble and powerful to these, he did not inform the queen, the Lady of Ngangbam, for he knew that the queen no longer wished to attend royal events. Moreover, he was a little cowed by her ever since that day's incident. He could not forget what the queen had said to him: 'She cannot be involved in a scandal with you, she cannot get a bad name.'

He had been very embarrassed that day, but he had wanted to ask—Sanatombi, why did you come running to me, did you resent me for calling your mother and handing you over to her? But he never found out, he had not had the time to ask her. All these questions, and Sanatombi, tormented him but her name never crossed his lips again. He remained silent.

Maxwell went to the hills all the time. How beautiful were the hill ranges of Manipur. Wherever he looked he saw the ranges, fold upon fold in many colours. A Meitei soldier pointed and said, 'That is why we say circled by our hills as sentinels, the golden heart of Manipur.' Spires of smoke rose from the widely spaced villages of the hills until they reached the heavens. The hillman porter said, 'Saheb, would you like to listen to our love song?'

Sang he:

> The smoke that rises yonder
> Is from your village.
> The smoke that rises here
> Is from my village.
> The smoke spires will join together
> Once they reach the heavens.

Maxwell did not understand the song in their Kabui language. The Meitei soldiers who were with him helped him understand using a mixture of Hindi and Meiteilon. After he understood it Maxwell said, 'I see, very beautiful.'

He had a wonderful time in this way, and the forests of Manipur had been beautiful. It was the spring month of Sajibu.

Who knew what foreigner had planted them but among the flowering trees native to this land blossomed rhododendron and azalea. How bauhinia flowered red upon red and white upon white to blanket the hills, and bonsum trees grew straight and tall. And many, many ironwood and magnolia. The men of the hills who laughed all the time, the men of the valley who always enjoyed themselves, he loved them all. Their simple, lovely homes, with groves of bamboo, rows of banana trees, little ponds, duck, pigeon, chicken coops, and pigsties—all of them were new to him, new and beautiful.

He loved to travel among the forests of Manipur in this way, and he thought—How beautiful, how beautiful. I am going to return home with love for this land. He remembered Sanatombi when he thought this. He remembered, and felt a pang in his heart.

He climbed Mount Koubru one time. He climbed up as far as the Cow Hump. And what pleasant company were the Meiteis he went with. They never said they were tired. They joked, and laughed, and sang as they walked. He was not the Big Saheb then, and they too were not his subordinates working for him. They were all men together. One soldier pointed at a skinny fellow and said, 'This guy has three wives. They don't give him any food at home. The three of them gang up and beat him and that is why he is so skinny … … … .'

They all laughed loudly. Maxwell also laughed uncertainly. There was much laughter on this journey. One time he went and spent the night in the little shack in Kangchup Village that the one-time Political Agent McCulloch had built. His travelling companions said quietly, 'This Saheb has gone crazy.'

Once when he was staying over for the night, seeing the chief of the village give Maxwell a hornbill as a gift, a Meitei solder said, 'Give this bird back to him, Saheb.'

'Why?'

'It is not good to keep this bird. Bad luck.'

'Who says so?'

'There is a story, Saheb.'

'Tell me.'

The soldier was pleased that he was getting a chance to tell the story and he began to tell the tale. Maxwell lay flat on his back upon the grass and listened to the story: 'Once upon a time, there lived a young girl called Ngangbiton, they say. She was brought up by her stepmother as her father was in the service of the court and so he never got to stay at home for long. And how nasty her stepmother was. She tormented the young girl, beating and scolding her. She gave her so much work to do that the young girl did not even have time to comb her hair. She was not allowed to be with her friends, nor was she permitted to go to any festivals. One day Ngangbiton's father said, "Daddy's little girl, your father has to go to the hills, you stay here nicely with your mother. I will bring back many things for you, I will bring you silk yarn to weave … … … ."

'Every day Ngangbiton would look in the direction her father had gone, and she counted the days until his return. She thought of how evil her stepmother was, how she would beat her, pleased now that her father was not around. Ngangbiton wept—

Where are you, my father?
Oh, my dear mother,
Where are you?

'Every evening, flocks of hornbills would fly by, headed who knew where. Ngangbiton called to the birds and said—

Oh, hornbill birds,
Are you going to my father's land?
Please tell him Ngangbiton awaits him.

'A little later, she said once again—

Oh, hornbill birds,
Please drop me a feather each
So your child may toddle behind you.

'The hornbills each dropped a feather for Ngangbiton every time they flew by in a flock. Ngangbiton picked the feathers up one by one and stitched them on to an old piece of cloth. One day Ngangbiton wore the shirt that she had made from the hornbill feathers and waited for the hornbills to come flying. And then she turned into a hornbill and flew off, following them—Saheb. And that is why we revere the hornbill. We must not keep it at home.'

Maxwell looked up at the blue sky as he listened to the story. When it came to parts that he could not follow he made the soldier tell it slowly, and if he did not follow at all he made him repeat it. Maxwell listened to the story, and a cuckoo sang in the distance—'Ting-kong kang-kong.'

When they were ready to leave after the sun had come up, Maxwell said, 'Let the hornbill go.'

'That's the way, Saheb, who knows, the bird may be Ngangbiton.' The soldier who told the story was pleased that his word had been taken seriously.

As they walked down the hill, one sang out—

Oh, flower of the rains
Blossoming in the hills.
You dropped off the branch
Before you could adorn me.
What regret, oh what regret,
Oh, how filled with regret am I ...

When he returned from a wonderful trip to the hills such as this, Maxwell found a letter waiting for him. He laughed when Bamacharan brought in his papers and said, 'Bamacharan, I had the most wonderful time. I have decided that I will start looking into the hills starting next year ... ...' He said one thing after another, but Bamacharan did not answer; he sat silently. He handed him the letters file. A letter from the Indian government headquarters waiting for Maxwell said, 'Maxwell is required back for some important reasons— another Political Agent for Manipur will be sent. His name is A. Porteous, ICS.' But Maxwell smiled a little. His superiors had recently given him several assignments. He had not

believed he would be needed back so soon. Well, he would
have to go. There was much that he had thought of taking up,
that he had to finish. He was a bit surprised at his untimely
recall, but he would have to go. He met all his friends. He came
to pay his respects to the queen one day but his lips could not
bear to ask to see Sanatombi. He had wanted to meet her just
once as he was about to leave.

'Chonjon, Sanatombi is staying in Wangkhei, right?'

'No, Saheb. She is staying with the queen.'

'Still!'

'Yes, sir, she has been staying at the queen's for quite
some time.'

Chonjon knew why she was staying at the queen's. He may
have mentioned it one time but Maxwell was uncomfortable
about asking him any further and so he was not aware that
Sanatombi was staying with the queen. He had also thought
she would be at Manikchand's. He remembered the incident
from before and suddenly felt unhappy. He strongly
suspected that Sanatombi's still living with the queen and
the incident of the other day were connected. He wanted to
see her even more; he wanted to say to her just once—Please
forgive me. If I have been the cause of your unhappiness,
please forgive me … … … .

'Pheijao, bring out the horses, let's go for a ride,' said Maxwell
to Pheijao.

The day of his departure was nearing. He had started
packing his belongings. He had already started sending most
of them ahead. Pheijao and he came out on horseback, riding
out southward.

When they approached the residence of the Dowager Queen, the Lady of Ngangbam, Maxwell brought his horse to a halt and said to Pheijao, 'Pheijao, tell the queen I am about to leave. Would it be all right if I give my salaams to Sanatombi just one time?'

Pheijao came back from the queen and said, 'Saheb, Her Highness Sanatombi is indisposed, it would not be convenient.'

'I see,' said Maxwell to himself sadly. He also felt embarrassed in front of Pheijao.

CHAPTER 16

No one knew where exactly Maxwell's new job was. There were all sorts of talk that he first spent some time at Fort William, some said he went to Shillong, others said to Silchar, there were those who also said that he had reached England. People talked about him for some time and then slowly they forgot about him. Even though those who had associated with him murmured about him, Maxwell's shadow faded slowly in Manipur.

About two years passed, then one day news began to spread that Maxwell was going to return as Political Agent, it was from reliable sources, and so on ... ... Even though it came as a bit of a surprise, people who liked him were pleased and said, 'Come to think of it, he really would be better.' It was also said that he was being called back because the previous Political Agent's wife could not get used to Manipur.

Quite unexpectedly one day, Maxwell, who had been gone for more than two years, came back. The people rejoiced but one could not say whether he himself was happy about it or not. As soon as he arrived, he dropped in on all the people he knew and was friendly with, like the royal grandfather the king of Moirang, Little Majesty, and so on. Even though there was one person he knew he should meet, he did not, thinking he would meet her after some time—and that was the widow of Maharaja Surchandra, the Dowager Queen, the Lady of Ngangbam. He remembered Sanatombi. The prospect of meeting her was remote but he thought of Sanatombi— any time there was talk of Manipur he had remembered Sanatombi. But it was a hopeless thought, merely the shadow of a distant dream. He got down to his work—and he worked very hard. He looked up the tasks he had left unfinished, he tried to apply new thinking to his work.

After considering it from various angles he decided that keeping the residency at Kangla Fort was not right and that he would build a new brick building at its previous location at the Konthoujam homestead. This time he would have to build it properly for during Grimwood's time there had been a crisis when the Meiteis had burnt the residency down, and on top of that, he felt that Manipur, now ruled by the British government, should have a residency that projected an elevated image. He soon began to make plans for the building of the residency. He had new blueprints drawn up in Calcutta. Papers went back and forth frequently with his superiors. He himself went to the Konthoujam homestead frequently.

The construction at the Konthoujam homestead began. A master builder skilled in brick work was brought in from India but Maxwell thought he would make people from this land make the wooden items for the bungalow as much as possible. The sahebs thought the people of Manipur were very clever and quick learners. He knew this from what he heard during discussions with the Meiteis when they were making roads and bridges, for example. The sahebs had great confidence in the Meiteis. He thought he would import as little as possible. He had always said too that 'Manipur is a country with many wants and poor income', and he was a very careful man who tried not to spend funds unnecessarily. So, he thought he would hire Meitei woodworkers, and he would instruct them himself and he would get them started on making the furniture for the residency. That would save money, and there would be no issues of transportation. He had also seen the woodwork in the houses in Kangla Fort, their floral carvings, the meticulous designs on hookahs, and he was able to see from all this the quality of the craftsmanship of Meitei woodworkers. He thought it would surely be possible to work with them.

He called Bamacharan and said, 'Bamacharan, find me a Manipuri carpenter. I will make him do some woodwork at Kangla under my supervision … … … .'

The woodworker arrived and he got to work. Maxwell came out often to look and give instructions. Maxwell was very pleased with the man's woodwork, and he talked to him about sundry matters as with a friend.

One day, he said in Hindi, 'Carpenter, where is your house?'

'Near Ta'Pheijao's, Saheb.'

'And where does Pheijao live?'

'In Satpam Leikai, Saheb.'

'Satpam Leikai?' Maxwell did not know where Satpam Leikai was. The carpenter tried to make it easy for him and said, 'In the house right next to Her Highness Sanatombi.'

'Sanatombi?'

'Yes, Saheb, Her Highness and I live near each other.'

'Isn't her home in Wangkhei?'

'She is no longer in Wangkhei. She lives in Satpam Leikai with her mother.'

'Why is that?'

'Her Highness is divorced from Manikchand.'

'What?' asked Maxwell in surprise.

'Meaning they are living separately. They fought a lot. It's been about a year.'

The carpenter went on. Maxwell listened to him for a while and then quietly went inside his house. He felt the desire to know the real story. He would not be able to rest until he knew it. Had Sanatombi broken up with her husband at this young age because of what had happened two years ago when he was here? He remembered many events from the past. He felt blows strike at his heart as he remembered. He saw Sanatombi's face as she rebuked him when they first met, Sanatombi in the moonlight as he took her on his horse, the woman who had fainted in the porch. But he did not think, he had not really thought, that matters would come to such a pass. He had thought that had been the end of the episode with Sanatombi, but it turned out it was not so. This time Maxwell really thought about Sanatombi, wondering—What should I do, what could I do? Have I been the cause of the break-up of her marriage? He loved Sanatombi but he had not thought this would happen, he thought remorsefully. In his long life as a soldier, in the midst of his many important duties, he had met Sanatombi in this distant land in all its green beauty. This bright spark

was a flower that blossomed among the thorns—forbidden
to touch, forbidden to get close to. And then he remembered
too how she had looked hard at him that day when she was
taken away by the Lady of Ngangbam. She had seemed
to say—Are you going to do nothing? Shall I just have to
leave? Maxwell remembered all this and thought—I must
meet her. Now that I have heard of this, it would not be
right to avoid her. He must know the truth.

'Chonjon, is it true that Sanatombi has split up with
Manikchand?'

Chonjon told him everything but narrated it indirectly—
Sanatombi's marriage broke because of your scandal. This
distressed him all the more; it was more bearable when he
only suspected but did not know. He decided inwardly that
he would meet her.

He said to the carpenter, 'Carpenter, does Sanatombi
know I have come back?'

'Yes, she knows, Saheb. She asks all the time.'

Maxwell said no more.

One day the carpenter gave him directions and Maxwell
went to Sanatombi's house. When Jasumati saw the Saheb
had come, she ran in and said, 'Sanatombi, the Saheb is here,
Mesin Saheb. Don't come out.'

Maxwell waited outside the gate for someone to come out.
It could not be said that the household was very prosperous.
He had seen how Sanatombi had lived at Manikchand's, he had
seen the house of the Lady of Ngangbam. And he realized—
Jasumati did not live well. She led a hard life. Maxwell was
pained when he saw this.

Jasumati came out as far as the gate and said, 'Saheb,
Sanatombi is not in.'

Maxwell did not know Jasumati, he had never seen her before. But from the way she looked, and some resemblance to Sanatombi, he knew she must be her mother and saluted her. He was a little taken aback when the easily panicked Jasumati said Sanatombi was not in even before he had asked for anyone. But when he looked he saw that Sanatombi was leaning against a pillar on the small porch—and that she was looking hard at him. She was even thinner, and a little paler, but he thought she looked even more beautiful.

Maxwell did not know what to say or do. After talking with Jasumati about the paddies and one or two other things, he saluted them both and left.

Maxwell could not sleep that night. He got up and wrote a letter home. '... ... ... Fate has brought me here again to suffer and to see suffering. I don't know what the future holds for me. ... ... But I love this painfully beautiful country. Perhaps there is no way out for me ... ...'

As he had thought, the matter of the paddies was where he had left it. They had asked for a report but it had remained unsent. He saw little indication that the ones who were to receive or take it had shown much interest. He saw before his eyes—Jasumati's little house. And Sanatombi, thin, her marriage broken. He thought he would take up this matter without any further delay. But he wanted to meet Sanatombi by herself just one time. He wanted to say to her just once all that he had wanted to say as he was leaving—Sanatombi, forgive me. He wanted to say this just one time even today. This thought began to torment him incessantly.

One day he put aside his embarrassment and asked the carpenter. Who knew if this simple man would misunderstand him? The carpenter was very devoted to Maxwell. He also knew Maxwell was very unhappy that Sanatombi was living in her mother's house. The 'Maxwell–Sanatombi' scandal was one that had shook the land and so he agreed to help arrange a meeting between the two of them—So, what was wrong if they wanted to clear the air, let them meet … … … So what if they met?

There was a small woodworking shed near the carpenter's gate where he stored some foodstuffs, his finished carpentry, and where he would stay overnight to guard his belongings. This kind, simple man not only took messages back and forth between Maxwell and Sanatombi but also arranged for them to meet one day at the shed. How it poured that day; there had been blinding rain since the morning. But as agreed, Maxwell came on time, walking by himself along the muddy road. It was after twilight. The royal market had closed shop early. Not many people were on the road. Looking at the rain the carpenter had been taking it easy, thinking that the Saheb would not show up after all. As he had just started stretching out on his small bed with his dinner, he heard a knock on the door. When he opened the door, he found the Saheb standing there tall at the doorway. He stooped as he entered and he took off his large raincoat and hat, and after putting them down, he sat on the loom seat that had just been finished. He did not say a word. The carpenter did not say anything. He left quietly, perhaps to tell Sanatombi.

Maxwell was left sitting, a single lantern facing him. The room was not well lit. He sat, but he was restless. He wondered if

Sanatombi would not come, or if it would end badly. He got up, but it was not a place he could pace. He sat down again nervously on the little loom seat, the Big Saheb of Manipur, Maxwell. He rehearsed what he was going to say to Sanatombi, he rehearsed what he would say in Meiteilon.

Sanatombi opened the door slowly and came in. A single cloth covering her head. Her stray wet hair glistened from the rain.

Sanatombi stood by the doorway. Maxwell rose to his feet; he thought she was about to fall. She had collapsed in Kangla one day. He went to her and sat Sanatombi down on the small bed and said, 'Come, rest awhile.' He forgot the Meiteilon he had rehearsed to say.

Sanatombi looked hard at him and said suddenly, 'Why have you come? Why did you come back to Manipur?'
Sanatombi had spoken harshly to him not only on one occasion but again and again, but it was not a rebuke today. It sounded different. And he forgot what he had planned to say, his string of words that he had come to recite. He held Sanatombi tight. He did not let Sanatombi's lips say a word. That day, for the first time, Sanatombi was defiled by the Big Saheb.

After that there was no holding back the flood. Sanatombi did not think any more; the Big Saheb of Manipur did not think any more. Sanatombi's mother Jasumati beat her breast. But merely in a soft voice, for Jasumati could not raise her voice to discipline her daughter. Jasumati was not the Lady of Ngangbam; she was her mother but she was not a strong mother.

Sometimes Maxwell would come and tease Sanatombi's younger sister Khomdonsana. He enjoyed teasing the outspoken little girl very much. The twelve-year-old Khomdonsana said, 'Why do you keep coming here? Do you like my sister?'

'No, I don't like her. I like you,' Maxwell replied, laughing.

'You old baldy. … You think I would like you?' Princess Khomdonsana incanted a litany of choice words.

'Then take this.' He took out a posy of velvet from his pocket and gave it to her.

'No thanks, give it to your wife,' answered the little girl angrily.

One day Princess Khomdonsana was playing near the gate. Maxwell tapped her and said, 'Now you're unclean. I have to take you now. I will take you to England.'

'As if. I will just take a bath, that's all.'

Maxwell had left a daughter like her back home. She would be impudent like her. Maxwell remembered his home and family in England, but he could not walk back the road he had embarked upon.

One day Mainu came and said to Sanatombi, 'Your Highness, this is not good, what you are doing.'

'I don't know, Mainu, I don't know anything any more. I have tried so very hard, but I can't help it.'

People disapproved of what they were seeing but thought that the spells of Maxwell had indeed hit their mark—

Sanatombi, the royal daughter of Surchandra, has gone completely mad. What else could it be but witchcraft? These people who speak in foreign tongues are well versed in these ways they say.

One day Chonjon came to the Saheb and said, 'I would like to say something if I may.'

Maxwell looked up from his book and said, 'What is it?'

'I am saying this because I am fond of you, Saheb.'

'So, tell me what is it?'

'There are some people from the Sagolband area who are very angry with you. From what I hear, some royal clansmen are waiting to get you. If possible, please do not go towards Sagolband very much, it would be good to be careful.'

Maxwell did not reply. He knew what Chonjon was saying. He also suspected it, for one day a stone had been thrown at him as he was walking on the road. But he had not mentioned it to anybody as Maxwell had decided by this time that he would stand up for Sanatombi, come what may … … … .

But he did say this to Chonjon: 'I understand.' Chonjon had wanted to say more but as the Saheb cut him short he could not say anything else. Maxwell also was very busy these days, and he was out of Imphal frequently. One time after he had been away for about ten days, Chonjon came in and said, 'Saheb, I have disturbing news.'

'What news?' Maxwell was alarmed.

'The little house that was the carpenter's workshop burnt down the other night.'

'How did that happen?'

'It looks like someone set it on fire.'

'Was he hurt? Do they know who did it? Did he have any enemies?'

'The house, the neighbourhood, I mean—they said it was defiled... ... .'

'I see. Chonjon, do they know exactly who set it on fire?'

'They say they do. You can arrest him if you want.'

'Chonjon, I won't arrest anyone. Go and give him a hundred rupees for him to build a house. I feel terrible. Tell him I will be coming too. ... ... Chonjon, nothing happened to Sanatombi?'

'No, nothing happened to her, Saheb.'

CHAPTER 17

Word spread like wildfire—Last night on the tenth day of the lunar month, on Wednesday, Manipur's Big Saheb eloped with Princess Sanatombi, the daughter of Surchandra. No, it was Surchandra's royal daughter Sanatombi who ran to the Big Saheb Maxwell, and so on.

Jasumati wept. She did not know what to do. On one hand, it was a national scandal, on the other, there was defilement. She wept, 'Sanatombi, I am lost, I am lost. My sovereign husband, I am now lost.'

Maxwell gathered around his close men, Tonjao and all. He consulted with them: What should he do now?—What is customary, I will do it all. When they said the first thing to do would be to inform the Dowager Queen, they discussed who would go to her. It was decided that Bamacharan and some Meiteis would go tell the queen. When Tonjao brought this up, Bamacharan said, 'Why are you dragging me into this? Please do not involve me. I do not want to be part of this mess.'

The sahebs who were there at the time said, 'Ridiculous.' Maxwell got together some Meiteis and had them inform the Lady of Ngangbam. The queen said, 'No, not now. Sanatombi has not settled matters with her husband. I would like to meet the Saheb—but it does not mean I am accepting this; we will talk about that later … … … .'

Maxwell came to see the Dowager Queen after dark without further delay. He truly felt awkward about meeting her. He felt intimidated. He knew the Lady of Ngangbam was a woman who could sharply put a person in his place at the right time. And so, he came to her very deferentially, with his answers prepared.

The queen said to Maxwell, 'Mesin, even though we do not speak each other's tongues, you have today taken my child. You are now a son-in-law of our clan. I realize you are not an unworthy person to marry my child but this is not a custom amongst the Meiteis. It is not simply not done. So, you must conduct yourself with knowledge of the Meiteis. I commend you for coming back and taking my child as your wife; you have manned up. But I cannot recognize the two of you yet because Sanatombi is still Manikchand's wife. Watch yourself … … … Do not wander about much … … … .'

Maxwell understood what the Dowager Queen was telling him. He waited for the queen to sort things out.

The queen first took up the task of finalizing matters between Manikchand and Sanatombi. She sent word. But Manikchand replied, 'I have divorced her long ago. There is no question of needing to bring matters to a close.'

Some of Manikchand's friends urged him: 'Take a lot of money. Ask the Saheb for a price for Sanatombi, why should you let her go for free.' Manikchand did not agree with this either, and said, 'I will not take a price for my wife. She left because she wanted to, and I also divorced her because I wanted to … … … .'

It was all right then, it was clear about Manikchand. Then what was next? The Dowager Queen, the Lady of Ngangbam, began to think on the implications for the country and for the lineage. These must be thought through. All the while, the Lady of Ngangbam gathered information on what the public was thinking, who was saying what. She called the scholars and consulted them; she conferred with the royal grandfather, the king of Moirang. On one side there was tradition, and on the other it was already a done thing. The Lady of Ngangbam had to think it through.

A scholar said, 'There is nothing much to the union itself, Royal Dowager Queen. There have been many princesses in the past who became queens of Burma and Assam. Even now, the royal daughter of Maharaja Debendra is the queen of Tripura. Princess Sanatombi is a female offspring, so it is not as if she is bringing him into the lineage. Moreover, it has been clearly predicted in the manuscripts that the royal blood would be defiled by the white man. Please do not worry, Your Highness, who can predict the destiny of a man and a woman.'

'I don't know, pundit, I just can't let her go for she is my daughter. Her Sovereign Father is no longer around as we know. So, you pundits must please be on my side,' said the queen.

She called the elders of the clan one by one, she went to them and requested them to look upon it with favour, it was a deed that had already been done. If Sanatombi is clever, she could even be able to be of much use to Manipur.

The wise and eloquent Lady of Ngangbam contained them all. After Maxwell had been accepted as one of them there were even some who grew quite fond of him.

The Lady of Ngangbam had waited until this point, and now their union could be accomplished. Even though it was not done very publicly, she arranged for the recognition of their union and arranged for a gathering of an inner circle of people to be kowtowed to. She did not want the matter to be blown out of proportion, nor did she want to have people disapproving strongly of this affair, nor must it be seen as though this was a very desirable state of affairs. She called for Maxwell.

How Maxwell stressed out when the day came. And what with the Meiteis telling him all sorts of things: This must be done, that must be done. Maxwell got even more confused; he did not know what to do. If he went along he could become a joke, if he did not he could be violating something.

One person also said, 'If one has eloped with somebody's child one must do everything and anything to satisfy their every wish.'

But Sanatombi came to his rescue, saying, 'Mesin, I will tell you. Do not listen to every little thing they say, you will only go crazy.'

The matter was this. A Manipuri had told him he must go wearing a dhoti on this occasion.

Maxwell asked Chonjon, 'Is that correct?'

'It is correct, Saheb. If you can do it, it would look good.'

'Then you tie it on for me.'

But Sanatombi said, 'What's the point, Ta'Chonjon. He will look like a fool if it falls off. Let him wear his usual clothes.'

Maxwell came with a few of his people to kowtow to the Dowager Queen. Bamacharan, Tonjao, and company also came along. They found Sanatombi's younger sister was also there. She giggled when she saw the state Maxwell was in. But Jasumati said she was not well and did not come.

Maxwell's relief knew no bounds when it was all over. He took off his jacket and tie as soon as he got home. He leaned back and stretched on the sofa and rested. But it was not over yet. The Meiteis were not done tormenting him yet. A Meitei fellow with little sense went and told him that if he married a princess of the royal clan he needed to give presents of clothes to all the elders. He agreed. When he sent Tonjao with clothes and velvet slippers and so on for the queen, she said, 'Who told him to do all this? The poor fellow must be bewildered by all of this.'

CHAPTER 18

Today Maxwell is no longer in Manipur; he has gone abroad. His life of fourteen years in Manipur is over. People gather around Sanatombi to save her. She is living without Maxwell. They all, including Little Majesty, try to make sure she does not feel sad. People would come to visit her, but she is surviving without Maxwell. She is alone.

Her illness has gotten worse again. She had recovered after Little Majesty had taken her to Calcutta for treatment, and for three or four months she had been able to go about around the house and out on the porch, but her illness returned once again. Her face is flushed and she has also begun to rave deliriously every time her fever starts. She mentions Maxwell often in her disconnected ramblings. This time she is suddenly physically ravaged. They treat her illness but everyone knows now that it is getting the better of her. The Dowager Queen, the Lady of Ngangbam, sent over witch doctors and shamans, and various offerings and prayers were made, but there was no sign of her getting any better. They consult her astrological birth scroll and see that she is entering her thirty-fourth year. Little Majesty is not in Manipur at this time either, he has gone abroad. What can be done? they worry—Should they send a telegram … … …?

Before he left he had entrusted her to Khomdonsana and Meino, 'Please look after Royal Sister well, keep me informed, I will dash back ... ...'

Sanatombi must not feel abandoned, she must not think 'I am abandoned', she must not be made to have any misgivings that she is bereft.

This time she mentions 'the royal son-in-law' very often when she is delirious. Everyone knows that she refers to Maxwell and not Manikchand. Mainu's eyes are heavy with tears all the time these days. She had heard Maxwell say to Sanatombi, 'My name is not Mesin.'

'I know that.'

'What's my name?'

'I don't know.'

'My mother calls me by another name.'

'We do not call our husbands by their name.'

'Our women call their husbands by their name. There is nothing wrong.'

'Then I will call you "*mamhak ibungo*".'

'What's that?'

Sanatombi had explained, a man who is married to the king's daughter is called 'mamhak ibungo', the royal son-in-law. Maxwell had said, 'Very tempting, I'll take that. Am joyful.'

From then on, she had sometimes called Maxwell royal son-in-law, sometimes she called him Mesin as before.

Khomdonsana and Meino look after Sanatombi even more closely while Little Majesty is away. They make sure

there are no breaks in her care. They send messages to Little
Majesty often—She is all right, don't worry.

It is winter. Christmas is over. It is foggy and very cold.
Maxwell had left Manipur on a foggy morning such as this.
Sanatombi asks when she sees her younger sister come in,
'Khomdon, is there a fog today too?'

'Yes, royal sister … … … Here, from brother-in-law in
England.'

Two Christmas cards. One to Sanatombi, the other—

To Princess Khomdon,
From her friend
Colonel H. Maxwell

He sends cards to many others like this. To his friends he had
left behind in Manipur, to Little Majesty. Chonjon, Pheijao,
even for Not Guilty; they each get a card with embossed
flowers. They say—I am thinking of you from across the seas,
I still love my beautiful, short and dangerous life in Manipur.

Sanatombi holds the card and looks at it. She puts it under her
pillow and says, 'There is no letter?'

'He wrote to your servant. It says if you would like, he will
also come.'

'What nonsense, one cannot come just like that.'

But Sanatombi knew Maxwell would do whatever he
decided to do, he would come if he decided to. He had said to
Sanatombi as he was leaving, 'Sanatombi, I will return, I will
surely return.'

Sanatombi says, 'Khomdon, tell Meino to write a letter and say I am all right. Let him stay on there for a bit longer; have Meino tell him not to come.'

Khomdonsana weeps secretly. She loves Maxwell dearly. He was truly her friend, and the day he left Khomdonsana had wept volubly.

There had been a time when Maxwell had teased her a great deal; how they had fought. She had hated him then, she had been angry, jealous. But after he had taken her older sister as his wife they slowly became friends. Over those long years, Maxwell had become a father figure and brought up the fatherless girl, the child with no older or younger brothers. He had shaped the career of her husband Meino, son of the Arambam family. But he could not help Jasumati openly. He had known that she would never forgive him and so he had made a gift of paddy fields to the gods Jasumati worshipped.

Khomdonsana is filled with sorrow today. She feels anew the emptiness Maxwell had left behind. Her foreigner brother-in-law Maxwell and Princess Khomdonsana were very close. She sometimes suspected her older sister was mean to Maxwell. In her heart, she took Maxwell's side. Now that he was gone she thinks of her foreigner brother-in-law often. Maxwell enjoyed teasing Khomdonsana very much. He would take chocolate out of his pocket and say, 'Open your mouth, eat.'

The little girl Khomdonsana tugged at Maxwell's shirt, pulled his tie, and touched him. She would say at home that they had not touched each other, and that she did not go indoors, and then she would go touch everyone else to defile them.

Princess Khomdonsana said to Maxwell, 'Open your mouth, here, come on, eat up.'

'Let me see what it is.'

'Cookie.'

'Nookie.'

'Eat it, you old thing. You don't even know how to say it. It is cookie, you fool.'

Maxwell did not eat what the little girl gave him. He was afraid to eat it, what if it was from the market.

One day he took Khomdonsana on his horse and rode southward at a gallop. He stopped the horse when they came to the foothills of Langthabal. After he had tied the horse in an appropriate place, they walked together, Khomdonsana holding his hand.

Maxwell said, 'What is that building over there, do you know?'

'Sure, I do. That is my Sovereign Grandfather's father, have you heard of the name Gambhirsingh? It is where he died, do you know.'

She told the story at great length: 'He died from a snakebite … … … .'

'Oh, I see,' Maxwell answered, feigning surprise.

Khomdonsana talked a lot. She never stopped for a minute. Maxwell occasionally said 'Oh, I see', 'Yes', 'Sure', and they walked together.

Suddenly the little girl cried out, 'Hey look! Look, at the chicken flying over there! Is that a chicken? What bird is it?'

'You don't know?'

'No. Shall we ask the man over there? Look, look there's another one flying, oh, there are lots of them!'

They went up to the man who was chopping wood and asked him. Maxwell mixed in some Hindi and said, 'What do the Meiteis call these birds that are flying a lot around here?'

The man knew a little bit of Hindi. He said, 'Chongaraba.'

He went on to say, 'This bird, very good price. Medicine, for medicine. Witch doctors like them a lot. Come one day with a gun. Let's make some money. Very good medicine.'

'What medicine?'

'*Iton, nungsung*, it can even dissolve stones.'

Maxwell said, 'Hold on.' He took out his notebook and wrote in it—

Hoopoe—Chongaraba
Cures—Iton (dysentery?) Nungsung (piles?)

Then after saying 'thank you' he walked on with the little girl. He said, 'Khomdonsana, I am tired, let's sit down.'

He was about to sit down on the grass.

Khomdonsana yelled out, 'Hey! You'll get bitten by *kakphei*!'

'What?'

'Kakphei, don't you know kakphei?'

'No, I don't know.'

'You don't even know that? Kakphei is, it goes like this. It bites, I'm also scared of them.'

'I see, leeches. Kakphei don't like old man. They like you.'

'What's with this crazy man? Did the leech say it likes me? Where am I going to find a bigger fool than you?' the little girl said impertinently. In this way, the two friends often went about together.

Today he is gone, he is far away. One could not say whether one would see him again or not. But Princess Khomdonsana could not forget this old man across the seas, and always thought he would come back. She asked her ailing older sister, 'Royal sister, my brother-in-law did say he would be coming back, didn't he?'

'Yes, he did ... ... Khomdon, where is that photograph your brother-in-law took of me at the residency? ... ... Khomdon, how is the residency?'

CHAPTER 19

As soon as the new residency at the Konthoujam homestead was completed Maxwell moved Sanatombi in and they lived together. Jacaranda, oleander, flame of the forest and the like grew among the long-lived sacred fig and mango trees. Many flowers from foreign lands began to blossom, in many colours, in many seasons. Ginger lily, the white patchouli, jasmine, star jasmine and stone orchid slowly learnt to flower alongside them. Attached to the tall trees, there flowered the golden *khongammellei*, the *iyonglei* orchid and *yerumlei* dendrobium, the foxtail orchid, and bunches of blue vanda orchids. How beautiful the new residency was, how lovely was the new household.

Not Guilty, who had studied pena ballads at one time, picked a spray of marsh orchids and gave it to Sanatombi, singing—

Flowers climbing among the rocks,
Green, green in their beauty,
Petals blossoming over the stones
Branches spread in comely profusion.

Oh, my precious beloved,
The flower that spreads upon the stones
Now blossoms in its fullest beauty.

Sanatombi and Mainu laughed. Maxwell also laughed and asked, 'What's he saying?' Sanatombi explained to Maxwell that the pena balladeer was singing a song of praise to flowers.

Not Guilty said, 'If you would like to hear, your servant will call my pena ballad teacher and have him sing for you.'

Maxwell liked to get on horseback and go riding in the morning. Sometimes he would take the two golden retrievers with him. The two dogs would run alongside him. Now Maxwell rode with a consort—Sanatombi. After riding a long distance, Sanatombi and Maxwell returned, each mounted on a horse. She could ride very well now. People watched the spectacle of the two of them riding. Sometimes Sanatombi would ride side-saddle. The chignon tied high upon her head dropped in a ponytail down to her waist. Tucked into her chignon, a single hibiscus that had flowered in the hedge of the residency. At other times, she would wear men's clothes, her hair tied loosely behind her. As soon as she rode into the driveway of the residency, she would, with a flick of her head let her hair fall loose. Her hair scattered, covering her shoulders. Sanatombi rode on ahead, Maxwell behind her. She brought the horse to a halt in the courtyard of the residency but she did not dismount. She would not get off her horse until Maxwell carried her down.

The residency was filled with Meiteis all day. Khomdonsana came bringing her friends. They played in the boats on the crescent-shaped pond at the top of the lawn. Lotuses bloomed there, many lotuses of a hundred and eight petals—lotuses red, lotuses white. The young Meitei girls came and made a lot of noise in the residency colony. Mainu was really living with

Sanatombi now. It was beginning to get hard to say what the residency in Manipur was, whether a Manipuri household or the household of a foreigner. Sometimes Maxwell would take Sanatombi to dinner at other foreigners' homes in Manipur. Sanatombi would wear a bright red sarong and a stole of raw silk embroidered in gold and come out sashaying in front of Maxwell. Not Guilty would sing giddily as they walked by—

Come, my lovely,
Come, let us go.
Many desire you,
Many covet you,
Come, come walk
In front of me.

Never angry with Not Guilty, they listened, laughing, and said, 'He has an excellent voice.' Once Not Guilty had pestered them so much that they had his pena ballad teacher come and sing. They made him sing the story of the hero's torture by an elephant. Maxwell listened intently and said, laughing, 'Where is that villain Nongban, I will arrest him and put him behind bars. ... ...' Not Guilty began taking liberties. He would take the tray from the bearer bringing in the morning tea and would stand outside their bedroom door and sing,

Divine King and Queen,
Dawn breaks and the world is astir.
The python rolls over in his morning sleep,
The wild wolf has cleaned his fangs.
Arise, oh Divine King.

Sanatombi would say, 'Oh, this fellow', and would turn over and go back to sleep. Maxwell would have been up a long time ago. He was an early riser. And so, they spent their days. They did not know how time went by. Maxwell would take Sanatombi on his travels when he had a chance. He taught her to climb the hills, and how to camp out under a tent in the forest. Sanatombi began to adapt to Maxwell's lifestyle, and Maxwell was no longer roundabout with Meitei lifestyles. One time Maxwell took Sanatombi abroad with him and stayed away for about three months. This was the first time Sanatombi had stepped outside Manipur. How she enjoyed it, how happy she was. The densely green hill ranges of Shillong, the susurrating pine leaves, the waterfalls and lovely houses, strange peoples, she marvelled at them all, she saw them all. Maxwell took her to the races, he took her to flower shows. Sanatombi whispered to Maxwell, 'I want this flower, let's plant it at home, can we buy it … … …?'

Sanatombi truly enjoyed their trip to Shillong. He took her to Shillong all the time. Maxwell said, 'Sanatombi, I am thinking I will retire in Shillong. Let us look for a house with some land.'

After a visit to Shillong like this, they brought back a piano. Everyone's astonishment knew no bounds when they brought it with great difficulty on a bullock cart along the newly constructed northern road into the residency. They had never seen anything like this before.

Mainu said, 'What is it? What is it for?'

'It's a musical instrument. It is called a piano.'

'So big! Who's going to play it?'

'I don't know. Maybe the royal son-in-law will. An old lady forced us to buy it from her. We did not want it very much as it is too big. But it was hard to say no to her seeing the state of the old lady. I don't know, he is such a pushover … … … .'

Maxwell seriously looked for a house with a plot in Shillong thinking he would retire and live there. He looked at many houses but there was not one that appealed to him. Having heard that a Parsi woman was selling her house, Maxwell had gone to look at it, and after a second look, he took Sanatombi along with him. It was not quite in the centre of Shillong, but a little way off, just where one started climbing up to Upper Shillong. The place was very beautiful, though there would be a bit of a difficulty with water, but Maxwell liked this house the best of all the ones he had looked at and thought that he just might buy it. The elderly Parsi woman came out and received them warmly. The woman, who was about seventy, still turned out in finery. She wore a sari of white muga silk, its long drape falling in front of her, its end tucked into her waist on the left. A scarf of maroon over her black pullover covered her back. One knew right away that she was a woman who came from a good and prosperous family, a woman who was used to dressing up well and looking presentable. She would have been a beauty in her time. To look at her, but for the sari she wore, she looked like a person from the West. Her complexion was very fair. All her children had got married and settled down. She did not live with anybody. This widow had tended to this house and compound with love for all these years. Now she was old and she had decided that after finding a suitable person to sell her house and compound to, she would go and live with her daughter in Poona. She proceeded to discuss the sale of the house with Maxwell, and she thought he might take good care of the orchids that her husband had so loved. The husband and wife had painstakingly gathered these orchids. There were even some from Manipur. The woman took the flower-knowledgeable Maxwell into the garden and said to him, 'This is *Cymbidium micolasianum* and this is *Paphiopedilum venustum. ... ...*'

She continued, 'Vanda from Manipur, I am sure you know it.'

'Perhaps.' Maxwell smiled.

When they were having tea in the living room, the old lady said, 'If you decide to take this house, I also have two valuable possessions. Please take them as well. Since I am about to leave I will let you have them for cheap.'

The old lady went into her house and she had her Khasi servant bring out a large box. She opened the box and showed, from what era she had liked and bought, a Manipuri dance costume with all its bracelets and decorations. One could but only call it a dance costume for it was aged beyond belief and painful to behold. The peplum was threadbare. The head decorations, the brace of bracelets, all were old. It must have got shopworn from showing it off regularly, surely not from wearing it. Sanatombi was amused no end, and Maxwell looked at Sanatombi and gave a small smile. The old lady must not even have known that the dance costume was from Manipur for she said, 'I am sure the young lady will like it. She can use it as an evening dress.'

Maxwell felt like laughing even more but he did not. He said, 'Good idea.'

The other was the old piano. It was still in very good condition despite being old, but what could one do with it? Of course, even if Maxwell had known how to play the piano at one time, he did not want to play the piano in the residency. As they came out to leave, they left the old lady saying over and over again, 'If you can, please take these two things as well or you will regret it later.'

Ultimately, he did not buy it as the land was not very well developed, but he bought the piano, thinking, 'It would be good to play it now and then. I might even teach Sanatombi how to play it.'

Not Guilty wanted to try out this amazing musical instrument just one time. He said, 'It couldn't be as difficult as the pena.'

But he never touched it out of fear for the Saheb, nor did he ever hear it played; it just kept sitting there in the drawing room of the residency. One day, hearing a sound coming from the drawing room after dinner was over, Not Guilty looked in and was taken by utter surprise. Maxwell, the dignified Political Agent of Manipur, was sitting beside the music box and producing the most astonishing sounds. Sanatombi was standing beside him. Not Guilty ran all over the place telling everyone, and all gathered to peep at the scene. They dispersed before long in fear, but they left Maxwell still playing the piano. Not Guilty said to Mainu, 'Wow, what a great man our Saheb is. This is why women fall for him instantly.'

Maxwell held Sanatombi lovingly in his arms after he had finished playing the piano and they sat together in the drawing room. The fire in the fireplace burned red. He said, 'Sanatombi, my mother played the piano very well, she also sang beautifully. We do not belong to the royal family like you do, we did not grow up in wealth, but we all used to gather around to listen to my mother play the piano after dinner … … … We thought the sounds of the piano made us feel as one.'

Maxwell talked about many things—about his native land, about his distant home, about his wild, unsettled life. Sanatombi leant upon his breast and listened to these stories.

Sanatombi felt very tender that day. Who knows, perhaps it was the sounds of that wondrous musical instrument, she loved Maxwell even more. She felt frightened that this man from a distant land might grow distant from her. She said, 'What would have become of me if you had not come? I would have died without knowing you exist.'

Maxwell felt restless after playing the piano, after playing the songs of his land. He recalled his life in the past, the life he had left distantly behind, and felt an urge to tightly hang on to it. His grasp seemed to slip wherever he reached out for a hold and he felt small and alone. He saw before his eyes his land of snows, his far-off home, the dearly loved people of his household. But Sanatombi was resting upon his breast without a care. Maxwell stroked Sanatombi gently upon her head and said, 'Come, let's go to bed, go change out of your clothes.'

Sanatombi went into the bedroom. Maxwell was left looking intently at her. He looked at the dying embers of the fire and saw many faces before him. He sighed deeply and he also went in the bedroom. He changed out of his clothes and went into the bathroom to wash up.

He came out to see Sanatombi in only a moss-green sarong standing in front of the mirror combing her hair. The well-built Maxwell quickly took off his shirt and put his arms around Sanatombi from behind. He said, softly, 'Come, let's go to bed.'

CHAPTER 20

Maxwell said, 'Sanatombi, can you help me out? The Viceroy is coming to Manipur. He will be coming with a lot of people. We have to host a proper reception. We have to put on a show at the polo ground. Tonjao and Meino will put up the pavilions. You look into that. I will go inspect the roads. There's a lot of work to be done. Talk to the king's grandfather about what kind of show to put on. Consult the queen ...'

The queen Maxwell referred to was the Dowager Queen, the Lady of Ngangbam. Sanatombi ran around a great deal for the tasks her husband had entrusted to her. She went to see the large pavilions being put up in the polo ground. Since the polo ground was not very far from the residency she came out on foot with Mainu. She carried in her hand a parasol with a long handle. One day she would wear an embroidered sarong of black and white with an easy fall and a red stole, on another day a limp sarong of pale pink and a small rose stole. In her loosely tied chignon she wore a spray of lantana she grabbed from the hedge as she came out. On another day a sprig of blue floss flowers, and yet another time, she stuck in her ear an out-of-season red chilli she found growing in the residency.

Sanatombi looked into where the Viceroy would be seated, where the king would sit, and where the noblemen. And how to arrange the entrance way ... ... Most of the people in the crowds who gathered to watch the tents going up had really come to look at Sanatombi. Sanatombi walked around giving instructions—she was actually very good at her job; she put her heart and soul into her work. The eyes of the people followed her wherever she went. But she paid close attention to the work; nothing could be left out. Because Little Majesty cannot be embarrassed. Her Maxwell cannot be embarrassed. And what about the entertainment? She consulted the Dowager Queen, she consulted the royal grandfather, the king of Moirang. She organized everything before Maxwell got back—a martial arts dance of sword and spear, a game of polo, a ras dance performance, a dragon boat race. She made her decisions swiftly but she said, 'We will wait for his opinion.'

A dragon boat race was an absolute must. One could enjoy other forms of entertainment elsewhere but where but in Manipur could they see the dragon boat race? Maxwell also agreed. He agreed to everything Sanatombi said. When he saw that Sanatombi had completed all the arrangements, he said, 'Good heavens, I never knew you were so efficient.'

At this point, Little Majesty Churachand came up with a proposal—he sent a message: 'We must have the Kabul Choir, please tell my brother-in-law too, it will be a lot of fun.' Sanatombi was not very supportive of this, but it was the word from the king. A royal command could not be shrugged off. Maxwell had no idea what the Kabul Choir was.

There was at around this time in Yaiskul, a group of accomplished dancers and singers who were fond of carousing and having a great time. They were very creative, coming up with all sorts of new things. They were a fun lot. Even though they did not have enough to eat at home, they spent their time hanging out together posing riddles to each other, making fun of people, and producing all sorts of new kinds of entertainment. They enjoyed themselves, giving the impression this was all there was to life. Even though people took them to be useless, lazy wastrels, these entertainers also could not be written off. The critics never knew when they would come up with a comedy that would eviscerate them. So even though they did not do any work but occupied themselves with useless stuff, the result always took on some form that people immediately liked and copied. They got together one day and said among themselves: 'Let's put together something called the Kabul Choir; we can sing during the spring festival and go around and make a lot of tips.' They gathered together right away and started to make up the songs and dances for it. The songs had no lyrics—they made up sounds that only mimicked real words. The dances were only in name; it was all nonsense and none could tell from where they got all their movements. People whispered from ear to ear that it was a salad of a performance. But the gifted, crazy young men entertained everyone to no end. They started during one spring festival and began to travel all over the place. People talked about the Kabul Choir. The main members were Yumlembam Gulap, Sanamacha, Mutum Chaoba, Phingang Selungba and so on. They were all unmarried young men, and all were charming. Their costumes were Afghan, with waistcoats and pointy turbans. They made up their nonsense lyrics and sang.

Maxwell asked closely about the Kabul Choir and said to Sanatombi, 'You go to the palace first and take a look at it. It'll be the end of me if it turns out to be a joke. I don't know what it is.'

Little Majesty Churachand arranged for an audition for the Kabul Choir at the palace one day. Sanatombi also came to watch. About thirty men started the music on the lawn. At first two men made sounds like bugles—

Nabon kaibong do nothing
Clang clang pettre pettre!
Pinao pinao little little
Clang clang napui clang …

Then the choir came out accompanied by the beating of two drums, and they sang—

Jhhangi is playing
Play the jhhangi!
For Allah pannaro
Yo ya naro …

After the choir was lined up, they launched into another song—

Touch mister not
Touch money not
Jump with spear!
Jump with spear! …

How Sanatombi laughed that day, she had to be helped up. She laughed till she had to wipe away her tears. And then she consented, 'Fine, let's have it, add a part of it just for fun.'

The young men of Yaiskul said loftily, 'So, we needed an audition, eh … … … Did you see how Sanatombi left with her head spinning.'

The Viceroy arrived. The chief commissioner of Assam also accompanied him. They came with many soldiers in attendance. Maxwell received them at the Tongjeimaril Passage. Sanatombi redecorated the residency. She began to hang paintings by Bhadrasingh in rooms that she picked out. Bhadrasingh the artist was really Maxwell's discovery. He sent the young man to Calcutta to study painting. He brought expensive paints for him from England, and he let him sit and paint in one of the rooms of the residency. The large painting of the dragon boat race that Sanatombi had asked him to paint was hung in the dining room. The painting of his lordship, her great-grandfather Chandrakirti returning on a brace of elephants, she hung in the drawing room. Manipur must not be shamed. Maxwell must not be shamed. She laid out in advance what her husband Maxwell would wear on each of the days that the Viceroy was there. Nothing must be amiss when anything was called for, there cannot be any running around. The Meitei peons in their dhotis and shirts began to pin on their shiny brass badges. They were made to wear their turbans somewhat in the style of their clans. It was deemed improper for them to wear them in the manner of service to the court. Maxwell said 'Fine, fine' as well. He could not pay attention to this and had left it all to Sanatombi as there were many more important matters that he had to think about.

The dragon boat race that was held on the second day of the Viceroy's visit was a wondrous affair. It was said that nothing like this had ever taken place before. Sanatombi had seen a dragon boat race during the time of her great-grandfather the Divine Majesty Chandrakirti, but she had been little at the time and had not understood it much. But this time she herself was involved in its organization and so she paid attention to it more closely. She would run over to the palace to see how Little Majesty was coming along, to see how the noblemen of the land would make their entry. She wanted to help Little Majesty get ready herself, she wanted to arrange his costumes and regalia herself. But that was forbidden—she could not touch, she had to watch from afar. Sanatombi the consort of the Big Saheb stood out in the courtyard and inquired about Little Majesty and came back. But nothing must go wrong; it had been entrusted to her.

It was the day of the dragon boat race.

The dragon boats were lowered into the green waters of Thanggapat Canal, boats with decorations in many colours: the boat of the Luwang Clan with its antlered deer head at its prow, the boat of the Khuman Clan adorned with the head of Kwakpa, the great boat of the king and the great boat of Lord Vishnu. The two racing boats waited at the ready. A new three-tiered parasol attended over the head of the king. The pena balladeers took up their procession penas and sang their ballads in praise of the king. The boat of Lord Vishnu floated about in the middle of the water. Brahmins in their pure clothes attended to Him. In the boat were drums, bells and cymbals.

The rowers of the two boroughs, ready in their costumes, waited for the cry of 'Shwa!' to set them off. People crowded on both sides of Thanggapat Canal to cheer on their teams. They waited anxiously, nervously. The boats were set off. Waves rose on the waters of Thanggapat Canal, muscles rippled on the bodies of rowers.

Two men on the boats raised their arms and urged the rowers on. Their supporters jumped into the water: 'Row! Row!' Married women supporters of the teams jumped in, not caring that they drenched their new *kum* sarongs and ruined them. The two mounted boats of the king and Lord Vishnu floated slowly, slowly, to and fro, in the middle of the water. Thanggapat Canal was brilliant. It was a spectacle; the dragon boat race was a spectacle to behold.

The Viceroy watched from the newly made thatched pavilion. With other white men. At the Divine Majesty's seat, with attendants with swords and spears, and laid out with long, velvet pillows, were a hookah of encrusted gold, a little gold chest for betel nuts, a spittoon, a napkin holder of gold, and the like. Wherever one looked, one saw a spectacle. And how handsome Maxwell looked that day. He wore his traditional uniform of his land, suitable for the occasion. He, too, was a man from a land ruled by kings, and he made his appearance as a warrior of royal Manipur. He seemed to be even taller than his usual height. No, he did not embarrass anyone; he rose to the occasion as he walked with the Viceroy.

Where would the crowds turn their gaze? Should they look at Little Majesty, or should they look at the Saheb? Should they gaze upon the great antlered royal boat, at the Meitei noblemen adorned with egret feathers, or at the foreign soldiers walking about in their midst? They did not know; their eyes were pulled in every direction.

'Look, look, there goes Sanatombi. Sanatombi, the native wife of the Big Sahib. Doesn't she look like the goddess Bishnupriya,' said someone in the crowd.

On that day, Sanatombi wore a sarong of vibrant pink. A long-sleeved shirt of velvet hugged her body, over which draped row upon row of necklaces—a string of marei, a string of bokul beads, a pair of smallish earrings glittered in her ears. But Maxwell did not look around him, and sat with dignity to the left of the Viceroy. Today he was a dignitary of Manipur. A woman in the crowd said as if she might be overheard, 'Doesn't the white woman with the red hair next to Sanatombi look like a doll? These white women are not very good-looking, are they, Auntie?'

Maxwell had arranged for a dinner for the Viceroy at the residency. Manipur's residency glowed with lights. The driveway was lighted with lamps of clay mounted on rows of young bamboo staves.

Maxwell said, 'What shall I wear? And what are you going to wear? Dress up to the nines and come out.' Seeing a sequined velvet shirt, he said, 'Are you going to wear this?'

'Yes.'

'Go bare shouldered. Do what you do traditionally.'

'Won't they laugh if I go bare shouldered?'

'No, they won't. Our ladies go bare shouldered when they really dress up formally. They wear their dresses across the breasts like you do.'

Sanatombi wore a finely woven sarong in black-and-white stripes with a hijam border. She wrapped it, tucked under her arms. She wore but a single gold kiyang strand embedded with emeralds. This necklace had been given to her by her great-grandmother. In her ears were stone-studded earrings of Indian make. On her feet she wore the red velvet slippers with the thin straps that Maxwell had brought for her from Burma. On top of them were fine golden chains, worn loosely like the women of Burma do. Red crêpe embroidered with gold covered her body. She wore in her ear a posy of spiked ginger lilies that Mainu had already kept ready, and a bunch of fragrant white patchouli blossoms in her chignon.

Not Guilty came in and said, 'My lady Mainu, why don't you give our land's son-in-law a posy to wear too? You really are so mean.' He picked out the smallest posy and, rising on his toes, tried to pin it on Maxwell's lapel as a boutonnière. But Maxwell took it from him and said, 'Thank you.'

Little Majesty came but left early without dining. Maxwell said to the Viceroy, 'Your Excellency, custom doesn't permit the raja to join us at dinner.'

The Viceroy left for Burma after two or three days. Maxwell accompanied him to the border.

Sanatombi said after they had left, 'Oh my, their affair is really exhausting.'

CHAPTER 21

Maxwell was transferred again from Manipur after a few years. This time he took Sanatombi with him, to a place called Silchar. As he had been posted there before, he was not upset, but having tasted the flavour of Manipur he did not enjoy it like he had before. He came for work; he had to work. But Sanatombi did not like it at all and there was not a day when she did not mention Manipur. She would have been happier if it had been a place like Shillong. She had nothing to do in this place; she would only wait for her husband to come back home, and she thought—It must have been really hard for Grand Queen Mother to have lived in India for as long as she did. So, this was the place that Manikchand said he liked and went to every so often. The crows cawed in the morning—Indian crows. How harsh was their cawing, and how hot it was. She was in a bad mood from the moment she got out of bed. The red flowers of the flame-of-the-forest trees hurt her eyes, she could not bear to look at them. Maxwell knew it too—Sanatombi did not like it here. But he said, 'Put up with it a bit, adjust a little.' 'I don't like it,' replied Sanatombi.

It was not just Sanatombi; he did not like it here either. If he had to live in a place in India, it would be Manipur. He said to his friends, 'It is Heaven on Earth.' But Maxwell still thought about how to make it more pleasurable for Sanatombi. He would take her out whenever he had some time.

It was the time of the festival of the Goddess Durga. Idols of the goddess began to be worshipped in bamboo shrines built by the roadside. Droves of people would come from villages afar, coolies from the tea estates, from the ghettoes. They wore whatever they had—bright reds, deep greens, heavy necklaces and bangles, wearing strings of beads; with babies on their backs and children in their arms came hordes of women. Their faces glistened with perspiration. Coconut oil mixed in with perspiration flowed down their faces. The crowds gathered around in front of the goddess. They ate snacks bought from the stalls. Four or five men sitting in front of the goddess beat vigorously on drums and gongs. How different it was! The choirs of Lord Govinda always dressed neatly, clay marks on their foreheads, and wearing combed strings of fine wooden sacred basil beads, as they sing the evening prayers—

When all is submerged in the Annihilation
The Ark assumes the form of the Lord …

The men began to bang harder on the gongs. Their beat became faster and faster. Their bodies gleamed dark with perspiration. Sanatombi could not bear it any longer. She elbowed Maxwell and said, 'Please let's go.'

The sun was hot, it was dusty, and there were a great many mosquitoes. But Sanatombi did not want to harp on how she was miserable in this place. Yet, she began to lose weight.

One day Maxwell said, 'I will take you to a great place next Saturday. A man from a tea estate has invited us. You will enjoy this one.'

They went together. The preparations were remarkable. Sanatombi had seen many big dinners at the residency, she had seen them at other people's places too, but such extravagant brilliance, such extravagant waste, she had never seen. Wealthy people from the surrounding tea estates arrived all dressed up. They came with many beautiful ladies—cleavage bared, in backless dresses, many tiny-waisted white maidens. Everything was shiny. Sanatombi looked at the crowd as people entered one after the other. She sat quietly and watched. Maxwell would come now and then to look in on her, he would ask after her and then promptly go back to join the rest. They talked to one another a great deal, turning to the ladies, then turning to the men. They laughed loudly; they were having a great time.

A beautiful white woman among them pealed with musical laughter, feigning surprise, feigning annoyance, feigning fright. Sanatombi continued to look on at their show. At the fully attired white men. The women lifted narrow stemmed glasses with drinks of many colours to lips as red as *tayal* fruit and sipped at them delicately. Maxwell brought over an Indian woman in a sari, sat her down near Sanatombi, and went off once again. The woman was also an outsider like Sanatombi. Musical instruments started to play. Wonderful instrumental music, airs from another land. The men and women in the room swayed to the music. One man with one woman, embracing each other in a dance; the ladies lowered their eyes, the men smiled. Sanatombi felt embarrassed; she had never seen men and women openly hold each other before. She turned her face to one side, she tried not to see. It would have been awful if the sari-clad woman had not been with her. Then she saw suddenly: Maxwell was also dancing with a lovely lady. His arm was around her narrow waist. Sanatombi's heart raced, she turned her face away so as not to see. But she saw—the two held each other very close, the woman's breasts seemed to be touching Maxwell's chest. They seemed to be whispering to each other, and Maxwell laughed.

They came back late together. Maxwell seemed very happy, but Sanatombi felt very small. She was miserable, she felt hurt. When Maxwell asked if she had enjoyed herself, Sanatombi burst out in sobs. Maxwell was alarmed and kept asking her, 'What is the matter, what is wrong, did anyone say anything to you … … …?' Maxwell understood and held her lovingly and only said, 'I am sorry.'

He held Sanatombi all night long and Sanatombi, remembering, drifted off to sleep after crying a little. She was sleeping on the breast of her Grand Queen Mother.

CHAPTER 22

But it seemed that a cord had bound Maxwell to Manipur, a knot that could not be undone. He kept going away, and he kept coming back—to this land, to the joys and sorrows of this land. Maxwell had come back once more. He was as happy as if he were coming back home.

This time Maxwell firmly believed he might get to live properly in Manipur for good. It would not be long before Little Majesty came of age and held the reins of the government. Maxwell thought to himself that Manipur would be his last post even if he had to retire. Little Majesty's schooling was coming to an end. He wrote up reports on the progress of the child regularly. He was pleased.

From the very first time he arrived in Manipur, he had loved the river Thongjaorok at Lamangdong. From the moment he set eyes on it, he had loved this river, sometimes unruly, sometimes calm, with boulders lying in great piles along its riverbed. He had often walked great distances along the riverbed when the water was low. Naked children piled up stones and played, they caught river crabs and played. He thought—I will build a small house only from these river stones, and if he had to live here he would live in this quiet house. And so, he began looking for a suitable site along the banks of the Thongjaorok. He would get permission from Little Majesty as soon as he had handed over the sceptre of the land; he would surely listen to him with favour. He had faced many a hardship and endured many inconveniences on behalf of Little Majesty. One time there had been a suspicion that they would kill the child Churachand and instal another child in his place, and that was why he had been taken to Ajmer on the pretext that he would be put in school there. He fended that off, and wrote to his superiors, 'In a gossipy place like Manipur rumours were abundant. ...' He went to Maharani Premamayi: 'Please bless Little Majesty in public when he comes home.' She demonstrated thus to the people that he was really Churachand, the king of Manipur, and none other. And so, Maxwell believed that he would surely be favoured, and that his request would be considered.

Maxwell resumed his work with even more vigour. He tried to take up what he had left unfinished in his restless, unsettled life. First, he took up his unfinished work and then he attempted various new projects. He tried to finish the more complex tasks first or Little Majesty would find it hard; for if he finished them during his term, Little Majesty would be able to properly execute his own undertakings after he had assumed his responsibilities. So thought Maxwell. He was very interested in starting tea plantations in Manipur but he failed repeatedly. He thought of sending tea grown in Manipur abroad but he was extremely disappointed when he saw his efforts had come to naught. He said to Bamacharan, 'I wonder why for several years in succession the tea plants failed to produce fruit ... ... We must get our tea gardens carefully protected to see to what cause this failure can be attributed.'

He had wanted to write two books about Manipur from the moment he arrived here. He had begun to gather material. They would not be like the scholarly books that his predecessor Political Agent McCulloch had written. He only wanted to write on two subjects: on Manipur's religion and rituals, its ancestral worship and beliefs; and the other on the orchids that were found in Manipur. He read many books on orchidology. Starting in the sixteenth century, people in the West had begun to be enamoured with the wonderful flower called the orchid. They had begun to traverse the hills and forests, and descended into gorges to look for this wondrous creation, and to discover new varieties. Maxwell, too, loved this remarkable flower. He went absolutely crazy when he saw them flowering beyond number in the forests in the interior. He brought them back whenever he went on his trips. He gave instructions for any new varieties encountered to be brought to him. But he had to be careful. He kept a close watch in case people from other lands who already knew about this came and plundered the orchids to the point of their extinction. Manipur's orchids and flowers must not disappear, they must not be lost. And so, he gave strict orders: 'Orchids must not be gathered from the forests of Manipur without the permission of the government.' For his book on religion and ritual, he consulted male and female scholars, he consulted with the royal grandfather the king of Moirang.

There were many other things that Maxwell liked as well; he was not a man to stay quiet. One thing that he liked among all the remarkable things in this remarkable land was *arambai*. The Meiteis had a mode of warfare called arambai. The cavalrymen who engaged in this warfare were called *arambai tendongyan*.

This warfare might have been amusing when pitted against cannons and guns, but its highly developed art could not be dismissed. It was an astonishing art of war. Bundles of darts with plumes of peacock feathers were carried in quivers. When the enemy drew near, the tendongyan cavalry would shower darts upon them. From under their horses, to the left and to the right, clinging tightly to the sides of their mounts.

And so, he thought he would teach this art of warfare to the soldiers of Manipur: let it be an entertainment for the eyes, but it would not be right to allow it to disappear. He called the accomplished Chancellor Namra Thambou and had him show it to the land. Flags ringed the inner polo ground. Many white men and important personages watched without blinking an eye. Maxwell thought he would also show this abroad when he had the opportunity so that people would know about Manipur. After he had become the Political Agent a Russian prince arrived in Manipur from Burma after having travelled through Siberia, Yunnan and Siam. He stayed with Maxwell for a few days. He regretted and thought about how nice it would have been if he had been able to show this to Vyazemsky, the prince from Russia. In this manner, he took time off from his duties of governance and took up many challenges such as this. His greatest support from among the Meiteis came from Tonjao and Meino. Tonjao and Meino the son of Arambam had now taken his sisters-in-law Princess Ombisana and Princess Khomdonsana as their wives. Today, Maxwell, Tonjao and Meino were the sons-in-law of Manipur's beloved king called Surchandra, Ruler and Victor of the Hills. These three men became well known as the strong men of Manipur. Thinking about this was a source of some satisfaction to the ill-starred Lady of Ngangbam, the Dowager Queen of Surchandra. At these times, it was forgotten that Maxwell was a foreigner.

Droves of Meiteis started coming to the residency now. They were able to air many grievances and make requests without misgiving. Even though the arrogant British did not like the Meiteis treating the residency so casually, no one could say it openly. The reason was that the person at the top approved it. Other sahebs in Manipur nursed their resentment secretly.

Princess Khomdonsana and Princess Ombisana came regularly to their older sister's home. Princess Khomdonsana went everywhere in the residency compound, and it was only its kitchen that she did not enter. Maxwell knew that Khomdon was disgusted by his kitchen and she could not bear its smell.

'Do you want to taste this dish, Princess?' teased Maxwell.
'Oh my, no no, I won't eat it. No, thank you.'
'Is it unclean?'
'I don't want to eat it.'
'You ate the chocolate I gave you.'
'That was when I was little.'
'Then you are unclean. Meino eats with me secretly.'
'I am telling you, my dear sir, I do not want any, you husband and wife can eat it,' replied the sharp-tongued Princess Khomdonsana.

But Jasumati never visited. She never came to say she needed something. She could never forget the sobriquet Sanatombi the Defiled, Native Wife of the Big Saheb. The affliction Sanatombi had caused in her Jasumati nursed to the day she died.

One day Sanatombi said, 'I was thinking … … …'

'What are you thinking?' asked Maxwell.

'I am getting old. I want to lead the dance just one time.'

'You are not old. Go ahead, lead it,' said Maxwell.

But it could not be done just like that. It needed to be discussed. She was an excommunicated woman. Would she be permitted to produce a dance, would the gods accept the ras she offered? What would the land say if the performance was in her courtyard? The Dowager Queen was consulted first. The Lady of Ngangbam in turn called wise men and experts of the land, including the royal grandfather the king of Moirang and the like, and conferred with them. They wrote a letter to Little Majesty who was away in school in Ajmer.

Little Majesty telegraphed back: 'I will come back in time for my royal cousin's dance.' So Sanatombi would produce a dance. The dance would be the *nitya ras*, and the place would be the courtyard of the residency. Rehearsals began. Many celebrated singers of Manipur, many ladies of nobility, the beautiful and the fine figured, were selected to take part. The second dancer would be Princess Thambalsana, daughter of Prince Pheijao. The dancer that Sanatombi really wanted to have as the second lead was Ibemhal, daughter of her royal aunt Princess Maipakpi. Although she was older than Sanatombi in age, ever since she was little, Sanatombi had been very envious of Ibemhal. These princesses of Chandrakirti had been always around the palace since they were small. They were loved by their uncles, in particular by Koireng. Sanatombi could not bear this. On top of that, at the time, Ibemhal, the daughter of Princess Maipakpi, was a beauty beyond compare. Sanatombi also knew Ibemhal was much more beautiful than she was.

She bewitched the eye. Sanatombi wanted to stand next to her in a dance just one time, but it was not to be. Sanatombi could not insist as the dance teachers said that, taking into consideration their height and build, the daughter of Prince Pheijao would be more suitable. Ibemhal did take part in the dance but as the next dancer in line. With a few more years on her, Ibemhal was now more mature and was even more beautiful. One could not take one's eyes off her. She had been a little slight before this.

But an important matter came up. The dance teachers, in particular Jhulonsana and company, approached the Dowager Queen and said, 'Your Highness, the princess is offering the dance with a pure heart, but perhaps the ras costumes that the Divine Majesty Bhagyachandra instituted ... ... might at least be spared in a ras performed in the courtyard of a foreigner.'

Then what was to be done! There was a lot of discussion. It was decided after much deliberation that they would wear the dance skirt but the head decoration would be taken from the manner of North India that the dancers' council was currently using, including their forehead amulets and hairstyles. Sanatombi agreed happily when they told her. She did not know of the private discussions. The costumiers were called again and told to make even more beautiful head decorations. Two butterflies were made to flutter on either side of the forehead amulet. They put great effort into the making of the new costume—perhaps the new might turn out to be quite attractive. It was decided that a large pavilion would be erected in Maxwell's spacious courtyard and Sanatombi's nitya ras would be offered on the Wednesday of the month of Ingen. The preparations were extraordinary. The large performance hall was completely covered. A new style for the ras performance area was designed. Bhadrasingh worked tirelessly to make the performance mandala in various styles. Maxwell came out regularly to look and gave instructions to Bhadrasingh, 'Bhadra, do not use a lot of colours, your ras costumes have a lot of colours. Too bright.'

How Not Guilty the peon ran around noisily at this time. He forgot his duties and got lost in the ras. Actually, he wanted to dance as one of the cowherdesses but didn't dare say it as he was afraid of Sanatombi.

He said, 'There seems to be a certain matter, Your Highness.'

'What matter?'

'This ras is going to be the talk of the land. What I am saying is that it is going to go down in the chronicles. If the son-in-law who is offering the ras does not wear a dhoti on this day people will laugh at him. As far as the Saheb is concerned he has agreed to what I am saying. When I brought this matter up he said, "I will do whatever you think is right, Not Guilty" and all. And the Saheb is a big man, so a dhoti for him is going to be a complicated proposition. So while there is still yet time would Your Highness arrange for one?'

'What nonsense. You are making a fool of the man. People will only laugh loudly at him; forget about the dance, he will become a joke. He does not even know how to wear a dhoti.'

'As for that, I can try it on him first.'

Not Guilty was using the word 'try' in English a lot these days. It was a new word he had learnt. Not Guilty the peon, always given to excess, had one day put shiny clay marks on his forehead and wearing a short dhoti of raw silk had brought a packet of fermented soybeans for the Saheb to eat. He did not bring it to Sanatombi but brought it straight to the Saheb.

Maxwell had looked at it and said, 'Yes. I'll try it.'

Another time, he brought some mustard sauce and Maxwell said then too, 'I'll try since you've threatened me.'

Not Guilty adored the Saheb. Hot green salad, fritters, aroids with fermented fish, fermented bamboo shoots, prickly lily pods—he wanted to feed them all to him. But Sanatombi always struck him down.

Not Guilty said, 'My lady Mainu, their food only looks good, it does not really have any flavour. If we could just make him taste our sautéed fermented river shrimp or fermented soybeans just one time, he would know. They would even send for the soybeans from England … … … .'

Even though Maxwell went along with all these absurd things that Not Guilty came up with now and then, Sanatombi never agreed and so Not Guilty harboured great resentment towards Sanatombi. And it was the Saheb that he loved the more.

Knowing this, Mainu teased him one day, 'Oh my dear man, you are in the side pocket of the Saheb.'

'Am I?' Not Guilty was pleased.

It was the day of the dance. The cowherdess dancers put on their costumes. Her younger sisters Princess Khomdonsana and Princess Ombisana and all the rest dressed in a room in the residency. Before she put on her own costume Sanatombi went around and asked everyone if they needed anything, chatting with them for a bit. She went in and started putting on her costume a little later. She stood in front of the large looking glass putting her dress on. Maxwell poked in his head every now and then, saying, 'Sanatombi, people are beginning to arrive.' 'Sanatombi, would you like some tea?'

How lovely Ibemhal the daughter of Princess Maipakpi looked that day. She wore a skirt of deep green. Over her shirt of green velvet, a green stole was raised to cover her head. The two butterflies trembled, her many necklaces glittered. How becoming it all was upon her fair face, how it made her glow. Ibemhal remained calm, she merely moved her head a little when she spoke. Her teeth showed but a little. Ibemhal was very composed.

And what of Sanatombi? Hers was a shirt of red velvet with a skirt of red. The skirt was studded with mirrors and sequins of silver. All the cowherdesses wore stoles of the palest rose but Sanatombi wore a sheer stole of golden crêpe. It was embroidered all over in silver. It covered a little part of her breast, a little part of her topknot. The ras was about to begin. All the cowherdesses went on. Sanatombi held Maxwell's hand and walked down the innumerable steps of the residency. They came down the steps lined with torches. She found it difficult to carry the skirt, and Maxwell led her by the hand.

As they walked down, Maxwell said, 'This could be a wonderful wedding gown … … … why don't you introduce it?'

The dance began. The dance offered by Sanatombi, the Native Wife of the Big Saheb. The audience looked on in wonder, the elderly wiped away their tears.

Sanatombi remembered her Grand Queen Mother, she remembered her Sovereign Father. Her Grand Queen Mother had once said to the dance costumier, 'A light skirt for my great-granddaughter. Do not cinch her waist too tight, it will be hard on her. She has a tiny waist naturally. ... ...'

Her father had come by and said, 'Oh how pretty, my daughter looks like a little goddess.'

Sanatombi's dance began. As Sanatombi made her entrance someone said, 'Ibemhal seems to look a little diminished today. How beautiful is this Sanatombi! What presence!'

When Sanatombi began to dance to the drums, the forehead pendant placed at an angle to the left slipped the thread holding it in place and fell right in the centre of her brow. The young woman costumier who had secured the pendant was panicked beyond words.

She ran up to the head costumier and said, 'Oh what am I to do, the pendant has slipped on my lady!'

'Be quiet. What can be done now?'

'Shall I fasten it when she comes out later?'

'Don't refasten it, it looks rather beautiful actually. It looks even better in the centre.'

As the dance offering neared its end, they began to sing the prayer of Surchandra—

Govinda, ruler of my heart,
With his lady Radhika.
... ...
My lord Chandrakirti,
To thee I have nothing to offer,
But this, your Surchandra's song.

Everyone wept. The dancers, the singers, the cowherdesses, all wept, remembering an age gone by, in the courtyard of the foreigner. Seeing the elders going up to the choir mistress and master of the ras, weeping as they kowtowed, the sahebs watching the performance were alarmed beyond words. They panicked. Some even started to stand up.

They asked Maxwell, 'What's the matter? What's wrong?'

CHAPTER 23

The Junior Sabeb's house was set on fire yesterday. This was the second time his house had been set on fire. It was suspected that the Meiteis were responsible for the arson because they hated the Junior Saheb. There were some who mocked him and called him the Nose Saheb. And as for him, he had the practice of beating Meiteis on the road—for not saluting him, for not folding their umbrellas when they saw him. There were a great many Meiteis whom he had smacked with his stick across the buttocks. The elders said that he could not have had much breeding. 'Just because they are sahebs does not mean all of them come from decent families, and that is why he wants to feel important.' Therefore, because the Meiteis did not like him, it was assumed that it could have been none other who had burnt down his house. But there was one even bigger reason, and that was—the Meiteis were still unable to accept the sahebs as their masters, and there was one incident that made Maxwell think this. The incident was a small one but Maxwell could not take its meaning lightly.

It had been a long time since a nobleman of the royal family had refused to pay the tax on a tap that supplied water for the neighbourhood, but neither sending the palanquin handler or intimidating him had worked. Thinking he would go himself and convince him, Maxwell went up to his gate and called out, 'Sanamatum, Sanamatum.' The nobleman who was sitting on his front porch pretending not to hear finally answered, 'I am not your dog, come in and talk to me, do not stand at the gate and yell.' He knew right away that controlling the Meiteis was going to be hard.

This time, the Junior Sahib was angry with the Big Saheb Maxwell. He had not taken strong action when his house had been burnt down the first time and so the Meiteis were not afraid of him, and on top of that he had taken a Meitei woman as his native wife. It was to be expected that he himself would side with the Meiteis. The Junior Saheb was not pleased and the other sahebs were also not happy. Even though Maxwell was not aware of what they were saying among themselves, he was worried, and it was evident from his manner that he was thinking about it a great deal. He was seen telegraphing back and forth frequently with the chief commissioner of Assam. There was a lot of activity inside. Sometime after the Junior Saheb's house had been set on fire, an order was issued by the Big Saheb: The security guard of Imphal would get the populace to haul in teak from Kabaw in Burma and they must rebuild the bungalow of the Junior Saheb. People from abroad and those working in the government were exempt. The hills would not be included, nor the villages. The people from the four boroughs wrote a petition to request that this not to be done. The royal family and the Brahmins, in particular, were very much against it, for this was not in line with their traditional calling. The people were furious. It was thought that, in particular, the noblemen—royal brother Megajin, royal elder brother Kalasana, Prince Thangkokpa, and others of the royal family—had instigated the incident. Suspecting that they might be arrested, these princes went into hiding for a while. But the Junior Saheb constantly reminded Maxwell: 'You are the head, you must work properly, or else … .'

The incident blew up. It was not going to be brought to a close quite so easily. Some approached the Dowager Queen— Please talk to the Big Saheb.

'I do not wish to talk to him about this matter at this point,' answered the Lady of Ngangbam. She thought that if her word was not heeded she would lose face.

The order for the people to rebuild the house remained in place. Nor did the people follow the order. One day, a man called Senggoi came to see Prince Thangkokpa, son of Maharaja Debendra the Feared and Talismanic, Settler of Dacca. Who knows how he found out where the prince was hiding from being arrested. He said, 'Your Highness, I will say that I set the house on fire. Why should the people bear the burden of blame?'

Prince Thangkokpa was surprised when Senggoi showed up, and he was even more taken aback when he heard what he had to say. The reason was that he had had a very unpleasant encounter with Senggoi a few years before. That, too, had been a national scandal.

Prince Thangkokpa was a nobleman who lived very well; he lacked for nothing. For a long time now, Senggoi, who loved dove fights greatly, would always come to the nobleman to borrow money whenever he went broke. Prince Thangkokpa could not bear to see his state and would give it to him now and then. He would say, 'This is the last time. Senggoi, do not ask to borrow money again in the future.' But he always came back, and Prince Thangkokpa always gave it to him. And what a run of bad luck Senggoi was having in those days. Baldy, his much-touted 'unmatched' dove, fled in a fight with the striped dove owned by Irom Haochoubi of Leichreng Khongjom. More than just losing money, this completely wrecked Senggoi's reputation. So, he had to buy another dove. He would have to train a new one. This irresponsible man was treated badly by his wife at home and she had also been stripped bare on his account. It had been a long time since the desperate Senggoi had taken an as yet unembroidered sarong from his mistress and had pawned it to Prince Thangkokpa. As a lot of time had passed, his mistress had begun to pester him to bring it back. As this was his mistress, Senggoi set aside all fear and shame and requested Prince Thangkokpa, 'Your Highness, may I take back my property, I will pay you back later. It has become a source of embarrassment for me. … Please believe me, as soon as I get some money, I will take care of this first.' Prince Thangkokpa was annoyed and refused. Senggoi left in a huff. After some time about thirty men came and turned Prince Thangkokpa's house upside down. They beat up Prince Thangkokpa's servants and men and taking nothing but the sarong, Senggoi said, 'Your Highness, I did not come because I was after your things, I came only for this sarong.'

Saying this, he set the sarong on fire in the middle of the house and left.

Prince Thangkokpa could have had Senggoi arrested for he did not come hiding his face. Instead, he said, 'I did not recognize anyone.'

He had not let Senggoi get arrested. Even though it came
as a surprise for a person such as this Senggoi to come forward
with an offer to go to prison on behalf of the people, it was not
entirely unbelievable.

He asked, 'Did you go and set it on fire?'

'I did not myself, Your Highness, but I know who did it.
But I was indeed involved in burning the notices. Actually, it
has been a long while since we have been waiting to show this
Big Nose Saheb. But I did not take part in the burning this time.
I did not come back home from the dove fight that night. There
was one man among us who had felt hurt and he was the one
who went and burnt it down. Now this matter has blown up,
may I just say that I did it? I will go to prison for the people.'

'That cannot be, Senggoi. We will step forward tomorrow. We
will let the Saheb arrest us. Why should you take the blame
when you did not even do it?'

'Why should the people take the blame when one culprit
has done it? I am upset that Your Highness is in hiding.'

'Well, you are not the one they are hunting down, are
you?'

The people were very displeased with Maxwell's orders this
time. They also found omens that something terrible was going
to happen. It was being said that spirits were heard singing
the ominous *ougri* chants in the evening at the marketplace in
Moirangkhom. It was also said that blood ran at the salt wells
in Chandranadi. Little Majesty was still a child, he still had not
taken the reins of government, so what then was to be done in
this interregnum? Who to plead to, who to go to? Sanatombi!

No, not this time—she was Sanatombi, the consort of the Big Saheb.

It did not look like the matter could be taken lightly. The flames would not be put out easily. One saw the people stand up to the might of the sahebs for the first time since they came to power. The people did not approve, and they were not afraid to oppose it however powerful the sahebs were. They first came in groups to submit petitions: 'Please remove the order.' Men gathered here and there to discuss with one another. Prince Thangkokpa and other royal men were also present at the large meeting held in the front porch of Hodam Chaoba. Soldiers came and put them to rout, and the fierce noblemen of Manipur were among those who were rounded up that day. Notices were hung: 'Anyone who identifies the person who set fire to the house will receive a reward of five hundred rupees.' But no one stepped forward, no one sold himself and put out his hand for five hundred rupees. Notices posted in the market were found torn up during the night. And then the women started. They came in droves and shouted at the Big Saheb: 'Release our men.' Sanatombi said, 'Remove this unreasonable order. This is a wrong order. Look for the man who burnt the house down, surely that can be done.'

Maxwell also knew it was an unjust order, but it was an order he had had to give. He was no ordinary person: he was the administrator of the land of Manipur, an important representative of the British government. There was no way to rescind it. The Junior Saheb, for one, was saying: 'You turned the other way when my house was burnt down the first time. You did not investigate it seriously. This time too, you spent your time carousing with the Meiteis, making your woman do a dance.' It was true, the burning of the house the second time came on the eighth day after the presentation of Sanatombi's ras. This second time the house was set on fire, the Junior Saheb believed, was because Maxwell had coddled the Meiteis. It was because he supported them that they had crossed boundaries this much.

The people shouted out loud: 'We do not agree. We should not have to rebuild the house … … … .'

For the first time, they challenged the might of the British government. Notices were put up in the market, in corners here and there: 'You are forbidden to congregate. You will be arrested if more than five people gather.' The market came to a standstill. But the people did not stop raising their voices, their anger did not subside. The police were everywhere, they stood guard in the four boroughs. No one could go out without a pass from the government but the women forced their way in—many angry women. They stood in clusters in front of the Big Saheb's bungalow; they would not leave, they stood there, shouting: 'Do not oppress our men.' They shoved the soldiers in the market; there were injuries.

Sanatombi said all the time, 'Why don't you do something. There is nothing wrong with taking back an unjust order. Do not give people a hard time like this.' Sanatombi was distressed: on one side were her people, on the other side there was Maxwell. She stopped eating. She paced the rooms of the large residency, at a loss for what to do. The foreigners were meeting in another room; they were discussing important matters. She must not listen in, she must not know. It was

the month of Thawan. It was raining. It poured ceaselessly.
The waters rose, the markets closed down. The angry women
came in the mud, their clothes drenched, and piled up outside
the gate of the residency. They shouted, 'We do not agree.
Release our men, expel the Junior Saheb. We do not agree
with your order … … … .'

Maxwell had the gates opened, and said, 'Let them in, I will
see them.' The women stormed towards the courtyard of the
residency. They were tired, they felt hungry, their breast milk
ran, but still they did not retreat as they waited for the Big
Saheb to come out. They would talk to him today. They waited
for a fairly long time but the Big Saheb still did not emerge. An
exhausted woman whose husband had been arrested shouted
out at the top of her lungs, 'Sanatombi, what are you doing?
You come out. Aren't these your fathers and uncles who have
been arrested? Why do you sleep in the Saheb's bed forgetting
your mothers and your children?'

Another said, 'Bring your husband out. Why are you holding
your husband back? Are you listening, Native Wife of the Big
Saheb Sanatombi … … … Have you no shame?'

Sanatombi heard these words in the large room of the residency.
She sprang to her feet. She came to the realization for the first
time—the room she was in belonged to the foreigners. She felt a
strange, unknown blow she had not known before, that she had
not realized all these days. Today she seemed to know its reason.
There had been a void somewhere, everything had come to a
standstill. There was nothing to hold on to—she was all alone.
The words of the women today woke her up: 'You are not by

yourself, you cannot live on your own, you cannot forget.' She saw before her eyes—Koireng, Thanggal, her Sovereign Father. The people beyond these walls were her people—the hurt people of her land. She heard in her ears what her uncle Kulachandra had said before he left Manipur, before he was sent in exile to the Black Water penal colony: 'Mother Manipur, you have become enslaved because of your unfortunate son.'

Without further delay she opened the door to the room where they were meeting and stood in the doorway. They were talking in their language. They were all foreigners. One of them and Maxwell were in a heated discussion; they did not have time to turn towards her. Only once did the foreigners' turn their heads and looked at her. Their blue eyes looked at the alien Sanatombi. They turned to each other again shortly—they did not have time, they did not have time to look at her for long. Then she saw—Maxwell. The foreigner Maxwell that she once had fought with in the bungalow. Sanatombi took a few steps forward. Maxwell jumped up and came towards her. When he came near her, she said, 'Mesin, remove the order immediately. Release them. They did no wrong. Why do not you understand that the Meiteis lie waiting in anger … … … .'

'Please Sanatombi, I will handle it, we are talking about it. Come, let's go in.'

Sanatombi brushed off his hand and ran out and she shut herself up in her room.

The meeting was over. The Big Saheb came out to meet the women. He said, 'We will make another judgment. We will

not remove the order yet. We will not begin the work either
… … … .'

Samujaobi called out, 'You must make a proper judgment
and remove the order. Why did you make the order first …?'

'Keep quiet. He's saying they will discuss it, isn't he?'

'He is lying. These people lie a lot.'

'Let us see. Let's see what he does.'

After murmuring among themselves, the crowd dispersed.
The mud-splattered residency was left silent.

That evening at dinner time Maxwell sat down alone.
Sanatombi's seat was empty. But he did not try to call her,
or persuade her. Sanatombi had not come out since she had
locked herself in. There was no use in calling her, she would
not come even if he did. In the large drawing room, he leant
back on the sofa and closed his eyes. He was resting, he was
trying to rest. Later, when he opened his eyes he saw Not
Guilty fanning the mosquitoes away from him. They did not
let mosquitoes into the residency but Not Guilty was fanning
him anyway.

'Go to bed, Not Guilty.'

Not Guilty said 'Saheb' and wept. He said, 'Saheb, I
cannot bear these people speak badly of you. Your servants
the Meiteis are innocent—this Big Nose Saheb is very bad, he
has made all this happen.'

The case was judged again. The security guards produced
some bamboo and wood and made it look like the matter
was settled, but the order was not rescinded. It remained in
place. The arrested noblemen were taken to India and they

were released once they reached there, free to go anywhere they wished.

The situation calmed down. It could be said to have calmed down but after this Maxwell felt a great aversion to face the aftermath of the crisis that would plague him. He had been defeated. He was defeated on both sides. He waited anxiously to see what his mistake would cost him. He waited: 'What is going to happen?' And then, the moment arrived. He had not thought that action would be taken so swiftly. He had believed that they would discuss his matter in great detail. Within a few months the order arrived: Maxwell the Political Agent of Manipur would have to leave Manipur. He was transferred to another place. He was to be replaced by a man called Colonel Shakespear. He knew right away his time in Manipur had come to an end. This time he would not be assigned to go back to Manipur.

He had no time to do anything. He had no time to think anything. He had no time to buy the house in Shillong. He had only begun to dream of his house at Thongjaorok. But after this he did not feel like working any more. Maxwell thought about important matters, about weighty matters. Manipur would not call him again—'Come back'—that much was clear. Shall I just quit my job? Shall I just leave?—He thought. But what about Sanatombi?

That night Sanatombi and he came back home together after dinner at another saheb's house. They sat together on the bed without changing out of their clothes. What had to be discussed had been discussed already.

So many things had been said. The first blows they had endured had subsided, and now it was a time of great weariness. It was a time of an unendurable weariness. The unknown road ahead made him afraid. But where did the road lead?

Maxwell said, 'Sanatombi, I have decided that I will take a year's leave and then retire. I had thought I would go home one more time. It is all right, I will give up my job. You come with me.'

Sanatombi did not answer.

To go or to stay, both were difficult for her. She knew the reserved Maxwell held in many hardships. A strong bond tied him to his homeland. A bond she could not break free from also tied her down, but Sanatombi was afraid. She was afraid to break the cord that tied her to this land. She also could not think of spending her days without Maxwell. She did not feel like thinking about anything. She endured her pain. She had not realized that this stranger foreigner had come to occupy such a large part of her life. Today she was not a child, she was not the princess daughter of Surchandra; she was a woman who must get to know life and live. What would she do now? What would be her decision at this great challenge in her life?

Maxwell said again, 'Sanatombi, come with me. Come, say yes.'

Sanatombi did not answer.

'Sanatombi, orthodox Manipur will never accept you.'

He also knew his mighty England would not receive her warmly. The weary Maxwell put his arms around Sanatombi and stroked her head slowly, lovingly. In this way, he had once put his arms around a young Sanatombi who had run in recklessly to him one day. It became late. They could not come to a decision. The time of the dawn service at Lord Govinda was approaching. The bell rang, heavy and distant— bong bong bong ... ...

Suddenly Sanatombi embraced Maxwell and wept, 'I cannot do it.'

'What can't you do?'

'I cannot leave Manipur.'

'Then why the hell are you crying? Sanatombi, if only you could realize how much I feel for you ... ...' He said a lot more after that in his language. Sanatombi put her arms around Maxwell and wept. She held him tight as if he might get away.

But he had decided that he must leave. The long time he had spent here, as like a hardy, desiccated tree buffeted by unruly winds, he had weathered it alone. An enormous pointless void trapped him as in a cage. One day he had been among the first who planted the Union Jack at Manipur's Kangla Fort. He was a soldier at that time, a mature soldier who had come with a shining vision of the future. He was a loyal soldier of the British government. He had come focused on conquering this land. It was true when he said that Lady Destiny had swept him here, and had beckoned him back here, time and time again. He had thought at the time—How clever of the British, how clever to pick this beautiful land. He had been to many lands in India but there had been none that had intoxicated him like this one. Lady Destiny had tossed him this land and he had caught it with open arms. He had wanted to build up this land with loving care; he did not want to lose anything, he wanted to pick up everything and cherish it. He had come to conquer this land without a thought, but this land had turned around and conquered him. It tied him with a powerful bond, a bond of love. There was no way to break free. He thought— What a tragedy! What use was it to us to trample this garden that exists by itself? What was the point of tearing it off and pasting it on to the Victorian Empire where the sun never set?

Today he was a bumbling, shallow soldier-guardian of the British government. He knew that the British government would be able to recognize him as an able, loyal officer but it would not be able to forgive him as an ordinary man. Arrogant England would not lend an ear to the story of this tiny colony. He must leave. Even if he were to return, he would be surrounded by suspicious eyes. It broke his heart to be torn from Manipur in this way. But he thought—I will go first. Who knows, sated, overflowing England may deign to forget him. But this he wanted to say out loud openly, 'Sanatombi, I love your Manipur; even if Manipur does not love me, I will not be able to stop loving it. The ties you have bound me with are not only the bond of happiness, but also the bonds of defeat.'

But he left without saying anything. Only this did he personally request his replacement Saheb Shakespear: 'Please do not oppress the Meiteis. Please cancel the order I gave to rebuild the house.'

Many memories came back anew to him before he left, many new thoughts came to him. The deposed queen of this little land had said to him one day, 'You must conduct yourself knowing the Meiteis.' She seemed to have said, 'You may be from a civilized land but we do not fear you. You may be a powerful race but your avaricious ways disgust us.'

Today he felt shame that he was the first man to have planted the Union Jack in Manipur. Let the Union Jack fly up to the sky—there was nothing that he coveted any more. He did not feel any pride today. But as a last word he said to Sanatombi, 'I will come back, Sanatombi, I will surely come back.'

CHAPTER 24

It is time. The awning spreads out over the courtyard. Prayers
are being held. The Brahmin was sent by the palace. Little
Majesty has been staying over. There are many others too.
Little Majesty had received a letter from Maxwell asking how
Sanatombi is. Sanatombi missed getting the message in the
letter. Sanatombi is intermittently awake, staring vacantly,
and it is uncertain if she understands when the news is given
to her—whether she hears the distant, distressed voice from
across the far-off seas. She lies there looking into the distance.
A woman is singing in front of her bed—

> When will I get to live in Vrindavan
> With my Lord, Resident of Vrindavan

Sanatombi is dreaming … … … The boat is drifting on the
Loktak Maxwell and she are in it the rower of the boat heads
home towards Thangga over the sounds of the women's oars
'splash splash' is heard a sound in the distance it is Not Guilty
singing his song he often sang—

> Oh, my precious,
> My mother-in-law's daughter!

I search and search today
For the trace of your footprints,
But I never see you any more
Oh, desired one.

The bed she is sleeping in is her Grand Queen Mother's she is lying with her Grand Queen Mother her mother Jasumati is holding her Jasumati weeps—I am lost I am lost—Maxwell and she are on the Irang River they are going to eat fish on the Irang people spread white clothes to dry—how tiring it is to climb the hill—from the top of the hill the song is heard—

Oh, my precious one,
My mother-in-law's daughter!
Have you left us here
To fetch the fire for the hearth?

How tall are the beasts of Kangla they grow taller and taller she plays at their feet she looks up at them and is suddenly afraid their faces are all torn … … … two teardrops fall on her forehead cold as ice she is running from the war how dark is the riverbed there are many fireflies Koireng gallops ahead on his horse she rides after him crying Uncle Uncle she is weeping I cannot come my Sovereign Father the woman calls out harshly Native Wife of the Big Saheb you come on out on the day when the lights of the ras performance shone brightly she holds Maxwell's hand and walks down the steps one by one in the chaos many people are running around the lights suddenly go out someone is singing—

Are you washing your hair
With gathered fragrant herbs

By the sands of your fathers' river dock?
Are you caressing your hair
As you comb your tresses
Inside your father's great house?

Oh, my precious one,
My mother-in-law's daughter!
Have you left us here
To join your maiden friends,
To adorn the swains yonder
Who teach you at play?

Oh, my precious one,
My mother-in-law's daughter!
I never see you any more
Oh, desired one.

It is the lunar month of Sajibu. The royal bier cleaves through
the curious throngs along the road in Sagolband. Five or ten
mourners walk behind it quietly. No one weeps loudly. The
bier is taken to the banks of the Nambul River coursing by
Nepram Menjor Leirak. The low waters of the Nambul River
flow slowly. The two or three foreigners among the mourners
stand around for a little while and then they go back quietly.
The people who have come bathe and hasten away. No one is
there to even bite the cremation bamboo tie and toss it in the
fire. No relative or close of kin carries the pot of water around
the funeral pyre. A stranger lights the pyre as but routine work.
She had wanted to be cremated. Everyone has left. Only four
men remain, sitting with towels wrapped around their knees,

their heads bowed. Whether they are weeping, or waiting for the body to be consumed, one cannot say.

The sacred white canopy over the blazing firewood flutters and flaps for a little while above the flames, then turns to ash. The story of the piteous cremation becomes one with the sands of the Nambul River. Her ashes, however, are forgiven by the flames.

EPILOGUE

MAXWELL

About Maxwell. I was not able to find out about his personal life properly. But this much I know—he was a man with a wife and two children. I might have been able to find out more if I looked, but let Maxwell be the Maxwell I know. And so, I have finished my book.

My mother had mentioned, when she told me the stories, that someone from England who was coming newly transferred to Manipur had told her that he had met Maxwell in England. At the time, he was busy getting news back and forth of Sanatombi's illness; he had seemed very agitated. I have not mentioned this in the book. But as I was getting ready to send the book to press a friend I had not met in a long time came running to me and said, 'I am glad to hear you are writing a book about Sanatombi. Maxwell came back to India again. When he heard that Sanatombi had passed away he turned back from Silchar without entering Manipur. My elders told me this … … … .'

I felt a desire to include this lovely episode in my book but that too I did not put in. Even though I wanted to believe it

I had a misgiving … Was this possible? But in my eyes, I saw a weary Maxwell looking at Manipur for the last time from the top of Laimaton Hill before he turned his horse around and went back.

Would he really have come? I do not know.

Sanatombi died on the 27 April 1906. Maxwell left Manipur in the February of 1905. There was not much of a gap. Sanatombi did not live without Maxwell for long. Thinking about this made me happy, and it also made me sad. The elders said, 'The Big Saheb gave her medicine to cut her life short and left.' They also said, 'The Big Saheb cast a spell on her, he made her go mad … … … .' We have always elevated Sanatombi. But Sanatombi did not live long after Maxwell's departure. Her burial stone poked up a mere span high above the ground at her cremation site on the banks of the Nambul River near Nepram Menjor Leirak. It had shouted out all these long years—I lived. Today, that bit of stone was a stepping stone for children at play. Around it the washerwomen dried their laundry, they tied their cows. How often I went to look at this stone. I had thought, I would take a photograph of it and request the Raj Bhavan to take this stone and keep it. It was in this place, it was in this house that Maxwell and she had lived. But I dawdled and could not do it. When I went back again, someone had removed the stone. I am sure, it was around here. I looked all around for it but it was gone! Yes, it was on that rise, right over there … … … . It is all right.

I was afraid to finish the book. Something unknowable had pushed me to want to write this book. One by one, I had

searched for the beads from a broken-off *liklu-pumhei* string,
fallen scattered among the grass. I had asked at many points—
How would it have been? And I always found the answer right
away. Time and time again, a mere word, a single word, would
come to my aid to build my story.

After the book was well into its printing at the press, there
came news that there were some documents about the
two, Sanatombi and Maxwell, in the house of someone
who lived in Keisamthong. I ran over without delay. And
I found the answer to an enormous question. It confirmed
the answer to a question I had asked before. At one point
in the book, Maxwell says, '... ... ... Fate has brought
me here again to suffer and to see suffering.' When I let
Arambam Samarendra, Sanatombi's nearest of kin, read my
manuscript he had said, 'Would they have believed in fate?'
But I did not remove these words from my book because
Maxwell had to say the word 'fate'. But I got my answer. I
was overjoyed.

Mr Takhellambam Prafullo's grandfather Mr Kirti Singh had
been a member of the village council in Manipur. It was during
the time of Maxwell. Among the papers that Mr Prafullo had
kept for a long time, there was a letter that Maxwell had written.
It was written to Mr Kirti on 27 May 1906, after Sanatombi
was no more. He said at one point: '... ... ... However, fate
has ordained otherwise, she has left many sad hearts behind.'
I had written that in my book—that it broke Maxwell's heart
to be torn from Manipur in this manner. Maxwell had said in
his letter—'I greatly regret leaving Manipur ... ...'

Maxwell had taught Sanatombi how to read and write. The proof was in a letter that she herself had written to Mr Kirti Singh. She wrote—

> My dear brother,
> I have received your letter and understood ... ...
> 11, 10, 98
> Sanatombi Rajkumari
> Bleak House
> Shillong.

Maxwell never interfered with Sanatombi's beliefs. He let her go to Vrindavan accompanied by Mr Kirti Singh. He was happy when he heard that Sanatombi had been cremated.

Maxwell loved Sanatombi; he loved the Meiteis. After he had left, an order issued by his successor Political Agent Shakespear said, 'In accordance with the wishes of my predecessor Political Agent Maxwell, I hereby revoke the order upon the Meiteis to rebuild the bungalow of the Junior Saheb.' And what is today Thanggal Bazar was also named 'Maxwell Bazar' during Shakespear's time. I am truly afraid to bring this book to an end. I don't know, I was made to feel misgivings that someone might suddenly come running to me with new information. But the book is finished. And I had received the answer to the enormous question that I had about Maxwell. I do not have doubts about him any more.

Binodini